ROBERT N. CHAN

Painting A Burning House

iUniverse, Inc.
Bloomington

Painting A Burning House

This is a work of fiction. All of the characters, names, incidents, organizations, and dialogue in this novel are either the products of the author's imagination or are used fictitiously.

iUniverse books may be ordered through booksellers or by contacting:

iUniverse
1663 Liberty Drive
Bloomington, IN 47403
www.iuniverse.com
1-800-Authors (1-800-288-4677)

Because of the dynamic nature of the Internet, any Web addresses or links contained in this book may have changed since publication and may no longer be valid. The views expressed in this work are solely those of the author and do not necessarily reflect the views of the publisher, and the publisher hereby disclaims any responsibility for them.

Any people depicted in stock imagery provided by Thinkstock are models, and such images are being used for illustrative purposes only.

Certain stock imagery © Thinkstock.

ISBN: 978-1-4620-7157-9 (sc)
ISBN: 978-1-4620-7158-6 (e)

Printed in the United States of America

iUniverse rev. date: 12/07/2011

To my fifteen year old son, Adam, whose imagination inspires me

I

A Lioness in Daniel's Den

DANIEL HUSTLED DAHLIA into his small, cozy den, shut and double-locked the door, then hugged her. His hugs had always made her feel safe, but now there was a slight tremor in his arms. And he'd never double-locked the door before.

"Thank you for coming," he said.

"Great to see you, Daniel." She kissed his cheek. "Really, wonderful."

He looked tired, his face chiseled with worry lines that hadn't been there when she'd last seen him, two years earlier, at her father's funeral. It was like the difference between a president's inauguration photo and one taken the day he left office.

His eyes scanned the room. Usually calm, he was twitchy like a rabbit.

Her stomach clenched. "What's wrong?"

With a sweep of his arm he cleared a wide swath on his desk—burnished aluminum designed to look like the wing from a World War II fighter plane. A gift from his ex-wife, the desk had outlasted his marriage by several years. Papers that had been neatly piled, corners squared, fell to the floor. His gaze remained fixed on her, as if he was unaware of the chaos he'd just caused.

"I need someone I can trust," he whispered.

"It's been a while since anyone has trusted me with anything that mattered."

He pulled the already closed blinds tighter, then unscrewed a standing brass lamp. As the lamp had provided much of the light in the now crepuscular room, she could barely make out his silhouette. He eased a rolled-up something out of the lamp's thick tubular column and carefully placed it on his desk.

"Come look," he whispered.

He unfurled two long sheets of pieced-together fragments of parchment,

1

each sheathed in serious-looking protective plastic. He turned on a flashlight, and the sheets appeared ancient, tattered, but still legible.

"Do you read biblical Hebrew and Aramaic?" he asked.

"Hebrew, of course, and I can almost fake my way through Aramaic."

"Take a look."

She studied the jigsaw puzzle of mounted parchment scraps, which might have been parts of a Torah, hard to tell from the gaps but maybe the story of Abraham. Whatever they were, they seemed not just ancient but holy; she felt lightheaded and awed.

"I found them in a cave near Qumran." Daniel spoke quietly but his voice trembled. "A freak storm… You know how the water pours out of those steep bare hills when it rains?"

"Dad used to take me hiking there, the views of Massada and the Dead Sea." The memory made her smile.

"Your father was a brilliant and righteous man."

"Funny, I never heard anyone call him *righteous* when he was alive."

She'd loved her dad more than anyone else in her life, a fact she kept to herself. He'd abhorred sentimentality and prided himself on his prickly sabra exterior, and Dahlia kept up the act. Anyway, she distrusted displays of emotion, since her own moods were so damn mercurial.

"Almost six inches of rain had fallen in less than three hours, a record." Daniel blew air through closed lips. "The wadi filled with a raging torrent, causing monumental erosion…. The entrance to the cave may have been hidden for more than two millennia."

She stared into the asymmetric face she knew so well. With his mismatched eyes, different sized-ears, and lopsided nose, he used to remind her of a portrait from Picasso's early cubist period. No one who'd ever gotten to know him, though, thought of him as unattractive. Both the green eye and the gray one revealed his empathy and fierce intelligence. Those gifts along with his extraordinary energy had assured that he never lacked for companionship.

"I'm afraid I'm going to end up like Joe Shustak," Daniel said.

"Who?"

"A former colleague, head of the NYU Archeology Department. I took the scroll fragments to him to ask his opinion. Too early to know for sure but he said they might predate the Dead Sea Scrolls by over a century! Three days later, I saw his picture in the *Post*. Dahlia, he *fell* in front of a subway."

"That's awful, but…" Questions so crowded her mind that she couldn't squeeze out even one.

"As you know, the Torah was hand copied, one from another for thousands of years. A good bit of work needs to be done before we can be sure, but what you're looking at might indicate that a mistake may have crept into the Torah during one of these iterations. A mistake in the Torah!" He extended his arms like a condor about to take flight. "Don't you see how big this is?"

"Still, killing the archeologist who found them would seem to be an overreaction, particularly with all these *mights* and all that work that needs to be done."

By now Daniel must've become accustomed to her flip tone or at least understood that if she was going to be able to help him, she had to maintain her emotional detachment—one of her few areas of expertise.

"Yes, but…this particular mistake, if proven out, would delete Abraham's blessing to his son Ishmael that his descendants—the Arabs—would be a great nation and instead condemn them to perpetually serve the Jews."

"Ouch! I can see how, if the media misreports and some rabble-rouser were to… That might piss off—"

"There's already been one murder!" he shouted.

"What can I do to help you?"

Whatever really was going on, she had no doubt that Daniel's panic was real. So she decided not to ask why he was so sure Shustak had been murdered because of the scrolls rather than having died an accidental death or even having committed suicide. Maybe all he needed was someone he could talk to, a caring objective ear. She certainly cared, but objectivity wasn't one of her strong points, even under the best of circumstances. With someone to whom she owed her life thinking he was about to be killed, this was anything but the best of circumstances.

"You were trained by the Mossad," Daniel said. "Your dad said you were top of your class."

"I hope you're not looking for a secret agent. I'm not licensed to kill." Her attempt at humor fell flat. "Did Dad also tell you they only took me because he pulled strings, told them I was fully recovered from my adolescent crazies. When they found out that wasn't true, they cashiered me?"

Daniel didn't respond.

"As I hope you know, there's nothing I wouldn't do for you, but whatever you have in mind, I'd probably screw it up," she said. "Why not go to the Mossad directly? I could arrange a meeting."

"The first thing the Mossad would do is confiscate the scrolls and have me arrested. I smuggled them out of Israel." He said, back to whispering. "The Israeli government takes that sort of thing *very* seriously."

"But you of all people know my… limitations."

"Looks like you're in top physical condition."

"I left Israel hoping to outrun my problems." Dahlia blew air through closed lips—exactly like Daniel had. "Since then I've had a lot of time with little to do but read, exercise, and run through my small inheritance."

Daniel reached behind the blackout curtains and checked that the windows were locked.

"I'm just using this lamp for today. I have better hiding places. After you leave, I'm going to move the scrolls."

Dahlia held up a palm: "Please, Daniel, this all sounds..." She wasn't about to suggest that Daniel—who she'd long thought of as the sanest person she knew—was paranoid, but... "I still don't know what you want from me."

"If something happens to me, take the scrolls to Yorum Ben-Ellisar at the Israeli Museum and have him verify them," Daniel said. "You know him, right?"

"He was at the funeral, but why don't you take them there now?"

"There are some...logistical problems, given how I smuggled the scrolls out. And I'm afraid I'm being watched." A heavy sigh. "But I should have phony export certificates tomorrow or the next day and be out of here within a day or two after that. Ben-Ellisar will make sure they're kept safe, and any danger to me will disappear."

Before she had a chance to comment, he silenced her with a raised hand.

"I should have brought them directly to him. But"—self-disparaging head shake—"I didn't want to share the glory, I'd hoped to use my discovery to leverage myself back into a professorship."

"Daniel, please turn on a light. You have blackout curtains."

He complied.

"How would anyone even know you have these?" she asked.

"Yusef, my assistant. A lovely young man, but..."

From a pile on a corner of his desk he extracted a photo of an adolescent with big dark eyes, full lips, cheekbones to live for, and a fetching curl of jet black hair on his smooth forehead.

"Very pretty, but—"

"We didn't *do* anything. It was a *Death in Venice* sort of thing for me, and anyway he's of legal age."

"In what country?" Dahlia asked, though she wasn't going to pursue a line of discussion that wasn't her business, not that she knew quite what her business was.

"My life's been a mess since I lost my professorship." Daniel again shined his flashlight on the scrolls, yet they seemed to glow with a light of their own. "These are my redemption. My legacy!"

Dahlia never saw him like this. His eyes burned with passion—the very thing her life lacked. Between her father's death and the mental problems it had exacerbated, she was barely been able to get out of bed by afternoon. She owed it to his memory to pull herself together. And redemption? If only that were possible. Her breath quickened.

"You said you wanted to use the scrolls to leverage yourself back into a professorship." She rested her hand on his forearm. "You can't be a professor if you're dead."

She wasn't used to being the calm person in the room.

"My mind is clearer than my words. I only learned of Joe Shustak's death the day before yesterday. I'm still shaken by it. He was a friend as well as a former colleague. And the answer to the question you had the courtesy not to ask before is *yes, I'm certain Joe was murdered because of the scrolls.*" He sat. "If you'll help me—"

She held up a hand: I need a minute. She went to the window and ignoring Daniel's guttural protest, slipped behind the curtains, so shaken by what Daniel told her that she was almost surprised to see the Queens neighborhood of modest but well-kept row-houses unchanged, normal, quiet. She returned to the desk.

"You know I'd do anything for you," she said. "You were there for me at the lowest point in my life. Without you I'd probably still be confined to Creedmoor."

"You shouldn't have been there in the first place. You're mentally ill not criminally insane, and with your heart and determination you're capable of much more than most so-called *normal* people—so much more than you think you are."

"Daniel, I suffer from schizoaffective disorder: I lose contact with reality, hallucinate, and suffer from extreme, sometimes debilitating, mood swings." Although she wasn't telling him anything he didn't already know, she spoke slowly emphasizing each syllable. "To use a medical term, I'm a fuck-up."

She'd always taken pleasure in his exalted opinion of her—one of several ways in which he resembled her father—but she couldn't allow that to lead him into a catastrophic mistake. Having let herself down so often, how could she possibly come through for him?

"Your extraordinary strength and resourcefulness trump your mental problems, and—"

Sensing what was coming, she raised a hand. "I can do without the canned lecture on the correlation between insanity and creativity and genius."

"And I can do without your selling yourself short. Because of the way you are, you have the ability to tap into and use a part of yourself most people can't access."

Before she had a chance to roll her eyes, he took her hands in his. She felt him shudder, or maybe it was her own trembling.

"Can't Yusef help?" she said. "He's your assistant, after all. I'm not copping out. It's just that…"

"Seems that at some downtown club he told the wrong person about my plan to take the scrolls out of the country and publicize them."

Daniel's mouth twisted as if he was considering saying something else. Dahlia waited.

"After that he had a visitor, sounds like it was the same person who threatened me."

"You were THREATENED?" So much for her being calm. "You called the police, right? What did they say?"

"Yusef's now so scared he barely leaves the house."

"Please hire a bodyguard. Don't put yourself in danger." Although she felt anger welling up, she kept her voice under control. "It sounds as if you *want* to be a martyr—a martyr without a cause. You do know the Torah condemns suicide?"

"I know I'm being irrational," he said. "That's how one achieves redemption, makes up for mistakes."

"By being irrational?"

"I've made my decision."

"Okay, so the next few days are crucial," she said. "You *will* hire a bodyguard?"

"I guess I should." He wrote Yusef's phone number and address on a piece of paper and handed it to her. "You might want to start by asking him who he told about the scrolls and what he said. He was too embarrassed or scared to tell me."

From behind the curtains, he pulled out a Safeway shopping bag—paper *and* plastic—and handed it to her. Dahlia looked under some cello-wrapped salad greens and saw well over a dozen neat fat stacks of hundred-dollar bills.

"If you end up not using this, give it to a charity that's fighting global warming."

"That's a lot of salad."

She wondered what she'd gotten herself into. While she still wasn't 100% sure that Daniel's situation was as serious as he thought it was, that money was certainly serious.

"I sold antiquities through backchannels." Dahlia thought she saw him blush but in the dim light it was hard to know. "If something happens to me before I take the scrolls to Ben-Ellisar, do whatever is necessary to get them to him, bring the truth to light, and make sure my killer and whoever hired him are brought to justice. Evil must be punished."

Yes! Here we go, like bats into hell!

Dahlia grimaced. Last thing she needed now was to hear that voice in her head.

"Ariella just spoke to you?" Daniel asked, his voice soft and empathetic.

Dahlia nodded. Ariella was the name by which she referred to the primary voice of her auditory hallucinations. Prior to naming the voice, at Daniel's suggestion, she'd thought it came from God and felt compelled to follow its directions, even when she knew the result would be disastrous. Now, she could resist it—except when she couldn't.

This'll be fun! You'll have my full support.

"Like how a noose supports a hanged man," Dahlia said.

Daniel tilted his head.

"Sorry," she said. "I meant to say that to Ariella, in my head."

She must've been more discombobulated than she'd thought.

Ariella laughed. *Life's hilarious to those of us who actually think.*

"But tragic to those of us who feel," Dahlia said in her head.

"If I don't get the chance to tell you where I've hidden the scrolls, get in touch with my sister, Suzie," Daniel said. " She'll know."

He took back the note on which he'd written Yusef's phone number and address, added Suzie's contact information, and handed it back to Dahlia.

"I'm still not sure I'm someone you want to rely on."

"You'll grow into the task. Your problem has been that you haven't had anything you cared about enough to truly motivate you."

"My problem is that I'm crazy."

He rested his hands on her shoulders, and she felt imbued with strength.

"I've no one else," he said. "But if I had a thousand candidates, you'd be the one I'd choose."

I know you feel like a single snowflake drifting toward a fire, but with me behind you, you'll be a blizzard.

Dahlia's experience with Ariella had been a mixed bag at best. But the combination of Ariella's encouragement and Daniel's confidence in her had made Dahlia feel like Alice just after eating a cake that made her grow several times her normal size.

"I'll do my best." Fist over her pounding heart. "*Nadar a neder,* I swear before God."

"I knew I could count on you."

Nobody else had, but if it came down to it she'd try.

She'd been yearning for something worth living for. Something worth dying for would do in a pinch.

Dahlia threw her quilt aside; to her astonishment, it wasn't yet nine a.m.

While she still didn't know what to make of her visit with Daniel the day before yesterday, the excitement of having a worthy task, even a nascent one unlikely to actually come into being, had woken her three hours earlier than usual. She bounded out of bed and even did without her customary hour-plus deliberation over whether to shower before or after breakfast.

She'd called Daniel twice yesterday, got only voicemail, then watched the news and checked the Internet. If something had happened to him, it hadn't made the news. Sure she was getting worked up over nothing, she nonetheless decided to again check the news sources and go to his place if there was nothing. At least she could help him with the preparations for his trip to Israel, take him to lunch, and nag him until he hired a bodyguard.

She turned on the TV, catching the end of international news. A pod of commercials, the weather, and more ads followed.

She paced the perimeter of her imitation Persian rug. Seeing movement out of the corner of her eye, she spun to face the intruder. Just her image in the mirror, but that morning at least, she liked what she saw. 5' 9", lithe, athletic, with long jet black hair and gold-flecked yellow-brown eyes—striking enough to cause men to lose the ability to think clearly in her presence. Unless they lacked that ability to start with, and her presence had nothing to do with it.

The anchorpeople reappeared, leaning forward, hands on their desks as if ready to pounce on their unsuspecting viewers. The camera zoomed in on a frowzy middle-aged woman who seemed to be giving some sort of news conference.

"David Shimek and Daniel Birnbach were both child molesters. I'm not sorry I shot them. The legal system failed to deal with them. I succeeded."

"What?" Dahlia said out loud—she must not have heard correctly.

But she had.

"You bitch!" She threw a slipper at the TV. "Daniel isn't a child molester."

Then it registered. Daniel was dead. Tears spilled down her cheeks.

Yippee! We have a mission!

Ignoring Ariella, Dahlia cried her heart out.

II

Le Petit Mort

MARC BLOCH TAPED shut the last of the cartons. Although the ceiling fan was going at full speed and he was only wearing a bathing suit, sweat slid down his chin and nose and plopped onto the corrugated cardboard. For the past two months, since the doctor ruled out further surgery for Lisa and pronounced another round of chemo and radiation a "hail Mary," pain had lodged behind his eyes, as if a rusty nail were scraping across his optic nerve. When busy he could ignore it, sort of, but now, with no more packing to distract him, the pain was—

"Daddy?"

Back from the walk she took to say goodbye to the ocean, Sophia shuffled in. She hadn't hosed off her feet and had left the screen door open, but Marc suppressed his Lisa-trained reaction to chastise her. So what if she got sand on the floor and a swarm of mosquitoes took up residence? At least something would enjoy the house before it was ripped down.

"I'm sad, Daddy."

"Me, too, honey."

He and Lisa had struggled over how honest they should be with their ten-year-old, but events had resolved that issue. The truth was too dreadful to hide. Her mother would soon die, and they could no longer afford the luxury of a beach house. Not that the two were comparable, but the latter was at least comprehensible. Lisa couldn't die. God—the One in whom he didn't believe—would intervene. Her cancer would go into spontaneous remission, and before he knew it, she'd be back to her beautiful, brilliant, vivacious self, better even, having grown emotionally and philosophically from her brush with death.

"This is our house." Sophia's voice was shrill. "We've been coming here since before I was even in Mommy's tummy."

"We still have our apartment in New York. That *is* where we live."

At least for now. The experimental procedures insurance declined to cover were horrendously expensive, and spending all his time with Lisa and Sophia had pulled the plug on Marc's already moribund law practice.

"I want Mommy—NOW!"

"You know she's in the hospital, trying to get better."

"She's not trying hard enough." Another petulant foot stomp, this time accompanied by a provocative grinding of sand into the white linoleum.

Every time Marc heard this new angry tone of hers, he winced.

"Come on, Soph, you know how much she loves you, how much she wants to be with you."

"If she didn't get sick, we'd have our house." Her lip quivered. "And I'd have Mommy."

Tears ran down her cheek, but she didn't break into full cry. Marc sat, pulled her onto his lap and reminded himself that seeing him cry would unnerve her. Lisa had ordered him to *man up*, and she had enough problems without having to deal with insubordination.

"It's not fair!" she shouted.

"It's not fair!" he shouted back. Manning up didn't preclude solidarity.

"Mommy says I shouldn't hate God because there isn't one, but I hate him anyway."

Nothing he could say to that. This wasn't the time for his canned lecture on hate always being wrong, particularly as he felt the same anger his daughter did. Not knowing what else to do, he kissed her forehead. *When stumped, show her you love her*: one of Lisa's childcare maxims.

"But Mommy might not die, right?"

From the way her eyebrows lifted and knitted, Marc suspected she was testing his credibility. He sometimes felt it difficult to determine whether she was speaking as the precocious child, capable of processing adult concepts, or as the one whose emotional development was on a par with the average ten-year-old's. Not that Lisa ever seemed to have any such difficulty.

"She's very sick, but cancer is unpredictable. She *might* get better."

"Mommy says she won't."

"She's been wrong before."

"No she hasn't!"

Sophia froze for a second—wondering whether it was worth getting down from his lap to stomp her foot?—then nuzzled her head into his neck and began sobbing. He stroked her long curly Lisa-like blond hair and since she wasn't looking at him, allowed himself some quiet tears. Lisa had forbidden crying in Sophia's presence, but if she couldn't see it happening, it wasn't in her presence, was it? Losing their summer house felt like a little death. If he couldn't handle this, how was he going to deal with the big one? He'd have to, somehow, be strong for Sophia. And cancer *is* unpredictable, miracles have been known to happen, even at this late stage. But watching Lisa deteriorate had destroyed his faith. B.C. she'd been a trim, athletic one hundred twenty pounds. Sophia—now tipping the scales at seventy-four pounds—would soon pass her mother's current weight.

Lisa's atheism remained steadfast throughout her illness. According to her, and David Hume, miracles were *a transgression of a law of nature.* A philosophy professor, even on her deathbed, she'd been arguing—dare Marc say *proselytizing?*—for acceptance of reality and clear-eyed planning for the difficult future without her. She had a more willing acolyte in her adoring daughter than in her equally adoring husband, whose faith was so shattered that he didn't even believe in the lack of faith. If Lisa could convince a ten-year-old to accept her mother's death as a normal part of life, that would truly be a miracle. Marc had consulted two respected child psychologists and—although he'd chosen not to mention him to Lisa—the rabbi from the synagogue he'd grown up in, but all he'd taken away from the meetings was that while there was almost nothing harder for a child to deal with than the death of a parent. Time and paternal love would help. It must be nice to practice a profession where all you had to do was state the obvious.

The front door opened.

"Hello, hello," said the short, slight man, who was knocking on the open door. "Is this a good time?"

With his urbane French accent, tan suit, striped pastel shirt, blue paisley ascot, and snake-skin loafers he seemed out of place in this Fire Island community, where dressing up meant wearing a T-shirt and flip-flops with a bathing suit.

"Mortimer de Saint-Juste."

"We've been expecting you. Come on in," Marc said, even though the man had already crossed his threshold.

As the sale of his beach house had been handled entirely by de Saint-Juste's Wall Street law firm, Marc hadn't met him before. The buyer hadn't checked out the house, which he planned to tear down and replace with a multi-million-dollar mansion complete with lap pool and air-conditioning. Marc wondered why he was bothering to visit now.

Fancying himself an old-time Fire Islander, Marc, even when sweating like a pig, considered AC an offense against mother nature and the ocean breezes she provided. Swimming pools were not only unnecessary, with the ocean and the bay both so close by, but worse, an excuse to close oneself off from the close-knit beach community. Although modest by Fire Island standards, the house sat on almost half an acre, a large plot for Seaview. Even in this depressed market, the sale brought in an astounding three-quarters of a million dollars, and de Saint-Juste's filed plans indicated that he'd put at least three million into building his beach mansion. Only someone with more money than sense would've sunk that kind of dough into a place on a barrier island that was only a few hundred yards wide and one hurricane away from oblivion. The Great Hurricane of 1938 cut a 4,000-yard-wide swath through the island, creating Moriches Inlet. These days, with global warming and increasingly violent storms, it was just a matter of time. But then what wasn't?

A few steps took the short-strided buyer through the kitchen and into the living room. He shook Marc's offered hand.

"Don't shake his hand!" Sophia said, her voice higher with each word until she was practically screaming at de Saint-Juste. "My daddy says you're going to tear down our house."

Marc feared she was going to kick him in the shin and wasn't happy with himself for wanting her to do just that.

De Saint-Juste bent so his face was level with hers.

"I'm going to build a nice big, *moderne* house, with a big-big pool, and you can come visit whenever you want."

"I don't want to visit *you*."

"Be nice," Marc said.

"No! Let *him* be nice and give us back our house." Sophia glared at de Saint-Juste. "You look like Mr. Burns."

"Well, I hope he's a nice man."

"He's mean. He owns nuclear power plants, has lots of big vicious dogs, and he kills people."

"Well, I'm very nice, and I work very hard to help the environment."

"He has the same hairstyle as you do, Daddy."

Both men smiled. Marc hadn't considered male-pattern baldness to be a hairstyle.

On this relatively high note, he stepped between his daughter and their visitor. The man's size, combined with his first name, brought to mind the French phrase for orgasm, *le petit mort*—literally a little death—and Marc was pretty sure he wasn't the first person to think that.

"Please, sit," he said. "I'm sorry we have nothing to offer except water, but we've got lots of that."

De Saint-Juste sat and crossed his legs, showing off bold-patterned socks.

"You're a lawyer, I understand. Once quite prominent."

"Sophia, please get our guest a glass of water," Marc said.

She glared at him. He glared back. She made her furious face but complied, putting on an imperious air as if further argument would've been beneath her.

"Davis & Stearling represents my U.S. interests."

"I know," Marc said. "They handled the closing."

"Just out of curiosity, what's your opinion of them?" De Saint-Juste's oh-so-casual tone suggested that he didn't expend precious words *just out of curiosity*, not that Marc could imagine any weighty reason for the question.

"They're the fourth or fifth largest firm in the country and the third most profitable, hauling in over three mil per partner. They must be doing something right."

After an enigmatic smile, de Saint-Juste said, "Sounds like you're not impressed with the quality of their work."

"Like any large firm, it's a collection of some fine lawyers, many mediocre ones, and some I wouldn't hire to clean my house."

"Just as well. You probably couldn't afford their rates." To show that his statement was an attempt at humor, he smiled, but it was the tight mirthless smile of a man who hadn't found anything amusing in a long time.

Marc shifted his weight from one foot to another. Wanting to cut the conversation short, he didn't sit, but his sixty-year-old knees made known their unhappiness with that arrangement. He wondered if it had been hubris to have a child at fifty. Lisa had been only thirty-eight when Sophia was born and now, barring a miracle, she wouldn't make it to forty-nine. He'd been a good father to Sophia, certainly he'd tried hard to be, but as a single parent...

Sophia handed Monsieur de Saint-Juste a glass of water.

"Thank you very much."

From the man's smile in response to her absurdly deep curtsey, Marc deduced that he'd missed the sarcasm.

"What kind of work do you do, Mortimer?"

De Saint-Juste's nostrils widened, and Marc realized he and his house's buyer weren't on a first-name basis—that smile had been a quite sufficient concession to American democracy, thank you.

"It's complicated," de Saint-Juste said.

Marc raised a hand: that's okay, better than okay. He didn't want to converse with this man. He wanted him out of his house—what used to be his house—and again wondered what why he'd come at all.

"Let me have your card," de Saint-Juste's too-casual-to-be-casual tone again. "I might be able to use you... for some of my smaller matters."

Marc suppressed his chagrin at the thought of being someone's cheap lawyer. Better to have *smaller matters* than none.

"I don't have one at hand." Back when he'd been building the firm that ultimately collapsed in scandal, he'd never gone anywhere without a business card, even keeping a few in a waterproof plastic bag in his swimsuit pocket. "But, Monsieur de Saint-Juste, I'll email you my contact information."

Marc felt odd so formally addressing a younger man who was visiting his house, but Monsieur graced him with a wispy smile, very *noblesse oblige.*

"We've got to make the four forty-five ferry." Marc looked at his watch. "The boxes won't be picked up till tomorrow, if that works for you?"

De Saint-Juste waved a seigniorial hand. "We don't begin demolition until next week."

"DEMOLITION?" Sophia yelled.

"Pack your backpack, Sophia, take one more look around the house with me to make sure we haven't forgotten anything, and I'll give you one final Fire Island tennis lesson. Or should I say lesson in humility?"

"You wish. I'm going to kick your very, very old butt."

"We'll see. I'm not going to go so easy on you this time."

"Yeah, right." Sophia grinned, then scowled at Monsieur, so he'd know he wouldn't be forgiven—not now, not ever.

III

A Circular Firing Squad

COVERING HER HEAD with a scarf, Dahlia said Kaddish for Daniel, her voice quivering but strong. Then, somewhat calmed, she willed herself to think clearly.

According to the Internet, David Shimek, LaPonte's first victim, was a recidivist child molester who'd gotten out of prison on a compassionate release and then miraculously recovered from his supposedly fatal illness. Certain that Daniel hadn't been a pedophile, Dahlia knew someone who wanted him dead had tricked LaPonte into killing him by feeding her false information. Dahlia had to find that person and bring him to justice. But how? The other prong of her quest, obtaining the scroll fragments, would be easier. Daniel had said he would tell his sister, Suzie, where they were.

She called Suzie, and in as pleasant a conversation as she could expect to have with a woman in mourning, told her about meeting with Daniel and promising him she'd see that justice was done. Dahlia didn't ask about the scrolls on the phone but instead suggested they get together for brunch. What with her grief and hosting the shiva, Suzie couldn't do it for two weeks, but they'd set a date.

Dahlia attended Daniel's funeral and made a shiva call. The room was crowded but not as much as it should've been—people willingly believed the worst about others, even, or perhaps particularly, their friends and relatives. Finally, she saw Suzie sitting on a folding chair and staring off into space as she responded in monosyllables to a pair of black-clad well-wishers trying to engage her in conversation. She waited until Suzie was alone, introduced herself, and said, "I'm terribly sorry for your loss. Daniel was one of the finest people I've ever met."

Enough with the platitudinal horseshit, Ariella said. *Ask about the scrolls and don't let her put you off with crapola about being in mourning.*

As shiva was neither the time nor the place, Dahlia left Suzie and drifted toward the door. The anxiety her insubordination spawned made her vision swim like dial-up video—or maybe that wasn't her anxiety but rather Ariella's retaliation. Dahlia started to leave without even saying goodbye, but before she was out the door an insurance agent and a stockbroker, who said they were Suzie's cousins, cornered her and without being asked to do so, handed her their business cards.

Whether real or not in the tangible world, the scroll fragments had taken on a virtual reality. A Christian fundamentalist group was offering two hundred thousand dollars for the scrolls on the Internet: "We have it on good authority that these scrolls definitively show that God hates Islam and commands us to do the same." Offering twice as much, a posting from unidentified Iranians said, "These so-called ancient scrolls provide unimpeachable evidence of a Zionist plot to deny the truth of the Koran. The Jews are eternal enemies of Islam and Allah, blessed be His name. When we obtain these scrolls, we shall display them at The National Museum of Iran in Teheran, so the whole world will know the truth. Death to Israel! Death to the Jews! Death to America!"

Dahlia kept Googling. A Sunni post offered three quarters of a million but predicted that the scrolls would never turn up, because "they're a vicious hoax planted by Iranian enemies of Allah, blessed be His name." A posting by the NYU Archaeology Department stated, "In the wake of the tragic death of our colleague, Joseph P. Shustak, Ph.D., we beg all parties to remain calm, wait until the Shustak Scrolls are located and verified, and then view them within the context of their time and place."

Ariella threw a hissy fit.

The Shustak Scrolls! That self-promoting jackass! Shustak had posted that note on the NYU Archeology Department Blog to take the credit for the scrolls. He got Daniel killed. Resurrect him and kill him again, this time slowly and painfully.

Dahlia agreed with the sentiment but dismissed Ariella's direction as impractical. If only she'd been able to slough off some of Ariella's past directions so easily.... Maybe she was learning how to cope better with her disability.

Don't count on that.

While Dahlia long ago had stopped thinking of Ariella as the voice of God, she had no doubt that the voice had a Jehovah-like capacity for disdain.

Hoping to persuade the prosecuting attorney to aggressively interrogate

LaPonte until she admitted why she'd really killed Daniel, Dahlia met with the Assistant District Attorney assigned to the LaPonte case and told her about meeting with Daniel. After listening impatiently, he said, "Our office greatly appreciates citizens' input, and I'll certainly bring our conversation to the attention of the District Attorney."

"And he'll do what with it?" Dahlia asked, feeling every bristle of the brush-off.

Dahlia agreed with Ariella that the prosecutor had the attention span of a gerbil with ADD. Finally, though, he agreed that "it might be interesting" if Dahlia could persuade Yusef to testify that his relationship with Daniel had been platonic.

Dahlia called Yusef, only to find his phone was out of service. She decided to go to his home, 17½ Weehawken Street. According to Google Maps, the street was in the West Village, a block from the Hudson and only a single block long. Paved with cobblestones and lined with early nineteenth century brownstones, the street had an old-timey feel. Dahlia had no trouble finding 17 and 19 and 18 across the way, but not 17½. With no people in sight, she rang the doorbells at 17, 18, and 19 and got no answer.

While most buildings on the block abutted each other, there was a space between 17 and 19, probably once a driveway but now largely overgrown. Arriving at a tiny weed-choked backyard behind 17, she saw an automobile covered by a tarp and an ivy-clad, windowless brick building—probably a small garage or a large tool shed. A garage door took up most of the front of the structure. An open skylight in the roof provided the only indication that it might've been habitable.

Knocking on the door and getting no response, she sat on a small RustOleum-patched wrought-iron bench, plotting her next move, or rather trying to. The electric current that had been animating her cut off, leaving her feeling like an abandoned doll formerly vivified by a child's love. The wind rippled a black plastic bag, but strangely it stayed put. The sky darkened. Pigeons took to the air. A sudden wind blew sheets of newsprint in ever-expanding circles until they soared above her like albino vultures. Leaves showed their silvery undersides. Eclipse-weird light descended, along with a silence alien to New York City. A lightning flash, a bench-shaking explosion of thunder, and Dahlia was drenched. She told herself to move under an overhang, but she couldn't seem to manage it. The rain stopped as suddenly as it had started. A rat emerged from the rippling bag and scampered into the privet hedges that surrounded the urban excuse for a backyard.

The roll-up garage-type door slid up a foot or so, and a pair of dark eyes peeked from underneath. It opened a little further, and Yusef's pretty head emerged, from between his ankles, as if he was practicing an obscure yoga pose.

"Who are you? What do you want?"

"Hi, Yusef. My name's Dahlia. I'm a friend of Daniel Birnbach."

He started to pull the door back down, but Dahlia dove forward, stuck her hands under it, and shoved it upward.

"Please," she said, voice soft and unthreatening, in contrast to her athletic, almost violent, movement. "I just want to talk."

With only a few inches separating him from Dahlia, who towered over him, he stepped aside to reveal a single room, paneled in dark wood. A chest of drawers, an antique pigeonhole desk with a computer but no chair, and a couch that probably folded out into a bed were the only furniture. A small refrigerator/freezer like students had in their dorm rooms and a two-burner stove occupied a corner. A curtain, to the right of the appliances, presumably sheltered a bathroom. Ancient-looking brass and glass oil lamps and menorahs shared wall-mounted shelves with reproductions of statues of David in various stages of nakedness by Michelangelo, Donatello, Bernini, and several Dahlia didn't recognize.

Yusef closed and locked the door—an older locking mechanism augmented by a shiny new-looking brass lock. Taking a damp towel from a pile on the floor, he handed it to her. After she dried herself as best she could, he put it back on the floor, taking pains to ensure that it covered the exact spot it had occupied.

"The damn skylight. I can't close it, and when the wind comes from the north…" He bent his head toward the steady drip onto the towels.

"Other than that, this is quite a cozy place you have."

"It's Daniel's. He'd bought it to use as a *very private* office, back when he taught at NYU."

If Daniel had had a trysting place, it wasn't her business and couldn't have been less relevant now.

Yusef flipped on a light. Red eyes and the tracks down his cheeks showed he'd been crying.

"The owner of number seventeen is retired and traveling around the world. No one knows about this place, particularly not the authorities, as Daniel never bothered to get a certificate of occupancy. I've *really* got to do something about that skylight, though. Someone skinny enough could…" He shivered, even though Dahlia, still damp, was the one who was cold. "They killed Daniel to suppress knowledge of the scrolls."

"Why would anyone want to—"

"I could be next." His hand shook so that Dahlia lit his cigarette for him. "I liked Daniel very much, but just so you know, we didn't have a physical relationship, not that I'd have minded, and I'm older than I look." With peach-fuzzed cheeks, he looked as if he'd yet to start shaving. "The police found my picture and address among Daniel's effects. LaPonte's lawyer asked me to testify. After that I tossed my phone into the river."

Dahlia tilted her head toward the couch. After his apologetic nod, she sat at one end. He took the other.

"A man paid me a visit, possibly the same one who threatened Daniel and persuaded that lunatic LaPonte to kill him. He wants the scrolls, doesn't seem to believe I don't know where they are."

"This man?"

"Tall, dark, and ugly. He had a reddish…*thing* on his cheek."

"A birthmark? Can you describe it?"

"I don't know, maybe it looked like three balls stacked on top of each other? I really didn't get a good look at it, might not even have been there. His appearance wasn't what I was thinking about."

He tilted his head, revealing a round burn on his neck that looked to have been caused by a cigarette.

"Ouch!" Dahlia said.

Yusef took another long drag and exhaled, decorously turning his head so none of the smoke reached Dahlia's face.

She said, "So, you think Daniel's death had something to do with the scrolls?"

"I told Ahmed that Daniel was planning to take them to Israel. A few days later, Daniel was dead." He covered his eyes. "This all has a bad feel, like a circular firing squad."

"Who's Ahmed?"

"An Armani-wearing club rat, grandson of one of the emirs who run the United Arab Emirates." He dropped his voice. "Rumor has it he was expelled from the place, a *really* juicy scandal, no one knows the details. Anyway, he's usually all cool, like he couldn't care less if you were there or not, but when I told him how the scrolls cursed the Arabs, he suddenly went all wide-eyed. It was like I was the sun in his solar system."

Dahlia leaned forward.

"According to Ahmed, the emir and his cohorts are all about maintaining the status quo, unrest being bad for business. He thought if he could persuade his father the scrolls might be dangerous, he'd want them suppressed, which Ahmed could use that to his advantage. He'd return home as a player, part of the emir's inner circle."

"You said *he thought*. What did he actually tell you?"

"Um…" He stared at his cigarette as if trying to read a message in the swirling smoke. "The conversation didn't follow a straight line, but at one point… I don't remember exactly what he said, but in light of the political situation over there…"

"Yusef, are you sure—"

"I'm very intuitive, and as I said, when I started to tell him about the scrolls, he got *really interested* and encouraged me to keep talking."

"Encouraged?" Dahlia asked.

"Usual way. Coke and meth." Pathetic attempt at a smile.

Blow the putz off, he's flakier than a breakfast cereal.

Although she knew she'd pay for it later, Dahlia ignored Ariella.

"You said something about the political situation?"

Yusef sighed. "The only thing I know about Middle Eastern politics is not to express my opinion when talking to people who have a personal interest, particularly if they're the ones who control the drug flow. But he was all about how to use the story of the scrolls to benefit himself and his family, tribe, whatever. It's like the Republicans and Democrats. You think any of them give a sparrow's fart about unemployment, the budget, or anything else beyond getting reelected?"

"They don't kill people."

"Ever hear about the wars in Iraq and Afghanistan?"

Yusef attempted a smoke ring but produced only an arthritic crescent.

"A few days later, the Internet traffic started, then that NYU blog. That really did it." Yusef gritted his teeth, pearly white despite his tobacco habit; his angelic appearance seemingly acted as a charm, rendering him impervious to the effects of his vices. Maybe he had a painting in an attic that showed him old, face cut with craters and channels. "Daniel did his best to stop this from blowing up. He told Shustak to keep the discovery quiet. He didn't. Daniel, Shustak, and I are the only ones who've actually seen the scrolls, and I'm the only one still alive. I'd like to keep it that way."

Dahlia decided it wasn't in her best interest to mention that she'd seen them, too. She quivered with excitement. Yusef seemed to confirm what she'd already known—that Daniel wasn't a pedophile. Daniel having been being murdered to suppress the scrolls *was* worth investigating.

Quiver away, my sweet; more people will die, but we're going to have such fun.

"Can you put me in touch with Ahmed?"

"He's gone back home and won't speak to anyone. I'd hoped I could persuade him to get this thug to back off."

Again looking as if he was about to cry, Yusef directed excessive attention to grinding out his butt in a coffee cup. Grief and guilt swam in his big dark eyes. Dahlia squeezed his hand, but she knew from experience that the only thing anyone can do for the bereaved is to listen without judgment and be willing to get unflinchingly close to suffering.

"I loved him, too," she said.

"But you didn't get him killed."

"Shustak's blog may have set it all in motion."

"The *Shustak Scrolls*. Did you see that?" Yusef screeched. "The self-promoting scumsucker!"

"Let me bring you to the police, then to LaPonte's lawyer."

He stroked his hairless chin.

"I guess I owe it to Daniel."

As it was late Friday afternoon and Yusef had weekend plans, so they made agreed that Dahlia would pick him up Monday morning.

Dahlia knocked on Yusef's door, got no answer and kept knocking to no effect.

She scraped her right thigh shimmying up a thick vine to look through the skylight. The drawers of his bureau were open and empty but for crinkled tissue paper lining. Like crime scene chalk body shapes, dust outlines showed where Donatello's statue of David and two menorahs had been when she was there on Friday.

Considering that Daniel had been murdered only a few weeks earlier, Dahlia's brunch with Suzie was remarkably pleasant—until dessert.

"Daniel told me you'd know where he hid the scrolls," Dahlia said over a shared crème brûlée

"All he told me was he'd found something on his recent trip to Israel that might turn out to be important." Suzie broke eye contact, her nostrils flared. Her smile didn't reach her eyes—and there'd been no reason for her to smile.

You see those facial clues? It wouldn't be clearer that she's lying if she hung a sign around her neck saying DO NOT BELIEVE THIS!

"Please, Suzie, we're on the same side here, tell me the truth," Dahlia said, fighting back the stress that was starting to singe her synapses.

"*What?*" No smile on Suzie's face now; she was angry.

"Please, Suzie, all I'm trying to do is help your brother."

Ariella was even angrier.

Gee, if I knew you'd be so polite to people who outright lie to you, maybe I wouldn't have bothered all these years to be truthful.

Suzie glared at Dahlia. She glared back.

Other diners spun around. One reared back, steak knife in hand, face neutral like that of a highly trained assassin.

Look out! He's about to throw that knife at Suzie to silence her before she can tell you where the scrolls are.

Dahlia jumped between Suzie and the assassin. Hands on Suzie's shoulders, she shoved her down and tipped the table over her to shield her from attack. The assailant and others began to gather.

"Suzie," Dahlia whispered as flatware hit the floor, "they have us surrounded, we don't have much time. Tell me where the scrolls are."

Suzie jumped to her feet, brushed the remains of their crème brûlée off her blouse, and shoved Dahlia away.

"You're crazy!"

That's the thanks you get for saving her life.

The maitre d' and customers closed in. Fear clutched Dahlia's heart. She was the intended victim, not Suzie. Suzie might even be one of *them*.

Dahlia bolted out, knocking down a waiter carrying a tray of smoked salmon and scalding herbal tea.

Out on the street, she was so mortified she could barely hail a cab. There'd been no assassin. Nobody was trying to kill anybody.

"You screwed up big time," she said to Ariella.

I told you to confront her at the shiva. You failed, so you had to be taught a lesson…. I the Lord your God am a jealous God, visiting the iniquity—

"Shut the hell up and stop playing God."

On the way home, she sorted through what happened. Dammit, she'd read Suzie's pre-hallucination facial cues correctly: she *had been* holding back about the scrolls.

The afternoon found Dahlia in tears. She called Suzie, and when she didn't pick up, left a voicemail: "I'm so terribly sorry about today." She paused, waiting for Ariella to tell her what else to say, then she repeated it into the phone—Ariella got her into this mess, she'd get her out of it. Maybe she'd even fulfill her obligation to Dahlia, but it was hard to know. Ariella prided herself on her unpredictability. "I've got some…well, mental problems. I imagined that one of the other diners… No, okay, right, no reason to get into that. Usually I'm able to keep myself under control—well, under *better* control. I've got this friend, Ariella, who looks out for me. No, never mind about Ariella. This whole… Daniel's murder, my struggle to make things right, my ineptness… Point is I don't handle stress well. No, the real point is…please forgive me. I want nothing more than to get justice for Daniel, find the scroll fragments, and have them authenticated, like I promised Daniel I would. Please call me."

Suzie didn't return her call, and Dahlia spent the next twenty-four hours in bed, sleeping and crying. Damn it, Ariella had made her sound even more crazy than she actually was.

"I should never have listened to you," she said to Ariella.

Oh yeah. Let's see how you do on your own. I forsake you.

"Thank God!"

You're welcome.

Over the course of the following day, Dahlia kept calling, leaving Suzie increasingly desperate—and possibly deranged—messages. Ariella's absence didn't make Dahlia any more sane or her voicemails any more coherent, just lonelier and more miserable. Two days later, Suzie disappeared, canceling her landline and mobile phone and leaving no forwarding address. Dahlia's subsequent frantic efforts to find her failed, but she realized that even if she were to track her down, she had about as much chance of reestablishing a rapport with Suzie as she did of unhatching a scrambled egg.

With nothing more she could do to find the scrolls, she had to concentrate on finding who tricked LaPonte into killing Daniel. The best place to start was to track down this thug who might or might not have had a birthmark on his cheek and if she couldn't do that, determine if there's anything to Yusef's story about this Ahmed and the emir. She knew just where to go for help with both: the Mossad, where she knew someone, via a friend of an acquaintance in Israel.

Let's call the thug the Snowman *in honor of the birthmark on his cheek.*

"Yusef admitted he didn't get a good look at it, said it might not even be there," she replied to Ariella.

Come on, the Snowman's just a nickname. Was Babe Ruth actually a babe? Was Old Hickory literally made of wood? Is Ozzy Osbourne the Prince of Darkness? Well, turns out he is, but that's another story. Point is you have to learn to be creative, to read between the lines.

"I wish I had an accurate description—"

Pouf! Wish granted. The Snowman really does have a three-ball port wine stain on his cheek and it looks just like a snowman.

"Wow, you've actually seen him?"

Of course not, if I had I wouldn't need to be creative, now would I?

"Wait, I thought you'd forsaken me."

Turns out you're too pathetic to forsake. I'd hate to have you out there continually fucking up without me.

"Yeah, I know how much you love to fuck–up *with* me."

Dahlia met with Ari Levi, an intelligence liaison to the Israeli U.N. delegation, and told him about her conversations with Daniel and Yusef.

"In light of Daniel's relationship with Yusef and his discharge from his teaching position at NYU for having an affair with a student," she said, "and with LaPonte already conducting her anti-child-molester campaign in his Queens neighborhood, it wouldn't take a genius to portray Daniel as a dangerous pervert and trick LaPonte into doing the deed."

Levi stroked a moustache.

That thing under his lip is so thin and dark it looks like a line of mascara, gives him a rodenty look.

"Maybe you ought to rethink your decision to unforsake me," Dahlia said.

"What?" Levi sounded pissed off.

Ariella laughed.

"Sorry, I was just talking to myself," Dahlia said. "Yusef told Ahmed that Daniel was just days away from taking the scrolls—scroll fragments, actually, they're just pieces fit together with large gaps between them—out of the country, the Snowman didn't have much time, and having murdered Shustak right after he published his blog about the scrolls, the Snowman undoubtedly feared doing anything that might raise questions that could lead to the scrolls and result in their being publicized. There's no better conversation stopper than accusing someone of being a child molester."

"Wouldn't it have been more efficient to torture Birnbach until he gave them up?" Levi asked.

Intelligence liaison? He's a stupidity liaison.

"He could've done away with him in an almost infinite number of ways, but that was how he chose to do it." Realizing she was speaking quickly, Dahlia slowed to normal speed. "I've told you my theory. Work with me, help get to the truth."

Levi raised his eyebrows.

Those eyebrows are so bushy they could provide a home for a family of rodents.

Taking a controlled leap of logic based on an intuitive assumption, Dahlia said, "Seems you're just embarrassed the Snowman isn't on any of your watch lists."

"Which would also be the case if he didn't exist," he said.

"You probably could find the name of the emir who's Ahmed's grandfather."

"I can't imagine it being in anybody's interest to have you, an Israeli citizen, running amok in the UAE. We may not have heard of this snowman, but we do have a file on *you*."

"Oh, that misunderstanding during my Mossad training." Dahlia tried to wave it away with a flick of her wrist. "Okay, I was mistaken in thinking the guy I shot was a double agent, but the bullet barely grazed him." At Ariella's prompting, she added, "Just my luck to pick the officer with the worst sense of humor in the place. That was reason enough to shoot the pompous jerk."

The look on Levi's face told her she shouldn't be listening to Ariella, who had a vested interest since, in retaliation for Dahlia's refusal to follow one of her dictates, Ariella had been the one who'd convinced Dahlia the guy was a double agent. Dahlia reminded herself that Ariella didn't exist, except as a voice generated by her own brain, but that only caused Ariella to giggle. *You know you don't believe that rational bullshit. Nothing exists except in one's own brain. Hell, you saw* The Matrix.

"Oh, but I do," Dahlia replied in her head, although she knew this wasn't the time to take her on.

Pain seared her nerve synapses, pounded her head, and expanded her guts until they felt as if they were about to explode.

You hurt, therefore I am.

Once able to move, Dahlia stood. "Well, Ari, no reason for me take up any more of your valuable time."

About as valuable as horseshit in a stable.

"Ever hear of Occam's Razor?" The creep's parting shot.

"Yeah, when you have two or more competing theories that make the same predictions, the simplest one is the better. When you hear hoofbeats, think horses, not zebras."

"Well?"

"Sometimes the hoofbeats actually do come from zebras," she said. "Particularly if you're on the Serengeti, metaphorically speaking."

"You're so committed to this theory of yours that you've stopped thinking clearly."

Her skin turned clammy and her stomach went sour. Maybe the agent had gotten the better of the argument, but whatever happens, and whatever stunts Ariella pulls, Dahlia won't be deterred from her mission.

Although certain Daniel hadn't been killed because of his sexual predilections, she was far from persuaded by the only alternative explanation she'd heard. In an effort to discover if there really was a basis for Yusef's theory, she researched the political situation in the United Arab Emirates. Finding nothing useful, she was becoming doubtful that his drug-infused run-in with the black sheep grandson of an emir had led to Daniel's murder, but she needed to know for sure one way or the other. Perhaps someone in the U.S. with Middle Eastern political connections could shed light on what was going on in the UAE and maybe even put her in touch with Ahmed.

The hours crawled by and her eyes went blurry. Then she came across an article in *Forbes* on someone with the unlikely name Mortimer de Saint-Juste that mentioned desalination projects he was building in Saudi Arabia and the United Arab Emirates. To have landed those huge contracts, he must have had connections at the highest level. Perhaps he was be the perfect person to verify the extent of the political infighting in the UAE. He might even have known Ahmed—after all, the UAE was a small country, there had to be a finite number of the emir's grandsons, even if, with their multiple wives, they did bred like rabbits. Did emirs still maintain harems?

Arrange to meet him and convince Ahmed to speak to you.

While Dahlia liked Ariella's suggestion, the article said he was fanatically private and focused on his work to the exclusion of all else. He was notorious for not returning telephone calls or emails. An angry T. Boone Pickens, who'd once tried to interest him in a wind-farm project, was quoted as saying, "It's easier to get an audience with the Pope than to get Monsieur de Saint-Juste to take a freaking phone call." She searched for a phone number or email address, found neither.

She didn't know how, but she knew she'd get to de Saint-Juste.

LaPonte was giving a news conference at the Best Western Plaza Hotel in Long Island City, her final one before the trial, which was scheduled to begin the following week.

Due to a subway snafu, Dahlia didn't arrive until midway through the event. She was distraught over being late, her skin tingled, and her hair chirped like a nest of hungry baby birds, but after her flip-out with Suzie she *had* to keep her crazies under control.

Let her have it!

"Why did you really kill Dr. Birnbach?" Dahlia yelled, then started to recede into the crowd. Damn Ariella.

You go, girl! You're on a roll.

"We both know he wasn't a pedophile!" She was walking right toward Daniel's murderer. "Admit it, you wanted to suppress the scrolls he found. Come on, admit it."

After a sharp little cough of disapproval, LaPonte pointed to a reporter wearing a plaid sport jacket and hand-painted tie. He lobbed her a softball question about the lasting harm pedophiles inflicted on their victims.

Someone bumped into Dahlia from behind.

"Stop this," he whispered, his voice seeming to come from in front of her. "I'd hate to see you do something that would get you sent back to Creedmoor Psychiatric Center."

"Who died and made you king?"

"Shustak and Birnbach, to name just two," he said. "Yusef told me all about you, before we mutually decided it was in his best interest to leave town."

He stepped forward, and Dahlia glimpsed a port wine birthmark on his cheek.

She gasped.

Before she had a chance to do anything, he disappeared in the crowd—literally. A minute later Dahlia saw someone that might've been him making a phone call. He flashed a ghostly smile and ducked behind a pillar. She ran to where she could see behind the obstruction, but no one was there.

One of the worst things about her illness was not knowing for sure whether what she saw and heard actually took place in the real world. Usually, she'd soon recognize her hallucinations for what they were, but occasionally, very occasionally, she couldn't be certain, and if she couldn't trust her own senses what could she trust?

Me, of course.

I trust you less than my congressman, whoever the hell that might be.

The conference concluded, and she attempted to speak to LaPonte, but security guards blocked her way, while LaPonte was whisked off like a celebrity.

When Dahlia reached the sidewalk outside the hotel, a burly policeman strode over to her.

"Let me see some ID, miss."

She showed him her passport.

"May I look into that bag, please?"

He pointed to the large over-the-shoulder leather handbag, whose makeshift false bottom contained the cash Daniel had given her—well over one thousand hundred-dollar bills.

"You don't have the right to just stop a citizen—"

Apparently having a decidedly different view of her rights, the cop's even burlier partner joined him.

"We have a report that you're carrying an unlicensed concealed weapon," the first cop said.

"Ridiculous."

But easily disproved. She held the bag open. A Beretta 92FS—an assassin's gun, similar to a gun she used to own but had misplaced around the time of her move to New York—was in full view. A cop made a give-it-to-me hand motion, and Dahlia handed him the gun.

Awfully nice gun to plant on someone. The Snowman's got more class than I gave him credit for.

An odd calm came over Dahlia. She intended to take advantage of the first opportunity that presented itself. Or to create one. She sensed Ariella departing to leave her to her own devices and uncharacteristically confident, Dahlia thought that a good thing.

"The ravens are raving!" she shouted.

The cops look confused.

"Caw! Caw! Caw!"

She flapped her arms furiously and jumped but didn't achieve take-off.

"Caw! Caw! Caw!"

A cop started to grab her. Eluding his grip, she tilted on her heels and twirled and wobbled like a bowling pin that wouldn't go down. Finally, she fell backwards, hitting the sidewalk hard, her head making a loud plonk. It hurt but was nothing compared to the agony Ariella from time to time inflicted on her when she wanted to make a point. From her stay at Creedmoor, Dahlia knew what a schizoid fit looked like. A crowd gathered, but this being Queens, it was a small crowd that showed no inclination to intervene. Once on her back, she repeatedly banged her head and feet on the concrete. Her eyes rolled back. Spittle drooled from the side of her mouth. One policeman called for an ambulance; then, seemingly content to wait until someone trained to deal with lunatics arrived, moved the crowd back until he'd cleared a space between the crowd and the street. Crouching, Dahlia scanned the road in front of the hotel but saw nothing useful. Then a pick-up truck came up the street, slowing as the traffic light turned yellow.

Snatching the gun from the cop's hand, she jumped onto the hood of a parked car. It provided all the spring she needed. Somersaulting, she landed on the bed of the moving truck.

"Stop!" one of the cops yelled.

Dahlia knocked her gun against the back window and shouted, "Go!"

Finding the firearm more persuasive than the policeman, the driver floored it through the light and took a left, burning rubber. Grinning, Dahlia peered over the edge of the truck bed.

I deserved to make the Israeli National Gymnastic Team, at least as an alternate, she told Ariella. And I would've if you hadn't persuaded me that the towel wrapped around the coach's neck was a burka and her fanny pack a suicide bomb.

She sensed Ariella's shrug.

At a stop sign, the vehicle slowed but didn't stop. Dahlia dove out, landing on a large pile of black garbage bags, and origamied herself into them.

The cops were prowling; she needed to lie still.

Her mood crashed. She was still an unredeemed fuck-up. She'd gotten nowhere with the D.A., the Mossad agent had made more sense than she did, her brunch with Suzie ended with a full-fledged attack of the crazies, she'd come off as a lunatic when she'd confronted LaPonte, and now she was wanted by the police for possession of an unlicensed firearm and resisting arrest. Worse, her nutso act just now, combined with her history, could land her back in Creedmoor. She felt like crying but didn't see the point. She'd promised Daniel. She was going to prove to herself that she could succeed and do something worthy of her dad's outsized pride. But a fuck-up couldn't do any of that. Never knowing when her crazies were going to sabotage her, she couldn't trust herself. And how could anyone trust *her* when she couldn't even trust herself?

The two people she'd truly trusted, Daniel and her father, were dead, and when she trusted Ariella, she often got into trouble. Lots of people in this world were alone, but at least they had got themselves to rely on.

She took a deep breath, then reminded herself that she could can rely on herself some of the time and perhaps, with added mental discipline, she could extend the duration and increase the frequency of those times. That went for Ariella, too. Didn't she sense, on some level, when Ariella was full of it or just toying with her? And Daniel had been right, she *is* resourceful. She'll just have to go with what she had.

What she *won't* do is give up.

IV

Arbeit Macht Frei

WHILE WALKING SOPHIA to school, Marc broke the long sad silence.

"See the red at the end of that branch?" He pointed toward the park. "The leaves are already starting to change."

"Is Mommy going to die today?"

"No."

"Tomorrow?"

"I don't think so." His throat constricted.

"Are you going to work?"

He sighed.

"All my friends' daddies work."

"So?" Their wives weren't dying.

Throughout July and August, Marc had maintained a flickering hope for a miracle, but now he knew Lisa was beyond the reach even of the miraculous.

"Mommy says that when she dies I'm going to want you there all the time, but that it's better for all of us if you work and make money so we can afford to live like we do."

If he could've somehow applied Lisa's uncompromising, hard-eyed attitude to the practice of law, he would have had all the clients he could handle. If only that had been what he wanted. Even before Lisa had gotten sick he'd started to hate fighting with people—not only adversaries but also stubborn, self-righteous clients and stupid, lazy judges. His practice had become a war and he a conscientious objector. If these feelings had arisen from newly embraced ethical principles, that would've been fine, but it had seemed to him that the root cause had been a precipitous drop in his testosterone level combined with an acute case of the I-don't-give-a-shits.

30

They reached the steps of the Ethical Culture School. He used to take Sophia up to her classroom, but now that she was a fourth grader they said their goodbyes on the sidewalk.

"Big hug," he said.

The hug made him feel better—for now.

"Have fun in school, honey."

"Have fun at work."

Her snotty tone reminded him of Lisa, back when she'd been healthy. Actually, his wife had lost none of her snottiness, and he'd come to relish it, like everything else about her.

He watched Sophia drag herself up the stairs. But then her friend, Talia, shouted hello. Sophia turned, half smiled, straightened, and after a second's hesitation, shouted an even louder hello back. She'd be okay, at least for that day, assuming Lisa was alive when she got home.

For exercise he speed-walked through Central Park on the way to the hospital on the far east side of Manhattan. He used to workout every day, competitive tennis alternating with swimming and weight training. On his fortieth birthday, back when he'd still had testosterone to spare, he'd begun an insane regimen and entered the Golden Gloves on a dare from his then best friend and partner, Peter Nichols. He scored a knockout and a TKO, against opponents half his age, before getting knocked senseless by someone who actually knew how to box. Marc missed the exercise and even more the bloodlust. He missed a lot of things.

Picking up his pace, he pushed himself to the point of pain and held it there, passing all the walkers and many joggers. He arrived at the hospital gross and sweaty, but Lisa had bigger worries. Not wanting to break stride, he raced across Fifth Avenue against the light, dodging speeding taxis. *That was stupid. For all intents and purposes, I'm the sole parent of a ten-year-old. But it was the only fun thing I've done in months.*

Bald, shrunken, and attached to tubes, his once-beautiful wife now resembled an extraterrestrial. He sat on the corner of her bed, listening to her breathe. After a while, she opened her eyes, still so wide and blue.

"What are you doing here?" Hostile tone, possibly the result of a morphine-induced nightmare but probably not.

"Visiting, hanging out."

"You should be at work."

"Coincidentally, I just had that very conversation with your daughter." He smiled—for less than a second. "I want to be here with you."

"Marc, man up, I'm a lost cause." Her voice was a trembling, breathy whisper. "You need to work. That's who you are."

Who I was.

"I brought a book." He showed it to her. "You like when I read to you."

"*The Bad Samaritan*, good title."

Pleased to be off the work topic, he opened the book.

"We need to talk," she said. "I want Soph to stay in our apartment and continue going to Ethical Culture. As little disruption as possible, okay?"

"Okay."

This wasn't the first time they'd had this conversation or some version of it. He considered suggesting that for variety, he take her side of it and she take his.

"Pretty much everything we cleared on the sale of the beach house went to paying medical bills." She frowned, unnecessarily reminding Marc that she'd refused experimental treatments insurance didn't cover. "Where will you get the money to pay co-op maintenance, our mortgage, and Sophia's tuition, let alone inconsequential fripperies like food and clothing?"

Fripperies. He smiled.

"I'm sure the school will work with us," he said.

She spit a bloody swirl into a plastic glass.

"You made almost a half mil a year for more than a decade—even while letting Peter take out twice that amount." Guttural sound indicating she was going to carry her hatred of Marc's ex-partner and ex-best friend to the grave. "My point is that in those days you were proud of yourself, confident, and happy. I can't imagine your being happy on the dole."

"Financial aid is hardly the dole."

This conversation would've been a hell of a lot easier if she hadn't known him so well. Financial aid, like food stamps, was great—for other people.

"You need to work," Lisa said, gently. "It's not just the money. Soph needs a strong role model, not a defeated sad sack."

"I'm hardly that."

"You keep up a good front, but your business difficulties and the alienation they engendered have taken a toll."

"That's the least of it." He rested a hand on her bony arm.

"I'm dying, get used to it. To repeat, Soph needs a strong, confident role model. Children are perceptive, particularly ours. You can't fake your way through it." Her voice sounded scratchy.

Marc filled a clean glass halfway with water and handed it to her. She tried to grasp it, but her hand shook from the effort. He lifted her head and held the glass to her lips.

"Work will make you free," she said.

"*Arbeit Macht Frei?*" He set down the glass.

"My sense of humor gets sicker as I do, but my point is—"

"Even if I could drum up some business, who'd take care of Soph while I'm working?"

"Martha."

"Her ex-babysitter?"

"I rehired her."

From her deathbed? Of course.

"You can take Soph to school," she said, "and Martha will pick her up and be available to stay as long as you need if you have to work late or have a date."

"A date?" His voice trilled up. They hadn't had *this* conversation before.

He'd used to occasionally fantasize about being with other women, not that he'd ever considered cheating on Lisa. But since she'd gotten sick—actually since the troubles at the firm—he'd not had any such thoughts. His lack of libido bothered him but it was nowhere near the top of his list of concerns.

"My God, the look on your face." She chuckled and Marc delighted in the sound. "You'd think I suggested you bite the heads off baby mice. I'm not being a martyr. I want the best for you and Soph, and suppressing your libido won't get us there. Time Marches on."

"Sixty years have Marched over me, and I feel each day's bootprint. But back to Martha. If we can't afford co-op maintenance or tuition, how are we going to pay for a nanny?"

"That's why you need to work."

"We've been over this, Lisa." But not more than a couple of thousand times. "My old clients have moved on, and new ones want younger lawyers who aren't weighed down by reputational baggage. All people remember is that my firm imploded and Peter went to jail. Some undoubtedly think I skated away on some technicality."

"Having done nothing wrong isn't a technicality."

Grimacing, Lisa pressed a button on her morphine drip and closed her eyes. Her breathing became regular. Marc stroked her bald head.

She opened her eyes. "What about de Saint-Juste?"

"What about him?"

"Soph said he wanted to hire you."

She always tells Lisa everything. Lisa's the confidant and disciplinarian. I'm the playmate and tennis coach. What's Sophia going to do when she's gone?

"He politely asked for my card. He's too arrogant and self-important to use anyone but the largest firms, wouldn't even tell me what he did for a living."

She sighed. Whether in reaction to his negativity or her pain, he couldn't tell.

"What else did Sophia say about him?" he asked, trying to sail the conversation into more placid waters.

"Referred to him as a pea-brained cretin."

He smiled. "How did she come up with that?"

"From *The Office*. Should she be watching *The Office*?"

"I find it hard to say no to her these days." His face felt like it was in a sauna.

She said, "And in the general scheme of things, with her mother dying and all, who cares if she sees inappropriate crap?"

Lisa's illness had had little effect on their ongoing disagreement about Marc's *laissez faire* childrearing versus her more hands-on style.

She again pushed her morphine pump and closed her eyes. When she opened them several minutes later, they were glazed but hard. *If morphine thinks it's going to knock her out before she's ready, it'd be well-advised to think again.*

"Call him," she said.

"Who?"

"Marc, I don't have time for you to play stupid."

"Okay, fine, I'll do it." When he felt up to it.

He picked up the book and started reading aloud.

"I mean now." She fixed him with her still-lethal stare.

He took out his phone, a four-year old BlackBerry. Once a smartphone, it now deserved to be sitting back of the class, wearing a dunce cap.

"Put it on speaker," she said.

After a crisp salute, he found de Saint-Juste on his contact list—he'd given Marc his number when he'd told him he would be coming to Fire Island—and made the call.

Dispensing with the conventional hello, de Saint-Juste said, "Mr. Bloch, if you have any issues with the sale, talk to my lawyers."

"I'm calling to follow up. You said you might have some legal work for—"

"You seem like a nice guy."

"Thanks."

"I've no use for a nice litigator. I'm looking for a tough son of a bitch."

"Blow it out your ass." Marc disconnected.

"That went well," Lisa said.

"See, I still have the magic touch."

"It's a pity I'm going to miss my funeral, by just a couple days, too."

His phone rang.

"What do you want?" Marc's turn to dispense with the conventional hello.

"You have a problem suing a large law firm?"

"I hate those pricks. They overcharge for inferior work."

"When can you be here?"

"I'll need to check my calendar, but I think I'm pretty free toward the end of the week. What works for you?"

"Ten minutes."

Marc looked over to Lisa, but de Saint-Juste had already hung up.

"Go," she said. "I need to rest. Sophia has tennis after school, and I promise not to die till you get back."

"And if you break your promise?"

She shrugged, grimaced from the effort, then grinned.

"Sue my estate."

After a uniformed security guard checked Marc's picture ID against a database and had him walk through a full-body scanner, Marc took an express elevator directly to the penthouse suite of 376 Park Avenue. The elevator opened onto a mahogany-paneled, marble-floored reception area lined with fine art. Seeing no receptionist, he faced a locked door resembling the gilded brass entrance to the Florentine *Duomo*. He rang the doorbell, then attempted to make himself comfortable on a black leather couch designed for someone twice his size.

After a wait of several minutes, a young man in a fitted Italian suit took him through the ceremonial entranceway and down a hallway lined with cubicles buzzing with activity. Then he led Marc through two sets of key-card-operated thick (no doubt bulletproof) sliding glass doors and into a huge L-shaped room with floor-to-ceiling windows on two sides. De Saint-Juste was sitting at an antique baroque desk, well suited to his diminutive frame. Not looking up from his paperwork, he pointed to a chair. Marc sat. The receptionperson bowed at the waist and exited, walking backward.

Framed photographs of a large construction site adorned the walls. The long wing of the office contained a series of plush couches roomy enough to accommodate several dozen people. By each couch was a silver-and-brass-inlaid table supporting a crystal hookah with multiple nozzles. The short wing featured a massive, ornate pool table, a collection of antique Arab scimitars, and what really caught Marc's attention, an elaborate set of armor with a coat of arms on the shield and a ragged hole in the chest plate.

"Worn at Agincourt by Sieur Guillaume de Saveuse, a distant relative. I display it to remind me of my fallibility." De Saint-Juste handed Marc a summons and complaint. "Read this."

While he did, de Saint-Juste turned his attention back to his work.

"So, Davis & Stearling is suing you for just north of ten million in legal fees," Marc said.

"One of my businesses is involved with green forestry in Indonesia. We had a contract with BP that allowed them to explore for oil under our land, but if they caused any damage, they had to repair it or pay us what the land had cost us, at our option. They did fifty-eight million in damage to land for which we'd paid only eight hundred thousand."

While Marc understood that de Saint-Juste was speaking in his casual tone, it would've seemed intense coming from anyone else.

"I gather BP was willing to pay the eight hundred K," Marc said, "but you wanted the fifty-eight mil, litigation ensued, and Davis & Stearling represented you, charging extravagant fees."

De Saint-Juste subjected him to the full force of his attention and seemed to dominate the now puny room. Marc sensed the concentrated energy that had made him such a success.

"The entire case turned on the one sentence in the contract that gave us the option to repair or replace, and the testimony of a couple of experts about the cost of repair. How complicated is that?" While he spoke quietly, his voice conveyed a fury that seemed to suck all other energy from the room. "I had to settle for twenty-two million, due to D&S's foul-ups. I want to counterclaim against D&S for the full thirty-six-million shortfall."

"But still you used them for the purchase of the Fire Island house."

"That was before they sued me for non-payment of their excessive fees. I still hoped we were going to resolve the dispute."

"I'll need a substantial retainer against my time charges."

De Saint-Juste had already failed to pay one law firm, and Marc wasn't about to let that happen to him.

"How substantial?"

"Hundred thou." Marc's voice raised only half an octave.

Even at the top of his game, $50,000 had been the largest retainer he'd ever received, but he figured $100,000 was a good place to start the negotiation. He would've been delighted with $50,000 and would've taken $25,000.

De Saint-Juste was already writing a check. He handed it to Marc: $100,000.

"I'll have my people send the file to your office within the hour." He hit a buzzer. "Abdul will walk you out."

"What's all that?" Marc pointed to the photos on the wall.

"We're building the world's biggest desalination plant in Umm al-Quwwayn, one of the United Arab Emirates, and an only slightly smaller one in Saudi Arabia." De Saint-Juste made no effort to conceal his pride. "Very exciting projects, entirely solar powered, totally green."

Abdul, the man who'd led Marc in, reappeared, and de Saint-Juste redirected his attention to the work on his desk.

"How are you feeling?" Marc asked, after showing Lisa de Saint-Juste's retainer check.

"Proud of you," Lisa said with what sounded like her dying breath.

"'I have a special practice. I handle one client, like Tom Hagen in *The Godfather.*" Marc frowned. "If I devote myself totally to it, do you doubt that I can do a better job with Sophia than Martha?"

"You've been great."

"But?"

"You and Martha will be better than you alone. You're a tiger trying to be a kitten." Her face showed the sort of tension that when she was healthy would've presaged a wise or clever remark. "You need to pull yourself out of your funk and relearn how to enjoy life."

"With you…"

"The word is dying. And dutiful and terrific though you've been, we both know you've been in a state of… emotional suspended animation, and that started well before I got sick. It's not only for you. Soph needs you to reanimate yourself."

He held out some ice chips, and voila! His hand, complete with sound effects, was an airplane coming in for a landing. She smiled…maybe, it was hard to tell.

"It's just amazing how great you've been dealing with all of this, but are you really not afraid?" He was unable to fathom her bravery. "Not even a little?"

"Emotions follow from knowledge." She spoke slowly and haltingly. "Since I have no knowledge of death, I don't know to fear it."

"Thank you, Socrates." He again stroked her skeletal arm. "Now tell me how *you* feel."

"Proud of you for picking up on my reference."

He wrapped a washcloth around some ice chips, and once it was cold, wiped her brow.

"Everything hurts. I'm either in great pain, addled by morphine, or both. Sometimes I think it'd be a blessing to just go to sleep forever… but that passes too." She took a shallow breath, undoubtedly intended to be a deep one. "I'm determined that three decades of studying and teaching philosophy count for something."

"Do they?"

Her fingers caressed the button on the morphine pump but didn't press it.

"They count for *something*. Just not as much as I'd like."

He folded his hand around hers and together they pushed the button, just once. He would've liked to press it again. Instead he plumped up her pillow and pulled up the sheet so it covered her bony shoulders.

"Walking over here, I was wondering…have you had any thoughts, however fleeting, about God, or some sort of an afterlife?"

She closed her eyes, and he thought she might've nodded off. But her eyes opened.

"If I were going to be a hypocrite, I'd have become one when it would've done me some good."

He laughed. Vintage Lisa.

On the way to his office from the hospital the other day, he'd been tempted to go into Central Synagogue and sit for a while, maybe even pray or speak to a rabbi. He'd considered joining that synagogue a couple of years earlier when his professional life blew up, but turning to religion when things got bad had seemed insincere. Not the type to be a fair-weather friend, he wasn't going to be a foul-weather congregant. And he didn't join this time because abandoning his agnosticism now would've felt disrespectful of Lisa's obdurate atheism. At least she believed in something, even if it was nothing.

"Tell me about this new case," she said.

That wasn't what he felt like discussing in what was likely one of their last conversations, but if it was what she wanted to hear and if it would distract her from her pain, why not?

He told her, concluding with, "Something about de Saint-Juste doesn't feel quite right."

"Last couple of years you've managed to come up with a reason to turn down most of the business that came to you."

"What little that did."

"Potential clients sense you're not… passionate about your practice. No longer have the killer instinct."

"I guess they're not as dumb as they look."

"That has to change. Don't go kitten on me now. Sophia and I need you to be a tiger."

"Most wives would be delighted if their husbands wanted to devote their energies to being warm, loving husbands and fathers."

"Very few wives want to see their families poor. You'll be a better father if you conquer your perceived failure as a lawyer."

"I don't think of myself as…" No point in completing that sentence; he couldn't fool her.

Her incipient coughing fit never got going due to lack of energy. Marc wiped her cheek with the cool cloth.

"De Saint-Juste could be your way back… into the big time," she said. "He's into a lot of things, all… environmentally positive *and* immensely profitable. These… desalination projects of his are the third and sixth largest construction projects in the world."

"You know this how?"

"Put my research assistant on the case." She smiled as best she could. "Sophia's better with the computer than either of us."

"For a moment, he focused entirely on what we were discussing, and I literally felt his intensity," Marc said. "I never experienced anything quite like it. I think the reason he came to the beach house was to check me out. He was already considering hiring me for the case."

"You always feared and distrusted success."

"Not success, but the overweening ambition it requires. I've seen too often how ambition destroys the soul."

She groaned. Pain or his soul reference? Both probably.

"You okay?" He leaned forward.

"Peachy." She gave her morphine button several hits. "Go to work. I've had enough clear thinking for a while. Got a date in LaLa Land."

He kissed her forehead. "You were kidding before when you talked about my dating?"

"What about Sabrina Corbin?"

"Talia's mother?" Marc curled his lip.

He ran an affectionate hand over her scalp.

"I love you," he said.

"I love you, too." Her eyes got glassy and her lids fluttered.

"You really don't have to be so tough and brave about it all, you know."

"I do." She said it so solemnly that tears sprang to his eyes. He squeezed her hand.

"Twelve years ago, when you said those two words… God, was I happy."

Her lips came together and made a weak whispered smooch.

"We had a great run."

"My life with you has been a gift," he said. "I'd never have turned it down even if I'd known it would end a month after we married each other. You delight me, even as you're dying."

"Go. I need to sleep. We've still got a few more days left."

She pressed the button several more times.

He kissed her parted lips and felt a powerful desire to kneel at her bedside and pray—a half-remembered Hebrew incantation from his bar mitzvah training—if only he'd believed. Instead he sat, holding her hand and watching her breathe. He hated feeling so helpless, but not as acutely as when he'd thought that somehow there must've been something he could do.

Once he was sure she was going to sleep for several hours, he left for the office to review de Saint-Juste's file.

V

No More Ms. Nice Girl

SURROUNDED BY LUMPY plastic and the odor of rotting food, Dahlia sat up. She shoved away garbage bags. It was already night.

What now? She couldn't go to her apartment, the police might be watching—if only she hadn't shown them her passport. The hell with that apartment; the hell with her old life. She had a quest, and more to the immediate point, over a thousand hundred-dollar bills and an assassin's gun. All she needed was a plan. And maybe a slice or two of pizza.

Hoping for an epiphany about what to do next, she walked. Nothing came, so she continued walking. Where was Ariella now that she could be useful? Epiphanies were one of her subspecialties, one of her few useful ones.

Feet hurting, Dahlia practically tumbled into the subway at Courthouse Square. She took the 7 Train toward Manhattan, her face buried in a copy of the *Daily News*. At the end of the line, Times Square, she changed to the downtown 1 train, exiting at Christopher Street. A block west, Ariella—where the hell had she been?—told her to turn around and go into the hair salon she'd just passed.

"Cut it short. Dye it red," Dahlia said to the beautician. "Make it spiky."

Looking into the mirror after the beautician had worked her magic, Dahlia barely recognized herself. Her gold-flecked yellow-brown eyes, however, were a giveaway. She bought green contacts.

Looking good.

"If it's good to look demonic and cat-like."

Continuing west, she scarfed down a mushroom-and-pepperoni slice and had her right nostril pierced and a gold ring inserted. Ariella suggested that, just for the fun of it, she get two small tattoos: one on her right butt cheek of a snowman, his head being shattered by a speeding bullet, and one on her left, a Baretta with a thin curl of smoke wafting from its barrel. Turned out it hadn't been much fun, but getting it done sent a message to herself: No more Ms. Nice Girl. Tired, she was ready to go home.

She shimmied up a thick ivy vine, squeezed through the skylight, and dropped to the floor at 17 ½ Weehawken Street. Nothing had changed. Drawers still open, there was no sign that Yusef had returned. No yellow crime scene tape.

"Welcome home, Dahlia," she said then opened the couch and fell into a long dream-free sleep.

The next day she took it easy, storing up energy for the tasks ahead. She explored the neighborhood, purchased groceries and cleaning supplies, and rid her new home of dirt, cigarette stink, and Yusef's cooties. The following day she bought a short leather skirt, sexy shoes, underwear, and a half dozen blood-red T-shirts. In a hobby store, she picked up a cleaning kit; intended for electric trains, it would work fine on her Beretta. The car under the tarp turned out to be more rust than steel, so she had it towed; she might want to put a vehicle of her own under there, once she determined what would be the perfect quest-vehicle—the *Dahliamobile*—and found a way to acquire it for a steal. She spent the balance of the day doing gymnastic floor exercises. The next day she woke up early to devote herself to her quest.

A week later, she was well settled in but had made no progress on her quest. She'd gone to Daniel's house, only to find an X of yellow crime scene tape marking the door—Daniel had been shot on his front stoop. Returning at night with a flashlight, she looked into the windows. Seeing the lamp in pieces and the drawers turned upside down, she knew that if the scrolls had been in his house, they weren't any longer.

She'd made several efforts to speak to LaPonte, who still refused to see her. She'd hired a private investigator to find Suzie. Since she wouldn't give him her own contact information, he told her to check back with him in ten days.

Turning her attention back to arranging a meeting with de Saint Juste, she found a small piece in the *Wall Street Journal* online about a lawsuit against him. After hours of eye-straining trial and error and stumbling though myriad useless sites, she came upon the site for the New York State Unified Court System. There, she found the summons and complaint in that suit and on it a business address for him.

The security system at his building was unbreachable. So, armed with a general physical description, she spent two fruitless days waiting by the door to the main entrance. Moving over to an underground garage and looking fetching in her red-and-white-striped tights, leather mini-skirt, and rakishly tilted blue beret, she held a bag of baguettes exuding fresh bread smell. However, she succeeded only in almost getting run over by a speeding tinted-windowed Rolls. Noting the license plate, she checked it through the Department of Motor Vehicles, only to find it registered to a Luxemburg corporation. She retuned to searching the Internet and finding nothing.

Finally, pay dirt! A blog: "Dr. Birnbach wasn't a pedophile. LaPonte killed him to suppress the scrolls he found." But reading further, she saw the blogger had only been referencing her own question at LaPonte's news conference and further down in the posting had referred to Dahlia as "a lunatic, later discovered to be carrying a concealed pistol."

Her mood crashed.

News reports indicated that the LaPonte verdict should come down today, two months after Daniel's murder. Some sort of record? But with LaPonte having admitted to pulling the trigger and no facts in dispute, neither side had much work to do.

Dahlia turned on the TV news: black-and-white-keffiyeh-covered heads of celebrating feyedeen, bobbing to horns and makeshift drums. "Hezbollah rockets fell on Haifa for the third straight day, one scoring a direct hit on an old-age home, killing eleven." The newsreader sounded bored. "In its strongest statement yet on the current crisis, France banned the importation of Israeli oranges."

Europe needs oil more than it needs Jews.

"You needn't state the obvious, Ariella."

Where was the verdict? What the hell did they have to discuss? Their deliberations should've taken ten minutes, an hour, if the jurors wanted a leisurely lunch at the state's expense.

She couldn't stand this. She should have been in the courtroom. No, even if she could've wheedled herself into the media-circus of a trial, waiting for the jury to conclude their deliberations would've made her so angry that she might've done something she would've regretted. Certainly others would've regretted it, and with the police looking for her, drawing attention to herself wouldn't have been smart.

She preoccupied herself, during the gazillion ads, field-stripping, cleaning, oiling, and reassembling her Beretta 92FS by touch, while staring at the screen. That ate up one hundred and three seconds. Now what?

She got through a series of anodyne stories about minor celebrity missteps and the following commercial pod by doing several dozen Marine push-ups.

"Breaking news! We take you now to Janet Parker in front of the Queens County Courthouse."

Media trucks lined both sides of Sutphin Boulevard, jackals waiting for their prey to breathe its last. The crowd erupted in ecstatic cheers—or perhaps furious protests.

"It's bedlam here, absolute pandemonium!" the reporter shouted. "Everyone, the press included, has been cleared from the courtroom for security reasons, but we've just gotten word that the jury has come back with its verdict."

The massive front doors of the courthouse swung open. A scrum of people exited. The mob parted, Red Sea-style. The camera zoomed in on a frowzy middle-aged woman, her frizzy blond hair secured by a double strand of flowers and a large silver crucifix swinging from her neck. *If only it were a noose.* (Ariella's most bloodthirsty tone.) Perched on the shoulders of a large man with a backwoodsman's beard and close-cropped hair, LaPonte waved enthusiastically, her fingers forming two V-for-victory signs, Nixon-like. The cheers, which had begun to fade, reached a crescendo.

Dahlia gasped. Her hand covered her mouth.

The reporter shoved her way through the tightly packed mass. Her microphone joined many others, straining to capture Ms. LaPonte's words.

"I thank God and the members of the jury, not that I had the slightest doubt about either. And thank you all for your heartwarming support!" LaPonte shouted. "Today's verdict is far more than a victory for me. In a literal sense it is the shot-heard-'round-the-world in the war against pedophiles. As the Bible says, 'The wages of sin is death.'"

To Dahlia's amazement, the crowd responded with raised fists and cheers.

"Ms. LaPonte," a reporter asked, "your second victim, Daniel Birnbach—"

"I condemn your use of the word *victim.* The only victims here are the children all over the world who suffer the most unspeakable atrocities while the authorities look the other way."

"What do you make of the story on the Internet that you actually killed Dr. Birnbach because he found ancient scrolls on an archeological dig in Israel that curse the Arabs?"

"Oh, please, that crazy woman's tall tale is so preposterous even the D.A. didn't see fit to present it to the jury. Has anyone even seen these supposedly history-changing scrolls? I couldn't care less about moldy old scrolls. What I care deeply and passionately about is ridding the world of these predatory monsters."

Another frenzy of cheers erupted, and Dahlia's stomach shrunk to the size of a cherry pit.

When the crowd quieted, the reporter asked LaPonte, "Is it true you just signed a contract for a two-million-dollar book deal?"

She threw her arms out like an opera singer about to launch into an aria. "Who will rid me of this meddlesome liberal?"

Nothing moved for several seconds. Movement and noise returned after the reporter disappeared into the crowd as if sucked into a vortex. Following a concert of kicks and punches captured by the violence-loving camera, the police linked Plexiglas shields, formed a phalanx, and waded in.

"As you can see," a shaken Ms. Parker said, "this case has aroused intense feelings and will undoubtedly continue to do so for a long time to come."

"If you want to see some *really* intense feelings, just wait," Dahlia said.

Feeling the warmth of Ariella's grin, Dahlia aimed at LaPonte's forehead. She pulled the trigger on her newly cleaned Beretta, heard a satisfying metallic click, and smiled. She loaded the weapon. Next time she pulled that trigger, someone would get hurt.

Dahlia returned to the online court file in the de Saint-Juste lawsuit. It listed his attorney as Marc Bloch. Checking him out on the Internet, Dahlia learned from a *Times* obituary that his wife recently passed away. Once an eminent lawyer, with a large firm, he'd gotten on the wrong side of a scandal and was now a single practitioner. Scanning online the list of cases filed in the past six months, she noted that he'd only appeared in the one he was handling for de Saint-Juste.

Good. He was certainly not too busy to see her.

VI

Open Your Mind Too Much and Your Brains Will Fall Out

As THEY LEFT the cemetary, the fast gray sky combined with the freakish early October dusting of snow to paint everything Marc and Sophia saw black, white, or gray. All in all, they were handling Lisa's death as well as could be expected—very badly. Even thought they'd had plenty of time to prepare, plenty is never enough. Her death seemed as shocking and sudden as if she had died in a terrorist attack.

Sophia stared straight ahead, her face a mask of misery. Marc struggled to come up with something to make her feel better but couldn't think of anything fresher than the platitudes friends and relatives had subjected them to for the preceding two days.

Finally he said, "Everybody was very nice. They all loved Mommy very much."

"It was a funeral, Daddy. They always say nice things."

"How do you know that?"

"Watching *General Hospital* with Martha." She returned to staring, then suddenly the dam broke and she started to sob. Gasping for breath, like Lisa toward the end, she said, "My mommy's dead."

He hugged her to his chest, stroked her hair, and tried not to cry himself. He had cried enough in front of her.

Once her crying jag lost steam and he pulled himself together, he said, "When we get home let's order in pizza, drink lots of Coke, and watch a movie."

"No." She sniffled. "You have to go to work. You already took two days off."

"Not on… Not today."

Lisa had said that if it made him feel better, he could say *Kaddish* and even sit *shiva* for her. Although deeply ambivalent, he'd declined, but some additional ritual seemed in order. Having turned his back on his Jewish upbringing, his current yearning for a spiritual something felt hypocritical, opportunistic, or… well, just not right—but his unfulfilled yearnings felt worse.

"Yes, *today*. You promised Mommy. Anyway Martha and I already have plans. We're watching *High School Musical*. She thinks it'll cheer me up. Isn't that funny?"

He didn't know if she wanted him to respond or even how to respond.

"I'll never cheer up. Even when I'm an old maid, like in that card game we used to play when I was little."

"Sweetie, you're not going to be an old maid, and believe it or not, one day you'll be just as happy as you used to be."

He reminded himself of his pledge—only occasionally broken—to always be honest with his daughter. He'd never recover from Lisa's death, how would she?

"Yes, I will. I don't want to have children and die and leave them all alone."

This had already been their longest, most rational discussion since Lisa died. Was rationality simply another word for denial?

"You're not alone. Martha and I will take very good care of you, and you'll always have Mommy in your head and heart. When you remember all the stuff she told you and all the good times you had together, you'll feel good and be happy." *Yeah, and the lion will lie down with the lamb, and nation shall not lift up sword against nation, neither shall they learn war anymore.*

That started her crying again. She cuddled into him, sobbing even harder.

Finally she said, "That wasn't nice, Daddy. You changed the subject, just like you used to when Mommy talked to you about something you didn't want to talk about."

She interlocked her fingers, rested her hands on her lap, and shot him a dead ringer of Lisa's hard-eyed stare. That accomplished, her eyes started to swell with tears.

He hugged her, stroked her hair.

"Sophia, Mommy told us what she wanted, but she knew we couldn't… What she said was an *ideal*. Yes, I should go back to work, you should go to school, and everything should be as normal as possible, but there are limits. We're human."

"Mommy wasn't human. She was perfect."

"Yes, she was, and so are you."

"Liar."

He shook his head.

"Tell you what, I'll watch the movie with you and Martha tonight. I'll take you to school tomorrow, then I'll go to work."

"And Martha will pick me up after school, and you'll stay at work?"

"If that's what you want."

"It's what Mommy wants."

"Okay then."

"Mommy said we have to take care of each other and in ways you need my help almost as much as I need yours," she said in the sing-song tone she used for reading aloud.

"We're going to make it through this. Not only is that what Mommy wanted for us, but also, the living go on living. That's what we've been put on earth to do."

The living just go on living? There had to be some better way I could've expressed that. I wish I could've said Mommy's in heaven and one day we'll all be together there and happy. Have we been put here for any reason or does human existence owe itself entirely to the indifferent random interaction of molecules?

Staring out the window, Sophia was too miserable even to cry. He stared out the other window, feeling the same way.

On the way to school the next day, Sophia said, "Maybe you should make friends with Mr. de Saint-Juste."

He tilted his head quizzically.

"Then we can get invited to the house he's building on top of where our house was and burn it down while he sleeps."

She smiled. Joking? Or proud of her idea? Like everything else she did and said those days, he wondered if it was a healthy or unhealthy reaction to Lisa's death, or in this case, how unhealthy.

Marc and Sophia shared their goodbye hug, and he watched her March up the school steps, a good little soldier carrying out her duty on her mommy's orders. In spite of the gray sky, he put on sunglasses to hide the tears he'd been holding back and trudged toward work, another soldier under Lisa's posthumous command, just not as good a one as his little girl.

Marc subleased a small office in a slowly shrinking law firm. The firm provided receptionist services and the use of a conference room, as needed. He did his own typing and filing. When he arrived, the receptionist interrupted her nail filing to say, "Hi, Marc. So sorry for your loss. I…"

"Thank you."

"How are you doing?" She reflexively covered her mouth. "I guess that's a stupid question."

He headed down a bleak hallway lined with law books that, with the ascendancy of computerized research, had been relegated to the role of decor. His office barely fit a desk, a chair, a client chair, and a filing cabinet. The one window looked out on an airshaft. The only decorative features were the framed photographs of Lisa and Sophia. He found it comfortable enough, even if it was a huge comedown from his palatial office back when he and Peter had been flying high—literally true for Peter, whose four-figure-a-day cocaine habit, somehow hidden from Marc, had been a big factor in the firm's crash-landing. At least Marc still had his well worn ergonomic desk chair, a long-ago present from Lisa.

He hung his suit jacket on the back of the client chair and forced himself to begin his normal morning routine: clearing his spam file of accumulated Viagra and penis-enlargement ads, checking to see that it hadn't ensnared any business-related emails, reading the *Law Journal*, and organizing his day. He intended to draft a demand for the documents D&S must produce in discovery, including the personnel files of each of the 105 D&S employees who'd worked on the de Saint-Juste case. Surely some had been reprimanded, gotten poor annual reviews, or had no relevant experience, yet D&S had charged $200 an hour for entry-level paralegals and $600 for third-year lawyers.

How could Marc pretend this was just another day? He stared at the photo on his desk of Lisa, gorgeous in her wedding dress. In another one, she was standing knee-deep in water, looking as if she knew just how hot she looked in that black bikini, unaware that the humongous wave forming in the background was about to send her sprawling. In the photo next to it she struggled to her feet, still looking amazingly sexy with her hair plastered to her head and bikini top slightly askew. In a large photo on the wall, she was balancing two-year-old Sophia on her hip; both of them had the same knowing smiles on their beautiful faces.

Enough of that. He went to the small kitchen, on the far end of the offices, where he microwaved water for tea. As soon as he returned to his office, he actually started to work.

A few minutes later, the receptionist's voice coming over the intercom on his phone shattered his fragile concentration.

"There's a Dahlia Birn here to see you."

"Tell her to make an appointment. I'm up against a deadline to get these discovery demands out. If you feel it appropriate, tell her I've been out of work for the past three days."

"I did that." Usually unflappable, she sounded annoyed.

In his head, Lisa told him never to turn down a prospective client without at least hearing about the case. If this Dahlia person were to retain him, it would double the number of his active clients.

"Fine, tell her I'll be out in a couple minutes—"

Too late. A woman sashayed into his office and without being invited to do so, took a seat, crossing long coltish legs that were enhanced by a leather miniskirt and short, high-heeled cowboy boots. With her athletic body, sea-green eyes, and spiky coppery-red hair, most men would've found her alluring. She might even have been a full-fledged knockout in spite of, or even because of, her outdated punk look. Or maybe that look was already retro; Marc had no idea. To him, she was ill-mannered and intrusive.

"The photo on your site doesn't do you justice," she said. "With your fit, wiry frame, intense blue eyes, and unlined face, you could pass for two decades younger, three if you had more hair."

"If you can't be bothered to call and make an appointment," he said, "you could at least wait in the reception area until—"

"Gotten to be a big shot since you started representing the *Comte* de Saint-Juste." Barely perceptible accent—Israeli?

"I was a big shot before you were born."

If he'd used that tone with Sophia…okay, who knew what she'd do, since he'd never have spoken to her like that. He wouldn't have spoken that way to Ms. Birn if she'd had the common courtesy to wait. Other than a slight hint of a smile, she showed no reaction.

He said, "Over the years, I've found that two percent of my clients accounted for ninety-eight percent of my problems, so I've become picky about who I take on."

Her cat-like stretch strained the seams of her blood-red *Carpe Mañana* T-shirt and demonstrated that she wasn't wearing anything underneath it. *Maybe she thinks her physical gifts entitle her not to observe normal courtesies, but sometimes a stretch is just a stretch.*

"I'm sorry about barging in. I'm not usually rude, it's just… My legal problems—anyone would be overwrought." She stood. "I'd be glad to make an appointment for a more convenient time. Whatever works for you. I'll dress more appropriately, too. I just happen to be wardrobe-challenged these days."

"No, it's okay. You've already broken my concentration. Sit, tell me what you're here for." He looked at his watch. "You've got four minutes."

He cautioned himself to dial back the antagonistic attitude. Not everyone was like de Saint-Juste, looking for a lawyer who was an asshole. She sat, again crossing her legs. Although he felt no erotic twang, he recognized that there was a time when he would have. Had she appeared in his office pre-Lisa, he might even have been intrigued.

"That was some piece on you in the *New Yorker*."

She sat back, crossing her arms, as if wishing she'd worn a less revealing top. Her warm, ingenuous smile conveyed an innocent sincerity he hadn't noticed until now, or had she realized her sexy come-ons weren't working and changed her tack?

"'In a law firm that believes the object of life is to kill one's enemies and enslave their women and children, Marc Bloch, one of the foremost litigators in New York, combines preternatural viciousness with unearthly compassion to achieve alchemic results for his clients,'" she said, quoting from the article.

"Odd that you made the effort to memorize that." He was pleased that his tone didn't convey any hint of annoyance but then realized, somewhat to his surprise, he was no longer annoyed. "Anyway, that was a long time ago. Lots of polluted water under the bridge. Now, please tell me about your case."

Will I ever again feel anything, other than grief over Lisa and love for Sophia? Sure, it's normal to be devastated when your wife dies, but his dead-man-walking sensation started even before she got sick.

"I'm Dahlia Birn," she said.

"So the receptionist told me."

"Née Birnbach," she said, voice heavy with portent.

"I'm sorry, the name means nothing to me. Should it?"

"My father was Daniel Birnbach."

"The pedo... I mean the guy that lunatic..."—he snapped his fingers—"LaPonte killed?"

"He wasn't a pedophile." She sniffed, and a tear drifted down her cheek. "Sorry, I... you're a lawyer not a grief counselor. I shouldn't be emoting to you."

"No, I was insensitive. She killed your father and became a celebrity of sorts. You have every right to be furious, distraught... Whatever you're feeling is appropriate."

Seeing how vulnerable she really was, Marc concluded that her earlier sluttiness and bad manners had been defense mechanisms. If she had a reasonable case, he should take it. In fact, he should be selling himself to her.

He handed Dahlia a Kleenex. She nodded her thanks, dabbed her eyes, and blew her nose. He made eye contact and thought he saw a responsive glint in eyes so deep, damp, and green one could drown a puppy in them.

"I didn't follow the LaPonte trial really closely. I...had my own problems at the time."

"I heard. I'm terribly sorry about your wife." Furrows materialized in Dahlia's forehead, highlighting her empathy. She reached across his desk and placed her hand on his. Perhaps fearing that her kind gesture was inappropriate or could be subject to misinterpretation, she withdrew it a second later. "Please accept my condolences."

"Thank you, and… accept mine, sincere if belated."

They exchanged the forced smiles of the bereaved, each emitting a strangled sigh, and the smiles that followed were tight but genuine. When she again placed her hand on his, he responded with a sympathetic squeeze. She pulled back her hand, but a connection seemed to remain between them.

"You started to say something about the LaPonte trial?" she said.

"The prosecutor could've tried a better case." If he couldn't sell himself he could at least have shown that he was capable of coherent legal analysis. "Rather than establishing Daniel's innocence, he contended that permitting citizens to take the law into their own hands would lead to anarchy. Given the general disdain for government these days, some jurors probably thought anarchy would be an improvement."

Dahlia nodded.

"LaPonte never took the stand," he continued. "Instead, her lawyer called a series of psychiatrists, who testified about the catastrophic harm child molesters inflict and how LaPonte's background as an abused child psychologically justified her actions. According to them, she believed her victims were serial child rapists who'd never be brought to justice and that her pulling the trigger was a public service. The prosecutor didn't counter any of that, since at least the first of her victims seems to have been just what she thought he was."

"I'd like to sue LaPonte. I'm told that in civil cases there's a lower standard of proof than in criminal ones."

"With her book deal and her already parading around on talk shows like a diva, it's unlikely a jury will like her much." He stroked his chin; he'd done a sloppy job of shaving. "You might have a shot at a big recovery."

"This may sound hokey, but all I want is justice for my dad. I want to know the truth. Why did she really kill him? He wasn't a child molester. She literally got away with murder."

"Truth and justice are philosophical concepts. They rarely occur in the real world and are certainly beyond my power to deliver."

"Are you always so encouraging?"

"I try not to oversell." *But for chrissake, sell a little more than you are.* "Litigation is an expensive crap shoot. I want to make sure my clients go into it with their eyes wide open."

She opened her eyes so wide her eyeballs seemed about to pop from her skull. Not able to muster a laugh, although he thought Dahlia's expression was probably funny, he responded with what he hoped was a confident smile. He wished he and Sophia had spent at least another couple of quiet days together. Given the weight of his grief, he shouldn't have been at work.

"I'm prepared to pay you and take my chances," Dahlia said.

For his entire career, he'd handled business cases. Truth and justice, right and wrong had been merely concepts he'd employed to win a money judgment for his clients or to block his adversaries from winning such a judgment. His clients had believed they were on the side of God in a great moral crusade, as did their adversaries. But for him litigation was a game, one he played well—or at least he used to. Now, sitting across from a woman whose father's killer had gotten away with murder, he had a chance to make a real difference in her life.

"Are you curious how I happened to come to you?" she asked.

"Usually I ask that up front. I'm surprised I didn't."

"I saw a mention in the *Wall Street Journal* online edition about your case for Mortimer de Saint-Juste and was impressed that you aren't afraid to take on the legal establishment. I'm a great admirer of his. That he's made a fortune while leaving only the slightest carbon footprint is nothing short of miraculous. In fact, I'm glad you brought him up."

"I didn't."

"He's a hard man to get to see. You could do me a huge favor by putting me in touch with him. Long story, but through his business connections in the UAE, he might be able to help me to understand one aspect of my father's death."

"Sorry, I don't do that. I couldn't, even if I wanted to. I hardly know the man."

She took a deep soulful breath and looked around his room, almost as if purposely searching for something, until her glance settled on his tea mug. She giggled in a way that Marc found odd. It was as if someone else in the room had said something amusing to her.

"Would it be possible to have your secretary get me a cup of tea?" she asked.

"I'll get it for you," he said, standing.

When he returned, she accepted the steaming mug with a grateful smile.

"One final question," she said. "What do you charge?"

"I bill my time at six hundred an hour."

Reaching into a black shoulder bag, she pulled out a thick wad of hundred-dollar bills, peeled off ten of them and laid them on his desk.

"This should cover today, some research and strategizing on your part, and another meeting. I can come say a week from Wednesday, so we can discuss your ideas for going forward. Would nine a.m. work for you?"

"A thousand for what's got to be four hours of time?" He pushed the money back towards her.

"Your office is less than half the size of the one you had at your old firm—a photo accompanied the *New Yorker* article." Perhaps reading the annoyed expression on his face, she added, "I'm Israeli. If we're not pushy, they revoke our citizenship."

He smiled.

"All I ask is that as you look into my case you keep an open mind."

"I've found that if one opens one's mind too much, one's brains will fall out."

"I sense this is the start of a beautiful relationship," she said.

"Funny, I sense nothing but trouble."

But why? He'd felt the same way about de Saint-Juste, so the problem must be with him, not his two clients, who could hardly have been more different.

"I wouldn't be hiring you if you didn't."

An unaccustomed sensation in his cheeks made him realize he was grinning—for the first time in who knew how long. While too depressed to be excited about the case, at least he found it interesting. He, and Lisa, had been upset when LaPonte had gotten off, but if Dr. Birnbach hadn't even been a pedophile, the injustice was so glaring it *must* be set right. Being the father of a girl, how could he not have been moved by a daughter's quest to find the truth about her father's murder and obtain justice? Dahlia's case was exactly what he needed to distract him right now. Soon as she leaves, he'd call Lisa and… Oh. So much for grinning, so much for distraction and even being interested

Dahlia stood, and he saw her out.

He turned his attention to the document demand for de Saint-Juste, and once he completed that task, he dove head first into his research for Dahlia.

He felt weightless, as if he'd just sprung off a diving board. He started by skimming a piece in *The New York Times* about the verdict, a smile again on his face, but then he came to something that stopped him cold.

Daniel Birnbach had no children.

VII

Tea-ed Off

WAITING IN DE Saint-Juste's mahogany-paneled, marble-floored, fine-art-lined reception area, Dahlia had no regrets about how she'd treated Marc. She'd paid him a grand for a half-hour meeting and some research that shouldn't have taken him more than ten minutes. She had no intention of returning for her Wednesday appointment. What would've been the point? Not being related to Daniel, she had no case against LaPonte.

When Marc had refused to put her in touch with de Saint-Juste, he'd left her little choice. While he was getting her tea, she'd sent de Saint-Juste an email from Marc's computer: "You'd be doing me a big favor if you'd spare a few minutes to meet with my valued client and dear friend Dahlia Birn. She has a matter to discuss with you that you'll find intriguing. It concerns some ancient scrolls, a murder, and a potentially lucrative business matter." Dahlia had also found de Saint-Juste's business and mobile numbers on Marc's contact list. By the time he'd returned, she'd deleted the email from his Sent file and had been sitting where he'd left her. Late that afternoon she'd called de Saint-Juste, who'd agreed to see her.

A handsome young man, Arab by the look of him, introduced himself and led her to de Saint-Juste's office, which was large enough to have its own weather.

De Saint-Juste glanced up from his desk, and a cold front approached.

"Thank you for seeing me, Monsieur de Saint-Juste."

"Get to the point. I'm quite busy."

He hadn't looked at his assistant and barely looked at Dahlia's face, let alone her legs or chest. His stare, as icy and intense as any she'd ever experienced, froze her mind so she couldn't think. Ariella had fled to warmer climes, and no ploy occurred to Dahlia. No amount of sex appeal, at least no amount she could command, would divert him, as he was too focused to have been beguiled or manipulated. With the seconds ticking off, she had to employ the most desperate of all strategies—the truth. Well, the truth flavored with just a touch of flattery.

"I came to you because I admire your work for the environment and because you're the most knowledgeable and sophisticated person around when it comes to the political situation in the UAE."

He unfurled his right arm: get to the point.

She told him about her meetings with Daniel and Yusef. He listened respectfully, though he did respond to emails.

She concluded, "I promised Daniel that if anything happened to him I'd take the scroll fragments to Israel and obtain justice for him. Yusef said Ahmed's grandfather and his political allies would want the scrolls suppressed because they'd be concerned about their being used to upset the status quo."

"What's that to do with me?"

Storm clouds formed behind the cold front.

"I'd hoped you'd give me some insight into the political situation in the UAE."

Deep breath. If de Saint-Juste supported Yusef's theory, that would give her a segue to her primary request—that he put her in touch with Ahmed.

"I'm quite sure these scrolls Dr. Birnbach supposedly found would be of little interest to anyone over there." Disparaging Gallic snort. "The contents of the Hebrew bible don't provoke much excitement in the Persian Gulf. Perhaps you ought to be directing your attention to places like Jerusalem or Williamsburg, Brooklyn."

The storm surge caused by his snort had washed away much of her hope, but still she pressed on, "Seems someone was sufficiently interested to have Dr. Birnbach and Dr. Shustak killed because of them."

"So you say." His clipped French accent conveyed that not only did he not suffer fools, but also if he'd had his way, they'd be obliged to visit Madame Guillotine. "Even if they had some concern about these scrolls, no one with any political heft in the UAE would do anything so convoluted as hiring a hit-man to hoodwink a fanatical lunatic into killing someone, and they *certainly* wouldn't do anything even remotely like that on these shores. All factions are keen on enjoying cordial relations with the U.S., and that's not accomplished by killing Americans, particularly with the current hysteria about terrorists."

"But..." Dahlia couldn't come up with a meaningful response.

"Did I miss something, or is this whole theory of yours based on a single drug-addled conversation in some downtown nightclub?"

"Yusef said Ahmed is the grandson of one of the UAE emirs. Maybe you know him or maybe one of the emirs you know does?" Her heart pounded. She was speaking so quickly that her words ran together. Stay calm! "Since Ahmed is over here and relatively young, I'd think they'd ask you to check in on him from time to time."

He tented his fingers.

"As a matter of fact, he did look me up when he came to this country. He's a serious person, with degrees from Oxford and the London School of Economics, not one to involve himself in an intrigue with some simpering little…*tante.*"

Another Arctic stare practically frosted the windows. No need for air conditioning in here, even at the height of summer, but the heating bills must've been gargantuan.

"I promised Daniel," she said. "He was threatened and killed, and I'm certain it has to do with the scrolls. I'm not going to give up."

"No, I don't suppose you will." De Saint-Juste shook his head, conveying what little pity he could muster for someone so pathetic and misguided as the poor creature befouling his chair. "Tell you what, I'll call him and see what he has to say, but if he fails to corroborate this *theory* of yours, please, for your own sake, take your amateur detective work in another direction."

"Thank you, thank you so much."

Dahlia mustered sufficient self-restraint to avoid falling on her knees and kissing his ring.

He pushed a button on his phone, then directed someone to get Ahmed on the line. Making a quizzical face, Dahlia pointed to the door: would you like me to leave?

He shook his head and spoke into the telephone receiver for a few minutes in French-accented Arabic, so rapidly that Dahlia couldn't make out a word he said beyond *Yusef.* When he hung up, he stared at Dahlia until she began to feel herself shrink.

"Ahmed did meet this Yusef fellow at a club." De Saint-Juste scowled his disapproval of such frivolity. "And Yusef did prattle on about those scrolls, but even if he sometimes keeps questionable company, Ahmed has enough sense not to take drug-addled rants seriously." He clicked his tongue. "Seems his interest in this boy turned on something other than his political acumen."

"It would be *really* helpful if I could speak to him."

"He has no interest." De Saint-Juste's tone couldn't have been more preemptory. "Whatever motivated that LaPonte lunatic to do what she did, I assure you it had nothing to do with the UAE. I suspect it also had nothing to do with Dr. Birnbach's archeological exploits and perhaps more to do with his exploits with people like this Yusef."

He directed his attention back to his desk.

"Thank you for seeing me."

"I'm delighted to do a favor for Marc. In fact, as soon as you leave, I'll call and thank him for putting me in touch with such a delightful person."

Dahlia sucked in air. "You really don't have to do that."

"That's what I suspected." His smile was cold enough to slow global warming.

"If you knew, why—"

"While you looked rather fetching in your tights and beret, I feared the next step might be wrapping yourself in a Tricolor and having someone roll you out at my feet naked."

A playful grin briefly illuminated de Saint-Juste's face, and she was struck by how handsome he looked.

"Yes, persistence is one of my better qualities."

"Abdul will see you out."

With his gaze fixed on his desk, it was as if Dahlia no longer existed to him.

De Saint-Juste's explanation didn't quite ring true, neither did his talking to Ahmed in front of her. She was further than ever from understanding why Daniel had been murdered. Seeing a Starbucks across the street, she decided a shot of caffeine might help her think things through.

She glanced to her right. Her Frappuccino fell from her hand. Two tables away sat the Snowman, dark glasses, fedora pulled low on his forehead, trench coat collar turned up to hide his birthmark. Easing her chair back, she walked backwards out the door. Four stores down the street, she ducked into a doorway. Not seeing him, she doubled back to look through the Starbucks window. The man was still seated. Having removed his hat, glasses, and coat, and concentrating on an iPad, she saw he had no birthmark on his cheek and looked nothing like the tall, dark, and ugly adversary Yusef described or the man she saw at the news conference. He seemed not to have the slightest interest in her.

Moving on, Dahlia had some questions she'd like to ask LaPonte. La Ponte's other victim had a well-documented history of child abuse, including three separate convictions, but why had she chosen Daniel, who'd had no such history? There couldn't have been an acute shortage of real child molesters in Queens, and if there were, there was always Brooklyn. And Dahlia *needed* to see Suzie again. The woman's too-adamant denial, coupled with her facial cues that she'd been lying, indicated that Daniel really had told her where the scroll fragments were.

Maybe LaPonte—and Suzie if she ever located her—would agree to meet with an intermediary. If only she could find someone who radiated integrity, gravitas, and charm. Hmmm. Yes! She already had an appointment scheduled with just such a person. Sure, Marc Bloch would be put out over having been lied to, but she'd smooth that over. After all he had bigger problems in his life than that. She'd learned, though, that the bereaved need distraction—without her quest to obtain justice for Daniel and recover the scrolls, she'd still be in bed—and if Marc let her, she'd provide him with plenty of that.

She'd made a classic mistake with Monsieur Grande Fromage: she'd told the truth. Truth was the last refuge of the feebleminded. It could always be spun, improved upon, or ignored in favor of something more seductive. The meeting hadn't gone badly but could have gone even better. Had she played it exactly right, she could've made de Saint-Juste her ally and had him persuade Ahmed to talk to her. She wouldn't make the same mistake with Marc.

Good thinking—finally.

At least Ariella was on her side, but was that a good or a bad sign?

Unfurled naked from a Tricolor á la Cleopatra, why didn't I think of that?

VIII

The Moment of Untruth

"WHAT SORT OF game are you playing?" Marc asked Dahlia, before she even sat down.

He'd have canceled, if he had a way to contact her.

"The hiring of a lawyer for a big, high-profile case game." She sat.

"I did my research as you suggested and—"

"I do hope I got my money's worth." Hard-eyed stare, presumably intended to be comical.

"You lied to me. You're not Daniel Birnbach's daughter."

Her facial expression didn't change. "Don't lawyers always tell their clients that if they're not fully forthcoming it makes the lawyer's job harder, the fees higher, and the results worse?"

"Your point?"

"If I wasn't truthful, it's my problem, not yours."

She jerked her head back. An odd movement, Marc thought, but then he got it. She'd attempted a flirtatious hair flip, but spiky hair doesn't flip. She'd recently had long hair.

He glared at her. Her conservative gray wool suit had the crisp look of an outfit being worn for the first time. The top two buttons of her pale pink shirt were undone.

"I consider myself his *spiritual* daughter, okay? Just the same, LaPonte murdered him and I want to see justice done. In fact, my not being his blood relative demonstrates that my concern for justice isn't distorted by filial love."

"But it does mean that you didn't suffer legally cognizable damages. Without damages you don't have a case." He spoke slowly, articulating each syllable. "Presumably you understand the difference between a *spiritual* daughter and a blood relative."

"I thought it better to keep the story simple until you got into it."

"That's transparent bullshit."

"Fine, from here on in, there'll only be opaque bullshit."

He didn't react to her playful smile.

"Okay, the truth. I knew if I told you he wasn't my father you'd tell me I wasn't your client."

"So I'll say that now."

"Two years ago, my real father was killed by a Hamas car bomb while eating at a Tel Aviv shawarma stand."

Marc tilted his head to look at her from a different angle.

"I'm sorry," he said.

"He was an arms dealer and a con artist, but it seems he was just in the wrong place at the wrong time," she said. "Not that that has anything to do with anything, I just thought you should know."

Marc nodded.

"But enough about me, let's talk about you," she said. "What you need is a case you can sink your teeth into."

"It's hard to sink one's teeth into smoke, particularly if it's being blown up one's—"

"Okay, I don't have a valid lawsuit. I get that." Her erect posture and clear articulation called to mind a not especially talented actress delivering a soliloquy, but Marc sensed she was preternaturally talented. He just didn't know at what. "From what I can tell, a lawsuit is a giant machine one enters as a pig and leaves as a sausage. I want to keep as far from the legal system as possible."

Marc said, "Best way to do that is not to hire a lawyer."

"I'm not going to let LaPonte get away with murder." Feral stare.

"My wife used to say all prayers come down to 'Dear God, please make one plus one not equal two.' You're asking me to change the math. I can't do that. Slews of lawyers, investigators, reporters have all—"

"That they've trodden over a patch of ground means only that it's been packed down, not that the worms have been forced to the surface. That takes the work of someone with a special skill set. Sure, you're skeptical. You see the world through shit-colored glasses, but with your first-rate mind and my incurable optimism we'll make a great team."

He felt the pull of intrigue and smelled a whiff of danger. But having no objective reason to be intrigued or sense trouble, he dismissed both feelings as curious byproducts of his emotional devastation.

"I have a sick sense of humor that emerges at unfortunate times," she said.

My sense of humor gets sicker as I do. Marc struggled to focus on the here and now.

"I'm sorry we got off on the wrong foot—"

"We didn't *get off on the wrong foot!*" Realizing he was shouting, Marc dropped his voice to an angry whisper. "You deliberately lied to me!"

"I said I was sorry, but really..." Inscrutable smile. "A client lying to you. What a shock! Ever have one who didn't?"

Her abrupt change of tone practically gave Marc whiplash, but before he could react, she made a face that reminded him of Sophia when she tried to avoid the consequences of misbehavior. He smiled, in spite of himself. He had to determine what exactly her problem was and whether he could solve it for her, and he hadn't the slightest idea of either.

"As a matter of fact I did," he said.

"Was he terminally stupid?"

"Comatose, actually."

She laughed. He also liked people who laughed when he said something he thought was funny.

"Lying to you was childish and stupid." Penitent head droop. "Please, let's start fresh."

"As we've ruled out a lawsuit, what do you imagine I can do for you?"

He glanced at the pile of papers on his desk that he needed to massage into interrogatories. Not only did he have work to do, but also he had a grieving daughter to go home to. He permitted himself several seconds of staring at the photo of Sophia and Lisa on his wall, long enough for the rusty-nail-scraping-his-optic-nerve feeling to take over. He turned back to Dahlia. Yes, he needed the money and would've liked to have more than one client, but...

"She got away with murder," Dahlia said.

"Yes, and my wife and I were outraged by the verdict, but that case is over, and whatever issues you have with LaPonte can't be resolved in a court of law."

"Come on, Marc. Where's your fighting spirit? Did Clarence Darrow give up on Leopold and Loeb? Did Johnnie Cochran give up on O.J.? Did—?"

"I thought you objected to people getting away with murder." He took the top document from the pile of papers for the de Saint-Juste discovery demands and began reading. Without looking up, he said, "You can see yourself out."

For reasons he didn't understand, he didn't want her to leave, but he had to show her that he wouldn't put up with any more crap. Her lying meant he couldn't trust her, but so what? He'd learned long ago that it was generally a mistake to trust clients. But he had yet to see how he could render a service to Dahlia that would confer a benefit substantially greater to her than the cost of his fees. Maybe if they talked some more and she was straight with him...

She leaned forward, as if she wanted to touch him but knew it would have been inappropriately intimate and placed her palm on his desk. In the process she bared yet more cleavage.

"Marc, I'm willing to pay you to do something that might expose a great injustice. Maybe you'll end up spinning your wheels, but I'm sure you've done that before." She smiled. "I just realized something: you need me more than I need you. You're emotionally dead. Representing me will make you feel alive."

Normally Dahlia's presumptiveness would've pissed him off but...

"I'm sad and out of it, my wife just died, but don't flatter yourself. You're not as clever or alluring as you think you are."

"I think I am." Radiant smile. "After a long dead period, I'm now full of life, and I'm passionate about my quest. You need passion, and second-hand passion is probably all you can handle. Three years ago you were at the top of every list of the city's foremost litigators, now... Except for the incidental fact that you're still breathing, you predeceased Lisa."

He rolled his eyes.

"After obsessively observing my own psychological defects over many years," she said, "I've become pretty good at reading other people's, and I'm all too familiar with the feeling of being dead. From the day my dad died until the day I took up Daniel's cause, I could barely get out of bed in the afternoon, forget about the morning."

"I'm sorry to hear that, but—"

"I looked up your filed cases. You should be delighted I came to you to fill the void." Her slight smile reminded him of how he felt when, on cross-examination, he'd close the trap on a hostile witness, but here there had been no trap to close...unless he missed something. "Instead, you're—"

"Hung up on a couple of piddly little details like you lied to me and have no case?"

She looked directly into his eyes. For some reason, he shivered.

"At the worst time of my life," she said, "Daniel did a huge favor for me. I owe him my freedom, and in a very real sense, my life, as he got me out of a place where I wouldn't have lasted another six months."

Her quiet sincerity differed from the kind people faked, but Marc told himself that this might mean only that she faked sincerity very well.

"I visited him four days before he was murdered. He told me someone wanted him dead and it had nothing to do with his sexual predilections. I gave him my word that if anything were to happen to him, I'd bring his killers to justice, and I plan to do that or die trying."

"Maybe that's a bit over-dramatic."

"Other than my real father and my mother, who died years ago, no one has been more important in my life than him." Her jade eyes glowed with intensity. "I may not be the most truthful person, but I don't make promises lightly. When I make them, I keep them."

"Why did he think someone wanted him dead?"

She spoke non-stop for several minutes, telling him about her background, Daniel's scroll fragments, and her conversation with Yusef. When she finally paused, Marc's throat was dry just from listening to her. He offered to get them a bottle of water, and unlike when he'd fetched her tea, she accompanied him. As they walked down the hall, he again felt a physical connection to her. She was sick, struggling heroically with serious mental illness. Maybe helping her would help assuage his guilt over having been unable to do anything to save Lisa. While de Saint-Juste's case paid the rent and held a certain interest for him, it was orderly and boring. Chaotic and interesting—and somewhat dangerous since there was a murder involved, at least according to Dahlia— might make him feel alive. And yes, damn it, he'd felt dead since long before Lisa got cancer. He yearned to feel alive. Now that he was Sophia's only parent he *had to* feel alive. She deserved a better dad than the *defeated sad sack* Lisa had said he was. Moreover, LaPonte had gotten away with murder. But could he help Dahlia? He would…somehow.

"So, what's next? Do I have to walk barefoot over hot coals?" she asked on their return to his office. "It's a wonder any clients successfully run the gauntlet of your cautiousness."

So Lisa used to say.

"While I'd never file a baseless lawsuit, I guess you're not asking me to do that, and you'd hardly be the first client I've counseled on issues that had both legal and psychological components."

She jumped up and clapped childlike, or rather Sophia-like, back when she'd been happy.

"You'll have to sign a retainer letter, confirming that I advised you that the chances of my coming up with anything useful are slim."

She gave him her address so he could put it into the letter, then took a dog-eared copy of *One Flew Over the Cuckoo's Nest* from her bag and read while he revised his standard form retainer letter.

After reading it, she said, "You not only covered your ass, you encased it in a bulletproof shield."

"If a lawyer doesn't know how to protect himself, he can't be counted on to protect his clients."

Using a pen from a paper maché holder Sophia had made for him, Dahlia signed the letter, then placed a wad of hundred-dollar bills on his desk.

"Now, let's figure out how to find Suzie and get the scrolls from her," she said.

"I'd like to have a better idea of why Dr. Birnbach was killed. If it really did have something to do with the scrolls—which I've got to tell you sounds unlikely—I'd like to know that before I get them and have someone shooting at you or pushing you in front of trains. Anyway, if the PI you hired couldn't find Suzie, I don't know how I can." He stroked his chin. He'd missed several spots shaving and left the house wearing two different-colored socks. "You think there's a chance LaPonte would level with me?"

"She's allergic to reporters and private investigators, but you reek of integrity, intelligence, and sensitivity." Mimicking him, she stroked her chin. "As a class-conscious striver who's insecure about her lack of formal education, she may respond favorably to that, which is one of the reasons why I'm so intent on hiring you."

She took a slip of paper from a leather holder on his desk, part of the deskset Lisa had bought him for Groundhog Day, picked up a Mont Blanc pen, a Memorial Day present, wrote something, and handed the note to him.

"Here's my number and LaPonte's. Don't lose hers, it's unlisted, and I had to squeeze through gasoline-soaked fiery hoops to get it."

"Another thing, this story about an emir being somehow involved doesn't ring true?" Marc said. "First thing we should do is find out more about the political situation in the UAE."

"I've been trying." She took a rubber band from his desk, wrapped it around her finger, studied her fingertip as it turned purple, then unwrapped it. "Anyway, I'm not so sure there's anything to it. Yusef wasn't the most reliable narrator."

"It didn't sound so credible to me, either, but... There are services that supply lawyers with expert witnesses on every conceivable subject. Some are whores who'll tell you whatever you want to hear, others are legit experts. I'm sure I can find someone who can tell us what's going on over there."

"Great!"

He countersigned a copy of the retainer letter.

"Marc, I fear I might've been too pushy. I know most lawyers would've taken my money without a whole lot of concern about my having lied or the quality of my case, and I truly respect your integrity. What I'm trying to say is, please, only set up the meeting and call LaPonte if you're totally comfortable doing it."

"I'm not the *totally comfortable* type, but I'll call you in a few days and tell you what I've been able to find expert-wise. I want to get that done before I speak to LaPonte."

"I'll be totally honest with you, from now on. Well, maybe not *totally*, but at least as honest as your average client."

IX

The Stench of Expertise

THE RECEPTIONIST LED Dahlia into the firm's conference room, where Marc introduced her to Matthew Vance, Ph.D, a professor of Middle Eastern Studies at the Columbia University School of International and Public Affairs. With his tweedy, suede-elbow-patched three-piece suit, non-Hitler beard—clean shaven only where the Fuhrer had had his moustache—and stink of pipe tobacco, the man looked and smelled professorial.

After apologizing for arriving a couple of minutes late, Dahlia showed Vance the posts she printed off the Internet. She told him about her meetings with Daniel and Yusef and shared her theory that Daniel and Shustak had been murdered because of the scrolls, possibly because an emir or someone else in the Middle East wanted them suppressed. She concluded, "Due to Professor Shustak's self-promoting NYU Archeology Department blog and Yusef's embellishments, a rumor spread that these scroll fragments may represent the original intent of the Torah, the currently accepted version being a mistake that subsequently crept into it."

"Maybe not a mistake," Vance said, "but the intentional act of a compassionate rabbi."

"A historical milestone," Marc said. "The earliest known example of political correctness."

Dahlia shot him a dirty look. "These Internet posts take the scrolls pretty damn seriously, and Daniel was killed because of them."

"Dahlia, you don't know that," Marc said. "And as for these scrolls representing the *original* version? It'll be years before any respectable scholar would be able to come to that conclusion, even if it's true."

"We're not talking about *respectable scholars*," Dahlia said. "We're talking about politically motivated murderers."

"I suppose that's possible." Vance's hand partially blocked his mouth as if he were holding an invisible pipe. "The Arabs revere Ibrahim as a prophet and trace their lineage back to him through Ishmael. They see him as the one through whom God's covenant will be fulfilled. If the Torah were shown to conflict with the Koranic account and say Abraham cursed the Arabs to suffer perpetual servitude at the hands of the Jews..." Vance put his invisible pipe down hard. "I suppose that if Iran, her fundamentalist allies, and her Hezbollah stooges were looking for a pretext for a jihad against Israel, the scrolls could be made to fit the bill. That would conflict with the interests of the moderate Persian Gulf emirs, but of course Israel wouldn't want that either."

Dahlia said, "But Israel wouldn't kill to—"

"At this point there's no way we can be sure of anything," Marc said, noting Vance's raised-eyebrow indication that he didn't fully share Dahlia's belief in Israel's benevolence.

Vance said, "Rumors about the Jews changing the Torah so it says the Arabs should be slaves of the Jews could be quite potent on the Arab street."

"Yes!" Dahlia shouted. "That's what Yusef said."

Giving her a look he must have perfected on interrupting students, Vance said, "Remember the riots some years back over a Danish cartoon depicting Mohammed? None of the rioters had seen the cartoons, so they, too, were acting on rumor, and those were far more placid times, politically speaking, than we're now living through. The cartoons, though, *actually existed*. I don't think there'd be disturbances in the Arab street unless the scrolls turn up, but if they do, politically motivated hawks could well make them a *casus belli*, even before they're authenticated. Keep in mind that ever since the successive collapses of the El-Abidine Ben Ali, Mubarak, Gaddafi, and al-Assad governments, the entire area has been a tinder box."

"Things have calmed down quite a bit recently, though," Marc said.

"It just seems that way because our media has the attention span of a hamster and has moved on to the latest celebrity meltdown," Vance said. "There's more intrigue than ever. Everyone in power now knows they're vulnerable. As a result, they overreact to provocations they wouldn't even have noticed a few years ago. That's particularly true in the UAE where, beneath a thin veil of stability, there's an increasingly nasty political fight for control."

"Yes!" Dahlia raised both arms, as if she'd just scored the winning goal in the World Cup finals. "Ahmed's granddad, one of these *moderate* emirs in the UAE, *is* behind Daniel's murder."

"You've taken several Olympian leaps of logic to reach that conclusion," Marc said.

"Since when has Middle Eastern politics been logical?" Vance said.

"While accusing a moderate emir of murder is wildly premature, I could see these scrolls causing a great deal of trepidation. A small inbred group controls everything. Such groups are incubators for rumors. And if political futures become tied to the scrolls…, Lord Acton's dictum about power corrupting and absolute power corrupting absolutely will be as true for the Persian Gulf as it does anywhere else."

Dahlia shot Marc a gloating grin. But Vance was, after all, auditioning for a job as an expert witness, and Marc was his potential employer, albeit with Dahlia's money.

"If I may make a suggestion," he said, "your next step should be to take these scrolls to an archeologist. Their bona fides must be thoroughly tested and carbon-dated. Then scholars would have to study the linguistic roots of the words in question and compare the scrolls to others from the time period—all of which would take years. In order to represent the Torah's original intent, the scrolls have to be older than the other versions we have."

"Professor Shustak said they were the real deal, and *he* was the *head* of the NYU Archeology Department." As if knocking on a door, Dahlia tapped her fist on the copy of the NYU blog.

"He said based on *preliminary review* they *might* be important, and *may* even pre-date the Dead Sea Scrolls," Marc said. "If you carefully read what he said, it's clear he was just speculating."

"We can't do any testing because we don't have them. And if the emirs have their way, no one ever will." Dahlia stood like a TV lawyer about to examine a witness, took on a deadly serious expression, buttoned a non-existent jacket and adjusted non-existent glasses. "So, Professor, in your professional opinion, is it possible that the prospect of these scrolls turning up sufficiently unnerved a UAE emir to cause him to want them suppressed?"

"Sure."

"And in the rumor-incubator you described, could that desire become so passionate as to turn murderous?" she asked.

"I suppose it's *possible*. These people have access to billions of dollars and are used to getting what they want," Vance said. "When they don't, they get tetchy, and they don't necessarily value human life as much as one might hope."

Dahlia turned to Marc. "Your witness, counselor."

"I have no cross-examination at this time. I'll save my questioning for the rebuttal case," Marc said, grinning at Dahlia's dead-on imitation of a lawyer examining an expert on the witness stand. He turned to Vance. "This has been a very useful first meeting, professor. Let us pay you for your time today, then we'll follow up with you as things progress."

"You think you can find the name of Ahmed's emir grandfather and maybe through him we can locate Amhed?" Dahlia asked. "I've been told Amhed has degrees from Oxford and the London School of Economics, but I checked the graduation rolls and found no Ahmeds."

Vance puffed on his imaginary pipe.

"I probably can, my brother-in-law works in our embassy over there."

After he left, Dahlia hopped around the room.

"In spite of your devil's advocate BS, he confirmed just what I've been saying! This *moderate* faction in the UAE killed Daniel!"

"He said jumping to that conclusion would be *premature*."

"Marc, he's a professor, he's going to be cautious, but he clearly said it was *possible*."

"Seems to me that it all turns on the scrolls themselves and a careful analysis by trained professionals, which would take years."

"Daniel was killed on the basis of *rumors*." She started to sit but too excited to stay still, she stood, occasionally stretching. "Professor Vance confirmed that the Arab street, egged on by fundamentalist agitators, could go bonkers if the scrolls were to turn up whether or not they've been properly authenticated. Politically motivated rabble-rousers, screaming about how the scrolls say that God wanted the Arabs relegated to the status of slaves, could bring down governments—governments like the one that so profitably runs the UAE. Vance affirmed that the emirs are scared shitless of the Arab street." Pausing for breath, she pointed at Marc. "I *guarantee* that more people will be killed."

"Dahlia, please sit," Marc said. "You have no way to *know* that."

"I *know* there'll be at least one more death."

"As Yogi Berra said, 'The hardest thing to predict is the future,'" Marc said, smiling in an attempt to defuse their pointless argument.

"Not in this case, because I'm going to kill whoever's responsible for Daniel's murder or he'll kill me, so there'll be at least one more death."

"Dahlia, you seem to have slipped into some sort of..."

"Manic phase, that's what it is, and it feels great!" She pumped the air with her fist. "And I'm sure I'm right."

"That's a pretty standard feeling for people experiencing mania, you know."

"Who are you calling standard, Buster?" Perching on the edge of the table, she stuck her face so close to his that her dilated eyes looked as big as half-dollars. "Them's fighting words. Or rather a fighting word."

She giggled. He pushed his chair back.

"That I'm sure I'm right doesn't mean I'm wrong."

"It doesn't mean anything," he said, rolling further back.

Sitting cross-legged on the table, she whispered something that sounded like, "Butt out. I'm not going to jettison the dead weight and go it alone. And they're not *dead weight*. And there's certainly no reason to *silence* them with extreme prejudice."

"What?" Marc asked.

She stared blankly at a framed photo on the wall. Her lips moved but no sound emerged.

"Okay, back to normal," she said a minute or so later, smiling. "Sometimes when I feel I'm losing it, I stare at a point on a wall and sing to myself— *HaTikvah*, the Israeli national anthem, if you can believe it—and that brings me back. It works, if I catch the crazy episode early. Once Vance gets us that emir's name, things will really start popping, you'll see."

"You'd said something about dead weight."

"No, just...I..." Her cheeks turned so red they practically glowed. "Sometimes I...talk to myself, nonsense words. It's nothing."

"It still doesn't make sense to me that an emir halfway around the world would risk the consequences of having someone murdered based only on rumor. There's something else going on, not that I have any idea what that might be."

She sat properly in the chair next to his.

"Would you mind if I follow-up with Vance?" she said.

"Not at all."

"Marc, I'm just so delighted that you agreed to work with me on this. I can't tell you how much I appreciate it. I even like arguing with you."

"I'm glad too."

"I love that you keep me grounded and don't get too bent out of shape by my crazy episodes. The other day, when I said you and I would make a great team, I was sort of teasing, but it might in fact be true."

"Hope so," he said, meaning *I agree.*

He realized, much to his surprise, that he was happy. Apparently feeling something similar, she squeezed his hand, causing an electrical surge of excitement to shot up his arm. Their eyes met, her head tilted, and her lips parted.

She stood. "I should go."

Thrown by the unexpected gush of good feelings, Marc neglected to stand when she did. Bending down, she kissed him lightly on his bald spot and started to walk out. Jumping up so quickly he felt dizzy, he accompanied her to the elevator but kept sufficient distance between them to avoid physical contact.

Several days later, neither having heard from Dahlia nor having been able to reach her on her phone, he called Vance to see if he'd made any progress in his effort to find the emir's name.

"He's not in," his secretary said.

"Please tell him Marc Bloch called and ask him to call me."

"I'm afraid he won't be back for awhile. He's in the hospital."

"Jeez, what happened?"

"He had a bad fall, ended up with a massive concussion, a subdural hematoma, and two broken hips." Her tone was inexplicably hostile, as if she blamed Marc.

"Well, if you speak to him, please wish him a speedy recovery."

"He left instructions that he doesn't want to speak to you or Ms. Birn, particularly not her."

"Why?"

"The police think he was pushed."

After trying in vain to clear his head, Marc called Dahlia and left a message on her voicemail to call him ASAP.

X

Suffer the Little Children

ALTHOUGH UNSETTLED BY his conversation with Vance's assistant and annoyed over Dahlia's failure to get back to him, Marc nonetheless decided to try to set up a meeting with LaPonte. To learn more about her, he bought her book, *Suffer the Little Children*, which had come out a mere three days after the trial. He felt guilty about running up substantial hours on what would likely turn out to be a boondoggle. He placated his conscience by deciding to read it quickly and only bill Dahlia for half his time.

Still it took weeks to get through it, and that wasn't merely because he'd been busy with de Saint-Juste's case and parenting demands and only had time to read between emergencies. The acknowledgement page credited—blamed?—an unidentified ghost-writer, but La Ponte would've done better choosing a collaborator from among the living. Although the book was only two hundred pages with wide margins, he could more easily have completed the collected works of Shakespeare. Marc bulled his way to page 152, which concluded the chapter on her killing Birnbach. Titled *What Would Jesus Do If He Had a Shotgun?* it explained how LaPonte had traipsed around Queens, hunting pedophiles with a sawed-off shotgun in a backpack. To avoid attracting attention she'd hollowed out the grip of a tennis racket and stuck it over the barrel, put a can of balls in the pack's webbed pocket and worn tennis whites. By the time he'd stopped reading, almost three weeks had passed. Annoyingly, Dahlia still hadn't been in touch.

As for why LaPonte targeted Birnbach? "I had unimpeachable evidence of his long history of acts so evil, monstrous, and disgusting that they're almost beyond the powers of imagination. I'm not free to reveal what I know or how I learned of it, but God knows I did right, and through His intercession on my behalf, so will the jury."

Making a LaPonte-like leap of illogic, Marc surmised from her final sentence—*Certain that Jesus has additional plans for me, I wait*—that with the trial over and her book out, it ate at her that the media had already moved on. If she thought opening up to him might lead to further publicity, she just might do it. People like talking about themselves, particularly people who'd basked in the limelight only to have that light all too soon focus elsewhere.

His call to LaPonte reached a recording, "Hi! How are ya? I'm not in now, but please leave a message. I'll be sure to call you back just as soon as I can. If you have information on a child molester, you can email me at Mary@ killsatansdisciples.com. May God bless you as He blesses me."

"My name is Marc Bloch. I'm a lawyer writing a book about how the justice system deals with high-profile cases. I'd appreciate it very much if you'd meet with me and talk off-the-record about—"

She picked up. "Mr. Bloch, I've talked to enough lawyers for three lifetimes."

"Perhaps there's something I can do to help with your battle against pedophiles. While I'm sure you haven't the slightest interest in courting attention for your own self-promotion, you must realize that publicity is always good for someone with a cause. We're planning a lot of PR for the book, and I'm sure any talk show I get on would welcome you as well. Perhaps you and I can clear the air about certain *ambiguities*."

He had written several chapters while his law firm was collapsing, so he told himself he wasn't really lying. If things slowed down, which they very well might at the conclusion of the de Saint-Juste case, maybe he'd get back to it. If any publishers are still in business and any people are still reading books by then, there might indeed be a PR campaign or more likely a Twitter or Facebook campaign. Sophia would explain to him how the hell those things worked.

"The air's crystal clear. Child molester prosecutions are up fifteen percent, acquittals have become rare, and paroles almost non-existent. All across the country people are uniting to keep these monsters out of their communities."

Her voice grated like the Borough of Queens anthem played on an electric razor. Had she not killed those guys, she'd probably be saying something along the lines of *paper or plastic*? Marc sighed, ashamed of his snobbery, particularly given the shakiness of his own financial future.

She said, "And just so you know, I haven't the slightest doubt that what I did was right."

"I'm sure you don't."

"Yeah, what makes *you* so sure?" she asked, tone bellicose.

73

It occurred to Marc that he might be able to use her hostility to his advantage. First, though, he had to establish his credibility.

"People have an almost unlimited capacity for self-righteousness," he said. "Almost every case I've had, both my client and his or her adversary honestly believed they were right."

As the silence stretched out, he thought he'd made a mistake and wondered how to bring the conversation back from the abyss.

Finally, she said, "I'm so sick of you liberals and your snobby moral relativism."

"Me too. Set me straight."

"You need to do that for yourself. Take Jesus into your heart."

"Please, if you can spare, say half an hour for me..." He smiled. "The liberal media didn't give you a fair shake with Daniel Birnbach, and truth is, you didn't make the best case for yourself in your book. I could help people to better understand—"

"People understand fine."

The intensity of her tone took him aback. He recalled one of Lisa's favorite Bertrand Russell quotes, *The whole problem with the world is that fools and fanatics are always so certain of themselves, but wiser people so full of doubts.*

LaPonte hung up. Hoping she hadn't slammed the phone down hard enough to break it, he called back, and she answered in person this time.

Playing a hunch, he said, "I've been speaking with Dahlia Birn."

"That little sociopath!" It sounded like she spit.

"I'm calling you to get a balanced view."

"If she were any more unbalanced she'd fall on her butt."

"I gather you're now living in Massapequa. Does the day after tomorrow work for you, say around three in the afternoon?"

"I'll tell you where to go."

He jotted down her address, while glancing at the clock—if he left the office right now, he could pick up Sophia at school.

Marc woke. Two a.m. His longing and sense of loss so intense that everything hurt, even his hair. As he hadn't slept through the night since Lisa died, he was almost used to it. The Chinese and the CIA used sleep deprivation as a form of torture, and he understood just how effective that must've been. His doctor had prescribed Ambien, but not wanting to sleep through Sophia's calls, if she had a nightmare or otherwise needed him, he hadn't taken any.

He turned on his light and picked up the book by his bed, but he was too despondent to read; except for LaPonte's, he'd made it through barely a dozen pages of any book since Lisa's death. He turned off the light and tried to plan for his upcoming meeting with LaPonte but no gambit came to mind. He didn't really care. Would anything ever matter to him again? He turned on the TV. He'd given up his lifetime habit of reading *The New York Times* in the morning and regretted that he was woefully unaware of what was happening in the world.

A mosque in Houston had been bombed. At the funeral of an American serviceman, a fight had erupted between mourners and a church-based group of protesters who claimed the soldier deserved to die as punishment for America's acceptance of homosexual fornication.

Marc unplugged the TV to guard against turning it on again when he next found himself in a despondent stupor.

He sat up in bed, surrounded by a 360-degree television screen on which LaPonte was riding a chariot out of the courthouse and through a triumphal arch as golden nymphs flew about, dispensing rose petals and dropping laurel wreaths on her head. He screamed, "No!" Sweat spurted from his body in pee-like streams. He rolled over and wrapped himself around Lisa, who was wearing nothing but a tight blood-red *Carpe Mañana* T-shirt. They kissed, and he melded into her. They were floating on soft, puffy clouds. John, Paul, George, and Ringo, tiny wings sprouting from their backs, were playing *Here There and Everywhere* on their harps.

She pushed him away and cried, "Mommy! Mommy, please come!"

No, that's not Lisa.

Marc ran to Sophia's room. She was crying.

"Mommy's dead. She's never coming back."

He laid next to her, holding her. She cuddled into him and sobbed.

After a while, he reached over for the book they'd been meaning to start—she didn't want him to read any that she'd read with Mommy—and read aloud, *In a hole in the ground there lived a hobbit. Not a nasty, dirty, wet hole, filled with the ends of worms and an oozy smell, nor yet a dry, bare, sandy hole with nothing in it to sit down on or to eat: it was a hobbit-hole, and that means comfort.*

Sunlight woke them, and they had to rush to get to school on time. They wouldn't have had to rush if they'd taken a cab, but their twenty-five-minute morning walk was a cherished family tradition. Did two people even comprise a family?

Having sold his car as part of the retrenchment that accompanied the collapse of his law firm, Marc took the Long Island Railroad to Massapequa. Crossing a parking lot, he headed towards a taxi stand. The dispatcher wore a Jets warm-up jacket over a Knicks T-shirt, and the brim of his Mets cap was turned to the side. Marc handed him the address he'd written down while speaking to La Ponte.

"There's no street named that in Massapequa or any other town around here."

Damn it! Just a few seconds on Google Maps and he'd have saved an entire morning, and saved Dahlia a couple of grand. Well, that one was easy. He couldn't bill her for his own stupidity.

"I was supposed to meet Mary LaPonte, you know, the..." Not knowing how she was thought of in these parts, he left his sentence unfinished. "Do you know where she lives?"

"Her place got more security than Fort Knox. If she gave you that address, you ain't getting within a hundred yards of her, unless you want a rottweiler permanently attached to your ass."

"Any idea where she hangs out, where I might just happen to run into her?"

He shrugged. "Chaise lounge."

"She lies down a lot?" Marc was confused.

"That, too, or so I hear."

Marc shook his head. What the hell was he doing representing a lunatic and playing at being an investigator?

"When's the next train back to the city?"

"An hour." The man pointed to a faded train schedule tacked to the wall.

Deciding to kill time before it killed him, Marc wandered around the blightscape. It wasn't a town, really, but rather a seemingly never-ending strip mall strung out along the road that ran parallel to the railroad tracks. The sidewalk went from cracked to non-existent to crumbling, but as he was the only pedestrian, it probably didn't matter. Seeing a bar down a side street, he decided his legs could use a rest.

The name of the bar drew a smile—Shay's Lounge.

XI

Pride in Prejudice

WITH ITS SPLINTERY wood floors, smell of old beer, missing tin ceiling tiles, and non-flat-screen TV, the place was like The Land That Time Forgot, or perhaps it was holding its breath, hoping time wouldn't stumble upon it. Marc used to hang out occasionally in places like Shay's Lounge, back before the city—and he and his friends—became gentrified.

He sat at the bar, leaving as much space as he could between him and the only other patron, an ancient malodorous drunk with a nose like a bouquet of booze blossoms. The man might've been Marc's age, but Marc looked three decades younger, or at least he thought he did.

"What can I get you?" asked a sandy-haired bartender.

After examining the multiple taps, Marc pointed to Sunfish Ale.

"Any good?"

"It's made locally, some swear by it, some swear at it."

"I'll give it a try."

The bartender filled a glass, expertly tilting it to keep the head to a minimum. Marc took a cautious sip. It tasted like it was brewed from club soda and sauerkraut.

"Fine," he said.

"Personally, I think it tastes like diabetics' piss."

"I wouldn't know," Marc said. "I'm hoping to run into Mary LaPonte. Hear she stops in here from time to time."

"Some days she does. Maybe in an hour or two. Some days not at all." He wiped the counter with a well-worn rag. "What's your interest?"

"I'm thinking of writing a book on how the justice system handles highly publicized cases."

"Handles them like shit."

"That's the premise. Publisher, though, wants a bit more detail. I was hoping to get a few juicy facts from her."

"You'll have to squeeze pretty hard to get any juice out of her." He looked over at the other patron, who had either passed out or died. "I don't approve of people taking justice into their own hands or anything, and all that Jesus talk of hers is a bit much, seeing as how it comes and goes depending on her mood, but she's good people, even if she is a bit..." He tapped his temple and rolled his eyes.

Marc sipped his beer, hoping to become accustomed to its taste. Like most of his hopes, this one failed to materialize, but his not liking the local beer was no reason to let the stuff go to waste. He dutifully took another swig. As someone who couldn't bring himself not to drink piss-flavored beer he'd paid for, he hated the idea of taking Dahlia's money and not giving her value for it. He'd missed the next two trains back to the city—even at half-rates, he was running through a lot of Dahlia's money with nothing to show for it. More urgently, he needed to prepare for a court appearance the following day in de Saint-Juste's case.

An extra-large man with a gun bulge under his jacket filled the doorway. He scanned the place with slitted eyes—a maverick Western lawman about to apply frontier justice. His face was like Mars, red, barren, and cut with dry canals, which in his case appeared to be knife scars. He strode in and planted his back against the wall at the spot where it met the bar. When he fixed his stare on Marc, Marc suppressed the desire to lift his arms and announce that he was unarmed.

A woman entered and took a seat at the bar. She resembled the book jacket photo of Mary LaPonte, only her hair was mid-length straight platinum rather than long, frizzy dirty-blond. She was thinner and had fewer lines in her face. Also, Marc hadn't remembered those large, firm-looking breasts from the news photos of the trial.

The bartender nodded to Marc, who slid over to the stool next to her.

"Hi!" He flashed his brightest smile. "I'm Marc Bloch. So glad I ran into you. Seems I wrote your address down wrong. I guess we're fated to meet."

The large man appeared between them, having moved so quickly he seemed to have apparated there, *à la* Harry Potter (Marc and Lisa had taken turns reading each of the seven volumes to Sophia). *No, don't go there.* The man crossed his arms in front of him, straining the seams of his burnt orange jacket. The bartender reached under the bar.

"It's okay, José, might as well just get it over with." The surgically improved LaPonte stood and motioned for Marc to follow her to a table. "You're buying."

"Of course." Actually, Dahlia was buying.

Marc pulled out a chair for her.

"Courvoisier, neat," LaPonte said to the bartender. "Make it a double."

She straightened her short black skirt, draped her thin black leather jacket over the back of another chair, and sat.

"Just for the record, Ms. LaPonte, I'm not looking to hurt you in any way. In fact, I hope to be able to enhance your reputation."

"Oh, that makes sense." She gave the bartender an impatient look. "Just not in this universe."

The bartender hurried over with her drink and looked at Marc, who pointed to his beer mug, and the hired muscle, who ordered a club soda.

"Ms. LaPonte, Mary, I'm just trying to get at the truth, and that's got to be in everyone's interest."

"And to think you're going through all this trouble just to help little old me."

He smiled. "With your ability to turn a phrase, you should've written the book yourself."

He couldn't tell if her tight hyphen of a smile indicated amusement or annoyance.

LaPonte gulped her cognac. She raised her glass, and the bartender brought over her new drink so quickly he must've had it already poured.

"Read my book, Mr. Bloch. That's all the truth you need."

"It seemed to gloss over the reason you were so sure that Dr. Birnbach—"

"Rachel Maddow spent almost as much time talking about that as my tits."

While Marc hoped she wasn't expecting a comment on the latter subject, several came to mind.

"She couldn't take her eyes off the twins. She may have been trashing me, but she was getting wet to the knees doing it."

They reached for and sipped their drinks at the same time. Their eyes met, and they exchanged conspiratorial smiles. Then, surprised, they composed their faces.

"Maybe you're not such a bad egg," she said. "They say the fags can't help being what they are, maybe it's the same way with you liberals."

"Jesus said, 'In my Father's house are many rooms,'" Marc said.

"Yeah, and Shakespeare said, 'The devil can cite Scripture for his purpose'."

Marc's head kicked back. She laughed heartily.

"So, what made you so sure about Dr. Birnbach?" Marc asked again. "That didn't come through in your book or the reports on the trial."

She took a dainty sip, spun her glass, watched the cognac swirl, and sipped again.

"On the phone, you told me you spoke to that spunk-bucket Dahlia Birn. A word to the not-as-wise-as-you-think-you-are: don't fall for her truth-and-justice whore's shit."

"She says she was quite close to Dr. Birnbach and needs the truth…for closure, to move on with her life," Marc said.

Her dyed-almost-to-the-point-of-invisibility eyebrows came together. "And you believe that?"

"Early in my career I learned not to believe anyone, particularly my clients."

"Must be a hard way to live," LaPonte said, her tone expressing genuine concern.

He'd trusted Lisa. That had worked out well, until she went and died. Fearing that if he spoke his voice would crack, he took a deep breath and put on his good-listener face.

"That I became a minor celebrity for doing what I did tells the perverts that it's open season on them and clues in the chickenshit politicians that there's votes in stamping out vermin."

"But why you were so sure about Dr. Birnbach?"

She again swirled her cognac, leaned forward, opened her mouth, and then closed it. They made eye contact, and he thought something akin to trust flowed between them. Either that or he'd had too much beer.

"I was first clued in when I received a photo of Birnbach and that boy Yusef. I checked Birnbach out and learned that NYU had given him the boot for fucking a student. Seems he wasn't particular about gender, any child would do."

"Both Yusef and the unnamed student were of legal age, and while their liaison may be revolting, it doesn't make Dr. Birnbach a pedophile."

Dropping her voice to a whisper, LaPonte said, "Someone sent me a file on Birnbach. Dates, photographs, the whole enchilada, enough to turn even your liberal, criminal-loving stomach, particularly as he got away with it all without so much as a hello-how-are-ya? from the cops."

She broke eye contact and yet again swirled her drink.

"This *someone*?"

"Never met her. She delivered the file by commercial messenger, I was allowed to look at it and take notes, then the messenger took it back."

"Didn't that seem strange to you?"

"The person who sent me the file was the mother of a child that freak Birnbach had violated. While she wanted him to get what was coming to him, the last thing she wanted was for her child to be forced to relive the experience or for what she went through to become public knowledge." She stared at Marc, as if daring him to make a cynical, smart-assed—or sensible or logical—comment. "But the information checked out."

She applied herself to her drink.

"How did you check out what was in the file?" Marc asked. "If it was a chronicle of past events, none of which resulted in conviction or even arrest, how could it be verified?"

"There were photos, sworn statements, witnesses so terrorized or traumatized that they wouldn't speak to me."

Having killed two people without a shred of remorse, this woman's so crazy she'd believe Santa Claus was a pedophile if she heard he slid down a chimney with a gift for a child.

"See, even you're shocked," she said.

"Why didn't any of that come out at trial?"

"My lawyer said we needed live witnesses, not just their affidavits."

"But if they gave *affidavits*, you had their names and there'd have been someone who notarized their signatures."

"Don't play lawyer with me. I meant *sworn statements*. They were anonymous. As I've been telling you, abuse victims tend to avoid the limelight. They don't want to relive the experience."

Marc saw no point in telling her that *anonymous sworn statements* was an oxymoron.

"Why didn't you take your evidence to the police?"

"They'd have chased their tails around until they turned into butter and slid up each other's asses." She made a face as if she'd swallowed a spoiled oyster. "I wouldn't be surprised if your friend Dahlia Birn had something to do with a couple of the disappearances, maybe even made them permanent."

"You *can't* be serious," he said but made a mental note to check out Dahlia more fully. Not that he believed LaPonte, but he would've liked to be sure. "Do you even know if the person who sent the file was a woman?"

"I didn't pull off her panties or subject her to genetic testing."

"Did you ever see her or even hear her voice?"

Her frown provided all the answer he needed.

"Is it possible the person wanted Birnbach dead, wrote the statements, and photoshopped the pictures?"

"No!" She slammed her palm on the table, causing the elderly drunk to wake with a start.

"Why?"

"God would never permit that."

"But if He permits child molesters... The problem of evil has baffled theologians since—"

"He speaks to me," she said, voice deep, quiet, and free of doubt or irony.

He took a sip while he tried to come up with a rational response. There *was* no rational response.

"He addresses you in an actual audible voice?"

She frowned.

"Ms. LaPonte, I just want to understand. Never having heard such voices myself, I'm most interested. Envious, too."

"Bullshit. Liberals like you think only schizophrenics hear voices."

"Ms. LaPonte, that's not what I think and I happen to be more a libertarian than a liberal. I'm for small government and lots of personal freedom. Maybe it's my legal training, but I'm plagued with the ability to see several sides of all issues."

A sharp little cough of disapproval—or was it a snort?

"You don't believe *me*, though."

"I have no doubt you're sincere and you believe what you say. It's just that, well, it can't be proven one way or the other."

"The truth doesn't need to be *proven*. It's just true."

She got the bartender's attention and pointed to her empty glass.

On the way back to the train station, Marc called Dahlia to report, got a recording. He sent an email. It bounced back.

On his return to his office, he did a computer search for Dahlia Birn. Nothing. He checked the address she'd given him to put on the retainer letter. If it had existed, it would've been somewhere in the East River.

XII

Treading Air

DAHLIA OFFERED THE scrolls for sale on eBay, describing them in detail. While she didn't have them, she hoped the Snowman or someone who could lead her to his employer would show up.

She sat by her computer all day but received no responses. Late afternoon, with the tilted skylight reflecting the sunset and bathing her room in a rosy glow, she had an epiphany, possibly due to Ariella's prompting.

It took her all night and into the morning but she finally succeeded in setting up an almost professional-looking website for ASH—the Association for Schooling at Home. The site promised to provide, free of charge and on a confidential basis, first-rate text books, tests, and curricula for home schooling. The home page copy explained that it was the brainchild of a billionaire who distrusted the school system as an arm of the government and since the material had not only been purloined from the nation's top private schools but also included actual upcoming SATs and New York State Regents Exams, mutual anonymity was required. All a subscriber needed do was provide an email address and a phone number, then the material would be sent electronically from a secure untraceable location.

She found several chat rooms for home schooling parents, entered under various handles, raved about ASH, and disseminated its link as widely as she could. Glomming stock footage of happy engaged-looking children, she created a video for YouTube. It was somewhat amateurish, but she liked the *cinéma vérité* style. It might not go viral, but even a minor bacterial infection would get Suzie's attention. As the conscientious mother of a school-aged child, she must've been educating her daughter and would surely appreciate assistance. Since she was on the run, the confidential aspect of ASH should have had special appeal to her.

Dahlia sent the information on home schooling from the ASH website to Suzie's pushy insurance agent and stockbroker cousins who gave her their business cards at Daniel's shiva. Perhaps they, or some other member of their family, knew where Suzie was and would forward it to her.

Dahlia would have to listen to a whole lot of phone messages, but she thought she'd recognize Suzie's voice. Would she provide a phone number? Sure, one from a pre-paid phone, why not?

Oh, gosh, she'd forgotten all about Marc. He'd seen LaPonte today. How did that go? She began to punch his number into her prepaid phone, but before she completed it, a wave of fatigue broke over her, and the undertow left her so tired and drained that her entire body hurt. It took all her energy and concentration to undress, brush her teeth, wash her face, and pull the couch out into a bed.

Waking the next morning, she realized she would need Marc to speak to Suzie.

Have him persuade her to give him the scrolls.

"NO! The Snowman might... It could get him killed."

He could die crossing the street or choking on a pretzel. You gave Daniel your word—that trumps everything else.

"But—"

With the police looking for you and the Snowman on your butt—literally as well as figuratively, given your tattoos—someone has to be your public face, and Marc's the perfect person for that.

"I don't like manipulating him and sure as hell don't want to put him in danger."

Dahlia practically heard Ariella shrug.

Every conscience has an off switch.

"Not mine."

Her brain shrank then expanded. Everything turned black, then bright white, followed by prismatic pain.

Sorry, I tend to overreact to abject stupidity.

Dahlia straightened and took a deep breath.

Don't worry, there's nothing we'll get him into that we won't get him out of in time.

"You sure?"

Really, Dahlia, would I have said it if I wasn't sure?

"Well..."

Next step is for you to get a better understanding of what makes Marc tick and learn just how far you can push him.

"But as far as him actually holding the scrolls—"

Okay, okay, enough with the whining. We'll cross that bridge after we come to it, or maybe I'll cross it and you'll swim.

Wearing a long coat, big floppy hat, and large sunglasses, Dahlia waited by the entrance to Marc's office building. She didn't see him but returned the following afternoon. At three o'clock, she spotted him leaving. She followed. At the Ethical Culture School he picked up a girl Dahlia recognized from the photos in his office.

Meet her, get to know her; she might turn out to be useful.

Dahlia hatched a plan that she knew any sane person would reject as convoluted and unnecessary, but if it worked she'd be even more confident that she could bring down the Snowman. Her confidence had been high since Ariella confirmed he was the killer and the instrument through whom the head honcho acted.

On her way home from spying on Marc and Sophia, she saw a man, handsome in a forgettable way, getting out of a beat-up green Ford Taurus. Car keys in one hand, a pair of shopping bags and a thick stack of headshots in the other, he was having difficulty locking his car.

After making eye contact and smiling, she asked, "May I help you?" and took the bags from him.

He returned her smile.

"You're an actor."

"How did you—?"

She pointed to the publicity photos. "You look familiar, have you been in anything I might've seen?"

His smile melted like a burned out candle collapsing on itself. "Tony's Trattoria? You might have seen me waiting tables."

"If you'd like to make some money, I could use some assistance in connection with an impractical joke."

XIII

Sultrily Dialectic

DEPARTING EARLY FROM the office, Marc picked up Sophia at school and took her to the Gap on a sweatshirt-buying expedition. She quickly located the style she wanted but couldn't decide among the colors. When Marc offered a suggestion, she called him "Sultrily dialectic," misquoting Lisa, who'd referred to him as *sartorially dyslectic*.

He asked why she was using her phone to take pictures of each color, and she said, "To send them to my friends and get their advice."

"This is a decision you ought to be able to make on your own. It's not a matter of what they like but what you like."

"I wouldn't have to do this if Mommy was here!" she shouted. "*She* had good taste."

He didn't remind her of the fights she and Lisa had when they'd gone shopping.

Later, while devouring the large salumi platter at Salumeria Rosi, a neighborhood restaurant that was their current favorite, Sophia said, "That wasn't very nice of me, was it?"

"What's that?" he asked, even though he knew.

"Playing the Mommy card with you."

She looked and sounded so much like Lisa. He felt like simultaneously laughing and crying.

Instead, he said, "I'm glad you realize that."

"I got the color I really wanted, not the one Talia liked."

"You chose right...but the process could've gone a little more pleasantly."

"Mommy and I used to always fight when we'd shop." She smiled. "Even if she did have good taste."

"Don't worry, Soph, we'll fight just as much as you like."

She grinned. "You know, you really are a very good daddy."

"Thanks." His voice cracked.

"Don't cry." She rested her hand on his. "'Cause if you do, I will."

He squeezed her hand. "Are you going to have enough room for bread pudding?"

"You better order one of your own. I'm not about to share." Sly Lisa-like smile.

"Deal."

They both ordered the bread pudding special—chocolate chip with crème fraiche—and a glass of milk for Sophia.

She made eye contact with Marc and tilted her head in the waitress's direction. He had no idea what she was trying to communicate but hoped she wasn't favorably impressed by the cobra tattoo snaking up the woman's right arm.

"Did you see how she smiled at you?" Sophia asked, after the waitress left.

Her dead-on imitation of the waitress's smile and flirtatious hair flip unnerved Marc.

"She'd like a big tip."

"I think she wants more than that." She fluttered her eyebrows in a way Marc might've found funny under other circumstances.

"She's half my age."

"Talia says old men go for younger women."

"I'm not sure her dad is someone I want to emulate."

"Is emulate like when the doctor gives a shot?"

"That's inoculate. Emulate means to copy."

Lisa had taught her to ask whenever she heard a word she didn't know or someone said something she didn't understand. The result was a vocabulary more appropriate to a high school student than a ten-year-old.

"You use big words when you want to change the subject. Mommy used them when she was angry."

He grinned. "Most people use short ones."

"You mean like *shit?*" To cut off an angry response, she said, "I'm just trying to *emulate* what some people say. The boys in my class say it all the time."

"I hope the girls don't."

"Talia can get away with anything since her parents split."

Her wise look turned sad, and he responded by stroking her cheek.

"Just because you can get away with—"

"I know, Daddy. I haven't acted up…not much, anyway. Mommy made me promise not to take advantage."

"You're a wonderful girl. I'm very lucky to have you."

"I'm trying hard, Daddy." Her voice cracked. "But sometimes…"

"I know. Me too. It's very hard."

Marc found Sophia's little-girl milk-mustache a soothing antidote to the unsettling effect of her precociousness.

"Daddy, do you like anybody?"

"Of course. There are lots of people I like, some very much. You're at the very top of my—"

She rolled her eyes. "You know what I mean."

"Actually, I don't."

"I mean *like*." Her face became Lisa-stern. "Didn't Mommy tell you to date?"

"But she didn't mean yet."

"When?" Piercing Lisa-eyes.

"Once you're out of graduate school."

"Daddy!"

Marc paid the check.

"Just curious, what exactly did Mommy say to you about my dating?"

She screwed up her face in an effort to recall her mother's actual words.

"That it would be natural for me to want you all to myself and be jealous if you go out with people, and…" She stopped to think. "Mommy also said that I might think you're being disloyal to her, but exactly the opposite would be true, you'd be doing what's best for you and me, and I need to push you to do it."

"How much of that made sense to you?"

"Everything Mommy said made sense."

"I know, but…"

"I didn't really understand, except for the part of wanting you always."

"So, *you* don't really want me to date?"

Her upper lip quivered.

"Yes I do! Mommy said—"

He placed his hand on hers. "I asked what *you* want."

"Mommy was smarter than me."

"So am I, older and more experienced anyway, and you don't do everything I say."

She smiled. "You're pretty smart, Daddy, but…"

"But I'm here."

They both traced their fingers over the wood grain in the tabletop. When their fingers met, they laughed.

In spite of the cold early January wind, they walked home holding gloveless hands. Turning off Broadway and onto 78th Street, Sophia, not looking where she was going, bumped into a woman.

"Oh, excuse—"

"About time you two staggered home. Isn't this a school night?"

"Dahlia, what are you doing here?"

Sophia approvingly eyed her mules, long legs, leather mini-skirt and blood-red *Life is a Cabernet* T-shirt. But for her open shearling vest and thin leather gloves, she'd made no concession to winter.

"I tried to reach you—calls, emails," Marc said. While pleased that Dahlia reemerged, he was less happy that she'd been waiting for them like a stalker. "I reached a recording that there was trouble on the line. My emails bounced back."

"Oh, gosh, you didn't fall for that, did you? Had I thought there was even the smallest chance that you'd give up so easily…" Dahlia smiled.

Palm on Sophia's back, Marc nudged her toward home.

"Call me in the office, Dahlia. I'll tell you about my meeting with LaPonte."

"That must've been some experience. I recommend a hot bath in a solution of Lysol, Drano, and sulfuric acid."

"Actually, it was quite interesting."

Dahlia stared slack-jawed, as if that was the stupidest thing she'd ever heard. Sophia grinned, knowing something humorous was happening, even if she didn't know what it was.

"If you found Mary LaPonte interesting," Dahlia said, "I recommend you rent that Warhol film of someone sleeping for six hours."

"Your reaction almost makes me wonder why you asked me to speak to her."

"No, not at all, I'd love to hear all about your meeting. How 'bout over dinner, say tomorrow night?"

"I…need to help Sophia with her homework, put her to bed."

"Martha can put me to bed."

"Tomorrow's not good." He turned toward his daughter. "Sophia, remember we agreed that if we went out to dinner, we'd go right home afterwards and you'd do your homework without distraction. If you ever want to go out to dinner again on a school night…"

Arms at her side, palms turned upward, Sophia shrugged her shoulders and rolled her eyes. Dahlia mirrored her.

"Dahlia, call me at the office to make an appointment."

"I'm never available during the day. If sunlight hits me, I spontaneously combust."

Between giggles, Sophia elbowed Marc and whispered, "You get it? Like a vampire, Daddy."

Turning his back to Sophia and dropping his voice to a whisper, he said, "Dahlia, I'm not happy with you stalking us, lying in wait—"

"Stalking?" Eyes slitted and head tilted, she looked at him as if he was the crazy one. "I just had dinner with friends down the street. How could I possibly know you'd be coming this way at this particular time?"

Marc didn't care enough to push it.

"Dinner the night after tomorrow?" she said.

"Is that when I have my tennis tournament?" Sophia asked.

Marc grimaced, not having wanted to share even that tidbit of personal information with Dahlia.

"A tennis tournament. How exciting! I bet you're really good."

"Pretty good, I guess. It's just the ten-and-unders."

Marc said, "We've got to be getting home."

"My daddy's really, *really* good. He played first singles at Yale. That's a college in Connecticut for smart people."

"Second doubles, actually, and George W. Bush went there so draw your own conclusions."

Dahlia bent to Sophia's eye level.

"So, where's this tournament? Would it be okay if I come watch?"

"No, it wouldn't." Regretting the harshness of his tone in front of Sophia, Marc added, "I make it a point of keeping my business and personal lives separate."

"It's at Alley Pond, right, Daddy?"

"Dahlia, that's way the heck out in Queens, just short of the Nassau County border. You really don't want to—"

Her upper eyelids rose as if she were afraid. The fear seemed to fade, but in its wake, her eyes showed confusion. For several seconds her expressions changed like random songs on an iPod shuffle before settling into an exaggerated, inappropriate pout—quite a contrast to her unusual poise.

Sophia looked at her, squinting, obviously trying to figure out what just happened.

"Sounds like these tournaments are something you and your father do together," Dahlia said, her voice halting and raspy as if she'd been woken from a deep sleep.

"Correct." Marc shot her the hardest look he could manage without tipping Sophia off that something was wrong. "By the way, the address you gave me—"

"I just made one up for that silly retainer letter of yours—you handed it to me, so the address was just a formality. I planned to pay you in cash, so you didn't need a billing address. I never get mail anyway."

"Are you in some sort of trouble?"

"No, and I like keeping it that way."

Marc shook his head, stunned at her equanimity.

A man came up the street. "Hi, Dahlia. Wasn't that a lovely dinner Jessica made?"

"Peter Fischer, this is my lawyer, Marc Bloch, and his daughter, Sophia. I just happened to run into them. Marc, Sophia, this is Peter, he and I just met at the cocktail party I came from. He stayed after I left, hoping to hit on the hostess." She shrugged. "It's not for me to understand the social pleasures of my species."

"Nice to meet you." Peter extended his hand, and Marc shook it. Peter tapped Sophia on the head, eliciting a scowl.

"Dahlia, may I drop you somewhere?" Peter asked.

"Thank you, but I'm not going far and I need to walk off the meal. It was great to see you again, though."

After a mock salute, to which Dahlia responded with a blown kiss, Fischer climbed into a green Ford.

Marc felt like a suspicious jerk for thinking she'd been lying in wait for them. Sure, she'd lied to him when they'd first met, but fish swim, bees fly, and clients lie. As for her mental problems, the troubled were entitled to counsel.

"Marc, when can we have dinner? Don't make me beg. It sends a bad message to Sophia about the dignity of women."

"I just…"

"I still have a credit balance on my retainer, right?"

"If I'd known where to send it, I'd have returned it."

"Don't be silly. So, Friday night? We'll spend some of it." Dahlia asked Sophia, "Where do you think your daddy and I should go?"

"Canard, definitely Canard."

"Where did you hear about Canard?" Marc shook his head. "Do you have any idea how expensive that restaurant is?"

"That's where Talia's daddy takes his mistresses, the ones he really likes. Talia says it's the most romantic restaurant in the whole city."

"This is a business dinner."

"Wonderful idea, Sophia. You know, you're very sophisticated for a girl your age."

"Nooo." She looked down at the sidewalk. "But I'm pretty smart, aren't I, Daddy?"

"Definitely."

"I'm the second smartest kid in the whole grade, not just my class. The smartest, if you don't count Ryder Benton, who's just weird. I have some sophisticated friends, though. Well only one, but she's my best friend, and she knows things some girls in middle school don't even know."

"Even if we wanted to, we couldn't get reservations at Canard on such short notice," Marc said, but he wondered why he was fighting this.

"You can do it, Daddy. Call Talia's dad. He and the Mattra Dee are like this." She held up two fingers, pressed together.

"He's among the last people I feel like calling for a favor."

He regretted speaking his thoughts out loud; he shouldn't have put down Talia's father in front of Sophia, no matter how well deserved it might've been.

"Actually," he said, "I do know someone who can probably get us in."

"Perfect!" Dahlia bumped fists with Sophia. "Shall we say seven o'clock?"

"Sure."

Dahlia raised her arm and a cab screeched to a stop as if called forth from another dimension.

"Mommy would be proud of you," Sophia said as they walked home.

"She'd be something, but I'm not sure proud is it."

"You mentioned a LaPonte. I think I might've heard of her. Is she on a reality show or dating Justin Timberlake or someone?"

"It's really late, and you have homework."

"Dahlia is very pretty and she really likes you, Daddy. That should be obvious even to you."

"*Even to me?*"

"You know what I mean," Sophia said. "That was great, though, how you played hard-to get."

"I wasn't playing, honey."

"Well, it worked."

Once Sophia was asleep, he called a former client, a celebrity chef whose clandestine affair with one of the major investors in Canard had received mention on Page 6 of the *New York Post* and *Access Hollywood*—much to her delight. The chef groaned about the Herculean task Marc asked her to do, but she called back a few minutes later crowing about getting the last table in the place. Among life's many mysteries was why a restaurant with a $149-per-person *prix fixe* was always packed and places that provide fine food, service, and atmosphere at a third the price struggled to fill half their tables.

On Friday, Marc began to review the discs containing the couple hundred thousand pages that Davis & Spalding had delivered in response to his document demand. Normally such tedious work would be given to associates or even paralegals, but he could do it much quicker than junior people and pick out those few golden nuggets to use on cross-examination to make the D&S lawyers look foolish, incompetent, and greedy. Most of what D&S had delivered was useless, sent over as part of a haystack in which the few needles of important documents were hidden. Although not relevant to the case, he found interesting de Saint-Juste's contract with the UAE for building his desalination plant. It contained a morals clause that allowed the UAE to terminate his services and confiscate the project if he did anything that damaged the country's reputation or ran afoul of sharia, Islamic law. While de Saint-Juste stood to make obscene profits, they had him by the balls.

Looking up from his desk, he realized that over four hours had passed. The time hadn't exactly been pleasurable, but it beat the alternatives of mourning for Lisa or being irritated with Dahlia.

Back to the de Saint-Juste case. While he'd yet to find a smoking gun, he uncovered documents that might have qualified as bullet casings with retrievable prints he could use to good effect at the depositions of the D&S lawyers. He'd gone through well under ten percent of their production and already found internal emails characterizing the work of several young lawyers and paralegals as "worthless," even though Davis & Stearling had billed hundreds of dollars per hour for that work. Another email called a pair of depositions, for which D&S ultimately charged north of $30,000, "a WPA make-work project we can put Bennett on." A month later, D&S fired Bennett for falling asleep in court. His personnel file referred to him as a "poorly functioning alcoholic" and contained a memo discussing whether firing him would violate the Americans with Disabilities Act, due to his alcoholism and dyslexia.

Marc planed to depose, under oath, each of the one-hundred-plus D&S time-billers, a task that would earn him as much as a couple hundred thousand dollars in time charges and keep him productively employed and distracted well into the summer. Being human and having humanly fallible memories, the Davis & Stearling lawyers were likely to tell stories with contradictions. On trial, he could use those contradictions to make it look as if they'd lied under oath. If their stories were thoroughly consistent, he'd use that to suggest they'd been given a script and told to stick to it. He sighed.

So what if he was engaged in game-playing with no benefit to society? No one criticized Roger Federer or Derek Jeter for game-playing. And Davis & Stearling had taken greed to a whole new level, but still—

His phone rang.

"I just settled the case," de Saint-Juste said. "Davis & Stearling is knocking four mil off their bill and giving me a million dollars in free legal work, so…"

"Why would you want lawyers who did such a terrible job working for you?"

"You do understand the meaning of the word *free*? Anyway, they've got two thousand lawyers, spread over thirty offices around the world. Their reputation opens doors you can't even get close enough to knock on."

"Yeah."

"Hey, *ami*, buck up, this has nothing to do with you. They've got offices in Abu Dhabi and Riyadh. I need them for my desalination projects. I just wanted to push them around a little, so they'd think twice about the way they bill me in the future."

"You could've been straight with me." Marc moderated his tone. After all, de Saint-Juste had treated him no worse than the way most clients had, he was just wearier of it now.

"I couldn't have gotten here without having an attack dog ready to go for the jugular. Tell you what, keep ten percent of the unused portion of the retainer."

"Right."

"Of course, you're not going to bill me for your document review."

"That cost more than the ten percent you're letting me keep."

"I didn't get any benefit from it, did I?"

"Our retainer agreement provides you pay for my time, regardless of the *benefit*. Wouldn't look good for you to have another lawyer suing you."

After a uniquely Gallic guttural sound, de Saint-Juste said, "Fine, charge for your time, send me the balance of the retainer, and we'll call it square."

Down to one client, Marc should have been glad he had dinner plans with Dahlia, and maybe he was.

Not having time to go home before meeting Dahlia, he called Sophia to check on how she was doing with her homework, tell her he loved her, and say goodnight in case he didn't make it home in time to put her to bed.

"Your first date. It's sooo exciting!"

"Really?"

Long pause.

"I'm not sure." Her voice quivered. "Mommy said… but…"

"It's not a date, honey. It's just a business meeting. She's a client."

"To her, it's a date. Women know these things."

"How long exactly have you been a woman?"

"I discussed the whole thing with Talia and her mommy."

"I wish you hadn't… No, I guess it's okay." It wasn't okay. "What did Sabrina say?"

Marc remembered all too well Lisa suggesting Talia's mother as a possible girlfriend candidate, or maybe just a friend with benefits.

Sophia flipped into her reciting voice. "'It's way way too early for him to date. But men are hound dogs, and this Dahlia's probably better than the alternative, at least you like her.'"

"It's not a date."

She giggled.

"What?"

"Talia says her mom would be interested in you, once you blow though your starter relationship."

"I'll keep that in mind."

"No you won't, Daddy."

"Probably not." He smiled.

"I can't wait to hear about your date."

"It's a business meeting. They're very boring."

"I don't think Dahlia knows how to be boring."

"That's what I'm worried about."

"You're funny, Daddy." Pause for effect. "*Funny looking.*"

They both laughed harder than the joke merited.

He began to sing a lullaby. Not exactly a lullaby, like Lisa used to sing, but one more in the classical tradition. "Ninety-nine bottles of beer on the wall, ninety-nine bottles of beer, if one of those bottles should happen to fall…"

XIV

How Not to Enjoy Fine Wine

Marc arrived at the restaurant, only to be told his reservation had been cancelled and there were no available tables. Mentioning his contact's name drew a look of disdain.

Dahlia, an ethereal vision in a short, backless black dress, drifted out of the elevator and seemed to float several inches off the floor. As an appreciated nod to propriety, she wasn't wearing her gold nose ring. In a quiet voice befitting a room with high vaulted ceilings, medieval tapestries, and crystal candelabras, he started to tell her about the reservation problem. She cut him off with a quick kiss on the lips, then said something in Parisian-accented French to the maître d'.

"So nice to have you with us, Mademoiselle Bruni-Sarkozy," he said with a deferential bow.

As the man led them to a corner table by a window, Dahlia whispered, "I hope you don't mind that I cancelled your reservation and made one of my own. I thought a better table would enhance an already-sure-to-be-enchanting evening."

"You made a reservation in the name of the wife of the president of France?" he asked through clenched teeth.

"Of course not. What kind of person do you think I am?" She pulled back, feigning surprise and disappointment. "I made it in the name of their daughter."

"They don't have a daughter."

"Then I guess she won't be needing a table. Turns out the restaurant's pretty lucky we came along to make use of it." Self-deprecating smile. "Having been born in Israel, I'm a sabra. Our contracts require that we be pushy, impolite, opinionated, and brimming with chutzpah."

"Mademoiselle Bruni-Sarkozy, really." He couldn't help smiling. "I'm flattered you made the effort to get us such a perfect table."

Abutting two glass walls and looking down on Central Park and much of the rest of the city, the table was sequestered from the rest of the dining area by a wall of flowers, their stems woven together over a barely visible bleached-wood trellis. Marc his companion, a sparkling young version of Carla Bruni, was staring adoringly at him. He intended to put a stop to that, just not quite yet.

The sommelier appeared beside their table.

Without looking at the wine list—a hefty tome bound in leather and glittering with gold leaf—Dahlia ordered a bottle of Pomerol, Château L'Evangile 1975.

"Do you have any idea what that costs?" Marc whispered.

He didn't but knew it was very expensive, and in a restaurant like this, that could've meant well north of five hundred dollars a bottle.

"All I know is that you're worth every cent of it." She reached out to lay her hand on his, but he foiled her plan by scratching his nose. "Sophia seems like a wonderful kid."

"Her mom did a terrific job bringing her up."

Returning quickly, as if concerned she'd change her mind, the sommelier showed her the bottle.

She studied it. "No obvious typos. Nice Chateau on the label. Hmm, you have any idea if the place is for sale? A little upgrade here and there, and it could make an appealing vacation home. Make a few calls, feel it out. If we close the deal, there could be a finder's fee for you."

Crooked smile. "I'm not sure I'm the right person…"

"With that attitude you're certainly not."

Her smile lit up the room, and the sommelier, now sure she was joking, laughed harder than politeness demanded. Marc joined in, out of relief that she'd salvaged the situation before it became embarrassing, not that he cared about being embarrassed but he didn't want the sommelier to be uncomfortable.

The sommelier poured some wine into her glass. She swirled it around, then tasted it.

"Mmm. What's the alcohol content?"

"Twelve and a half percent, Madame."

"Then we're good." She took another sip.

The fine line between charming and obnoxious was thicker for attractive women, but Marc was still impressed by how effortlessly Dahlia walked it.

The sommelier half filled their glasses, put the bottle on a side table, and withdrew.

"Am I trying too hard?" she asked as soon as he departed.

"Almost."

"When's Sophia's next tournament?" She leaned forward, eyes glowing with enthusiasm.

"Three weeks."

"Would it be okay if I come watch?"

"It's at the same location, Alley Park," he said, hoping that would dissuade her; if not he'd just have to tell her she wasn't invited.

She stared off into space, calling to mind her reaction the last time Marc had mentioned the place.

"Maybe it's a father-daughter thing I shouldn't interfere with." She refrained from making eye contact. "So, what did the murdering bitch say about me?"

"Other than referring to you as a *spunk-bucket* and a *little sociopath*, nothing much."

Her eyebrows rose.

"I hope you sprang to my defense."

"Absolutely. Told her in no uncertain terms that you aren't little."

"I am compared to her. Those implants of hers are so big she probably declares them as dependants on her tax forms."

The waiter brought menus. She waved him off and reverted to her adoring stare.

"This is quite good, well worth a tenth of what they're probably charging," Marc said.

"You're worth a multiple of—"

"This is a business dinner. I'm here because you're a client. I finally decided that if this is how you want to spend your money, I shouldn't object."

She raised her glass as if proposing a toast, and he touched his to hers.

"Perhaps you'd like to hear more about my meeting with LaPonte?"

"Of course, but let's wait till we're into our second bottle," she said. "One of my policies is not to talk about psychopaths sober."

"One bottle's plenty."

She looked at him as if that had been the stupidest thing she'd ever heard, the sort of look he'd have to get used to once Sophia became a teenager.

He observed the Central Park lights through his wine as he wondered why he was hesitant to ask any of the questions that flitted through his mind like hummingbirds on speed. Not coming up with a satisfactory answer, he started with an easy one.

"Why was it so important to you that we have dinner together?"

"Isn't it obvious?" Her tongue makes a slow transit across her perfect white teeth.

"Please, drop the sleazy come-ons."

"Okay, I'll stick to classier ones." She stroked her chin, an incongruously masculine gesture. "An absolutely divine new recording of Mozart's *Magic Flute* has come into my possession, via totally legitimate means, of course. Perhaps after dinner we can retire to my place for some champagne and caviar and listen to it. My great aunt will be in attendance, to make sure there's no funny business."

"My question?" Marc asked, smiling.

"You have an unfortunate tendency to see problems where there aren't any. I just wanted to get to know you better over some wine. If we get to know each other better, we might be able to head off misunderstandings before they develop." Her smile was so warm it melted his annoyance. "Marc, I know my delusions and mood swings make me a difficult client, but maybe you'll come to enjoy the challenge."

"I'm delighted to help you in any way that makes sense, but I'm not a psychiatrist."

"Phew." She wiped imaginary sweat from her brow. "I've never found them the least bit helpful."

The film-loop of Lisa dying, while he'd sat by helpless, ran through his head.

The sommelier refilled their glasses—amazingly, the bottle was empty. Dahlia ordered another.

"Dahlia, I told you one bottle's plenty."

"You also said something about not objecting if this is how I want to spend my money."

He smiled...again.

"Are you enjoying yourself?" she asked.

Strangely, he couldn't answer her without a moment's reflection.

"Yes, more than I have in some time. And you?"

"I'm enjoying myself. And you as well."

Feeling his cheeks grow warm, he broke eye contact and looked out the window for a moment. When he refocused on her, she blushed and looked down. Having never imagined that she was capable of blushing, he was at a loss.

"Marc..."

"What?"

She shook her head. The silence that followed seemed almost comfortable, and Marc wondered how much of what seemed to be going on between them was attributable to the wine.

"Silence is always good manners," Dahlia said, "and in social situations it's often clever as well."

"You have an uncanny ability to home in on my thoughts and translate them into an appropriate aphorism. If only you'd be so articulate in response to my questions."

She sat up unnaturally straight and placed her hands on the table in front of her, fingers interlocked.

"Having ordered our second bottle, I'm now ready for your tale of how my stout-hearted Ulysses took on the Circe of Massapequa."

Marc told her of his travails in getting LaPonte to talk to him and finally got to her *proof* that Birnbach was a child molester.

"Did she bother to tell you who dropped off that file?"

"She said someone sent it through a courier."

"The Snowman, undoubtedly. Maybe it's time to turn up the heat on him."

He smiled to acknowledge her pun but then realized, from her unchanging facial expression, that it hadn't been intentional. "I'll bite. Who's the Snowman?"

"A thug with a three-ball birthmark who threatened Yusef. I suspect he's the one who gave LaPonte that file and killed Shustak."

"Why didn't you mention him before?"

Was she squirming in her seat? He was mistaken; nobody could squirm in that little black dress.

"One would think that with such a distinctive feature," he said, "law enforcement wouldn't have much trouble locating him."

"But one would be wrong. I've tried, even going so far as hiring a detective and conferring with a Mossad agent, but it's as if I'm asking them to find the second shooter from the grassy knoll. They look at me like I'm crazy."

"You *are* crazy."

While he'd intended the remark as repartee, he was afraid it came out as judgmental. He was in over his head. A bad guy no one had seen but Dahlia?

"Doesn't mean I want to be looked at like I am."

"With you, one question just leads to another, like an endless series of matryoshka dolls."

"Might surprise you how much fun it is to play with dolls."

The sommelier refilled their glasses.

"I don't think I should represent you anymore."

"Because?"

"I smell trouble."

He opened the menu.

She took it from him.

"Fine, I'll deodorize it. Bring on your niggling little cavils, so we can move forward into the sunny uplands of further legal representation."

In their second meeting, she'd predicted he'd represent her because she was the only thing in his life, other than Sophia, that made him feel alive. He still wasn't sure if she'd been right, but he wanted to help her. Her struggle with mental problems only made him want to help more. But he knew he couldn't help and sensed that trying would lead to problems he couldn't solve...and risks a father had no right to take.

"I loved meeting Sophia, she's delightful."

"Her mother died four months ago. She's... fragile."

"I know, that's why I'm trying to help."

"Please don't."

Dahlia fingered the corner of the menu but didn't open it.

"Let's get it all out on the table," she says. "In *vino veritas*."

"Well, for one thing, it would make me more comfortable if I had an address, a way to contact you, but just so you know, even with an address I probably still wouldn't—"

She wrote a phone number on the back of his hand.

"I don't know how long I'll have this number. Unfortunately my circumstances are such that for now my address is in flux, as my personal life is...under construction." She ran a fingernail along his forearm. "It's... just a temporary thing, so please, Marc, don't read too much into that. It's no big deal."

He ignored the electric current of excitement that shot up his arm.

She asked, "What else is bothering you about me?"

He shook his head.

"Come on, Marc. I'm trying to clear the air here." She leaned forward. "Your being enigmatic isn't in the script—that's my role."

She took a drink and pointed to his glass. He had a sip. She waited wide-eyed with anticipation, but then her lips moved and her eyes seemed to focus on a spot on the wall over his left shoulder.

"Shut up!" she shouted.

"Dahlia."

"Oops." She covered her mouth. "Sorry about that, but she can be so damn annoying."

"Who?"

Dahlia bit her lip. "No, it's...nothing, just talking to myself, reliving a bad memory, like an acid flashback without the LSD."

Her eyes narrowed with anger and her lips started moving again as if she was having a conversation with someone else. Marc grew increasingly concerned.

"It's hard to explain."

He rested a hand on hers and looked into her eyes. "Try."

Attempting a reassuring gesture, Marc rested his hand on her forearm. She took a deep breath, followed by a hard swallow. "I sometimes get these... auditory hallucinations, but the voice seems real and can be so commanding that I'm not sure it's a hallucination. Anyway, whatever its source, I have to do what it says or all hell breaks loose in my head."

"Like when the Son of Sam heard a dog ordering him to kill?"

"No, you unimaginative twit, it's like God speaking from a burning bush, and if Moses hadn't had the sense to listen to Him, *you* would still be a slave in Egypt." Dahlia's face, contorted with anger, then relaxed. "Sorry, she made me say that."

"Seems the voice has a rather exalted opinion of itself."

"You don't know the half of it." Her attempt at a smile resulted in the bent lip of someone stricken by Bell's palsy. "I don't always follow the voice's commands. I'm fighting it more and more."

The waiter approached the table, but Dahlia again waved him away.

"I don't mean to be insensitive here," Marc said, "but if you know this voice isn't real, why can't you just ignore it?"

"Thing is I don't quite *know* that. Yes, I understand it intellectually, but it feels more real than anything." She sighed. "Some people claim to *know* God isn't real, but when things turn to shit, they're the first to go down on their knees and pray, and even the most atheistic among us would fall into line if some huge bearded guy started tossing thunderbolts from a cloud-mounted throne."

"You really believe God's speaking to you?"

"I call the voice Ariella, that makes her seem less fearsome, and I can sometimes think of her as sort of a deranged big sister, but still she has the power to overcome my will to resist. It just depends on how badly she wants me to do something. Sometimes she lets me get away with insubordination, sometimes not."

"Lets you? How can she stop you?"

Dahlia screamed in pain.

"Dahlia, what can I do?"

She shook her head but a few seconds later ran a hand through her spiky hair, and seemed fine.

"She controls me by the force of logic and reason," Dahlia's sing-song tone called to mind a political prisoner reading a coerced confession. "I've learned through hard experience that she's always right." False smile. "Except when she's wrong. Like when she told me to shoot a Mossad officer."

Pained wince.

"You've had quite a lot to drink on an empty stomach. Maybe you should—"

"No, really I'm okay, just a little glitch." She dropped her voice to a whisper as if about to disclose a deep dark family secret, "Ariella, though, has something of a drinking problem." Dropping her voice still further, she said, "No, Ariella, that's nothing at all like the pot calling the cocaine green, whatever the hell that means."

"Maybe we should get up and walk around a little," Marc said, more shaken than he'd like to admit. "Or at least go to the ladies room and splash some water on your face. Then we'll order dinner. No more wine."

"Or better yet, pull your head out of your ass and acknowledge that there's more to this world than what your four puny senses convey to your underused brain," Dahlia said, her voice a full octave lower than usual.

Marc wondered if she was about to spin her head 360 degrees and vomit green pea soup.

She stood and in her normal voice, said, "Sorry. Maybe I could use a trip to the w/c. Thank you for being so understanding."

But then she sat, pouty-faced, arms crossed.

He laughed—he too had had a lot to drink on an empty stomach.

"I'm not laughing at you, it's just that you look like four-year-old Sophia, refusing to eat her carrots as a matter of principle."

A sudden burst of light seared Marc's cornea. His first thought was that Ariella, playing God, had command of special effects. Then he realized that a family celebrating a milestone event at the next table had had a waiter take their picture and what Marc had seen had been the flash of the camera reflected off the window.

"You're the only one, other than Daniel, I've ever told about Ariella."

Touched, he found himself again leaning toward wanting to help her. A foolish consistency might have been the hobgoblin of little minds but his foolish inconsistencies had to be worse.

"You're so strong-willed and fiercely intelligent that it would seem you could—"

"You think child molesters can control their compulsions? Anorexics know that they're starving themselves to death and all they have to do to save themselves is eat. Yet a third of them die."

"Yes, of course, but—"

"I'm working on it and making progress. As you've seen, my insubordination can lead to psychosomatic pain, but in a weird way I consider that a good sign. These pain attacks are a recent development, and that they're happening now might indicate that Ariella fears her hold on me is fraying and she's getting desperate."

"That sounds—"

"Sure, it's an anthropomorphic oversimplification, but it's not wrong."

"I accept that." As if his acceptance or rejection meant anything.

"The real problem is that I also suffer from mood swings. When I'm manic, I'm particularly susceptible to Ariella's suggestions. When I'm depressed and she puts me down, the effect is devastating. It pushes me just a nanometer short of suicidal"

"That headache attack or whatever it was certainly seemed…"

"I said that happens infrequently. She was just showing off for your benefit. She has a jealous streak."

"You make it sound like…" He smiled reassuringly—well, he hoped it was reassuring. "It's almost like she's a separate person with her own personality."

"In contrast to an uptight lawyer without one?"

"Was that Ariella or you talking?"

"Hard to tell, but if it was me I didn't mean to offend, it's just that…"

"It's got to be frustrating for someone as articulate as you to be unable to explain your problems clearly to someone who doesn't suffer from them?"

Brilliant smile. She reached for her wine glass, but Marc held it down and shook his head.

"We've gotten sidetracked," Dahlia said. "There was something on your mind?"

"No." He studied his glass.

"Marc, don't humor me."

"Both times when I mentioned Alley Pond, you uncharacteristically lost your cool." His turn to swirl his wine. "Really, it's nothing. I just thought maybe you once lived near there."

He waved his arm: forget it.

"What's so significant about where I might have lived?" Her tone communicated casual curiosity—too casual.

"It was just…"

"A thought. Yes, you said that. We're now moving on to the part of the conversation where you put that thought into words."

"Is it you or Ariella who wants to know?" His smile and the accompanying tone made it seem as if he was joking rather than trying to embarrass her into getting off a subject that would not end well.

"She has a theory about you…that you don't have my best interests at heart."

"Do you share that theory?"

She grimaced. "I'd like to be able to completely rule it out."

"It should be a comfort to both of you that I'm considering not representing you anymore."

Disturbed by the ugly tone that crept into the conversation, he caught the waiter's eye, but before he took his second step toward the table, Dahlia shook her head and he receded.

"I asked you, 'What's so significant about where I might have lived?'"

The dangerous look on her face confirmed that he shouldn't tell her what he'd been thinking. But she'd met Sophia and he'd had more than a hint of how crazy she really was—her reference to Ariella's having her shoot someone sealed the deal—he needed to know.

"Stupid observation, but Creedmoor Psychiatric Center is pretty much across the street from Alley Pond. You told me you were institutionalized for a while. I'd pictured some sort of private sanitarium, but Creedmoor houses severely mentally disturbed patients, including those adjudicated to be criminally insane."

Her lip curled.

"No way I'm going to let you send me back there!"

She tossed the wine at his face and stormed out.

The maître d' handed him a napkin. "Is there a problem, sir?"

"I'll just take a check."

$2,770 for two bottles of wine.

At least she'd made easy the decision of whether to continue representing her.

XV

The Dirty Blonde

SINCE STORMING OUT of Canard, Dahlia had been walking aimlessly. By all rights her feet should've been cold and aching in her unbroken-in Christian Louboutins, but the pain of regret eclipsed her physical discomfort. She was deep into Central Park before she realized that she'd entered the park. Trying to pull herself out of dejection before it devolved into a full obdurate depression, she forced herself to concentrate on the nocturnal beauty around her.

She couldn't believe more people weren't out enjoying the park. It couldn't just have been that it was well past midnight and cold and windy. Perhaps their reticence was a throwback to the crime-ridden past, before New York became one of the world's safest big cities, and crime moved to the meth-infected suburbs and small towns.

Now that it was too late, she understood what had caused her descent into the full crazies. Although alcohol had eroded her ability to keep Ariella under semi-quasi-pseudo control, the primary catalyst had been her realization that she was beginning to have romantic feelings for Marc—she actually *blushed* when he'd caught her staring at him like a love-struck teenager. Knowing she couldn't allow herself to lose focus on her quest, she'd had enough sense to shut down such thoughts, but the tension between her desire for romance and her need to concentrate entirely on her quest had undermined her focus anyway. Ariella had jumped in to fill the mental gap.

And lucky it was that I showed up before the gap grew until it turned your entire brain into a total gapping void.

"Ahh, you are jealous."

Just that I'd rather see you fulfill your mission than fall into bed with a man twice your age with a hairy back.

106

"How do you know he has a—?"

Omniscience has its advantages.

"I could've done without you literally putting words in my mouth at dinner."

And I could've done without your carelessly revealing my existence and your institutionalization.

"I was being honest, not careless."

A distinction without a difference.

"I allowed myself to get sucked into one of your sadistic games." Dahlia punched herself in the thigh. "When you told me he was the enemy and was planning to send me back there, you knew I'd go nuts!"

You think he's fine with someone, adjudicated to be criminally insane, befriending his daughter? It would be easy enough for him to convince himself that having you committed would be for your own good. He'd admitted he was concerned about whether you'd been at Creedmoor and had already started telling you to stop drinking. The man's a meddlesome moralizer.

"I don't see him that way at all."

That's just one of the many reasons you need me around to look after you.

"So it's okay for you to be a meddlesome moralizer, but when there's the slightest hint that someone else might—"

I'm hardly a moralizer.

"An immoralizer is worse." Dahlia ground her teeth. "I feel awful about dousing him with wine. I'd give anything to go back in time and just change the subject."

Anything, hmmm. Too bad you don't have something more valuable to give than your life. If you did we might be able to do a deal.

"Screw you."

Ariella's cackling laughter echoed painfully off the walls of Dahlia's skull.

Next time she'll disregard Ariella's advice and suffer the consequences. A little psychosomatic pain would be preferable to the agony of fucking up.

Dahlia couldn't afford to be crazy; she had to keep control over her impulses and keep focused on her plan. But she couldn't focus on a plan until she actually had one. She forced herself to keep walking and formulate a course of action. Once she got Suzie's phone number via ASH, maybe she'd be able to persuade Suzie to speak to Marc. But would he do anything for her after tonight? Dahlia had brought him back around after she'd lied to him about being Daniel's daughter, perhaps she could do it again. Life was hard, but it was even harder if you were crazy.

At twenty-eight, it was about time she'd succeeded in something. It was a sin against God for someone so gifted to be a failure. Furthermore, someone evil enough to cause Shustak's and Daniel's deaths had to be stopped. So what if she's a little crazy? Lincoln and Churchill had suffered from depression. Joan of Arc heard voices and had visions. Schizophrenia didn't stop John Nash from winning a Nobel Prize or David Berkowitz from attaining his goals. Okay, so the Son of Sam wasn't the best example, but even if he'd thought a talking dog told him to kill people, he did succeed in carrying out his plan.

As she navigated a steep path in her high heels, a stone bridge caught her attention. It was a perfect classical arch, identical in form to those the Romans built to support their aqueducts. A cloud passed in front of the moon, throwing weird shadows. A brief snow flurry added to the general spookiness. Cold sank its fangs into her neck. She walked swiftly on. At the crest of a hill, she saw the rowboat lake through the leafless trees, the thin veneer of ice glowed with lunar light, and the boathouse—

Something sharp cut into her coat. A knife!

"Give it up to me." Deep male voice.

Her mule-kick, landing square on her assailant's kneecap, knocked him down. She spun, pulled her gun, and clicked off the safety.

"Oh my God. I thought…I'm getting paranoid in my old age." She helped the filthy blond man to his feet; he was four inches taller than her and a good seventy pounds heavier. "I'm sorry, you're just a mugger."

After several seconds of confused staring, the man made the universal two-fingered gesture requesting a cigarette.

She shook her head.

The wind shifted, and she was enveloped in his effluvia. He was such a failure at his chosen profession that he had to live on the street.

She took out her wallet.

"Would it hurt your professional pride if I gave you some money?"

She held out a twenty.

The man's bug-eyed look was all too familiar. Why did everyone think she was crazy, even when she was trying to be nice?

"Take the damn money," she said.

He took it.

"I came out here to work through some issues, things I can't talk about honestly with anyone I know," she said. "Mind if I run something by you?"

He bent to pick up a cigarette butt from the side of the path, when he saw it was a partially smoked marihuana joint, he flicked it away.

"What would you say if I told you that Daniel Birnbach was killed not because he was a pedophile but to suppress a valuable archeological find?"

"Since you're holding a gun on me, I'd agree."

"Sorry." She returned the gun to her bag. "If we were just friends talking?"

"I'd ask who Daniel Birnbach was."

"One of Mary LaPonte's victims."

"Oh, yeah, the guy who raped all those kids, right? He'd have lasted about a day and a half in the joint."

"If he never raped anybody, what should I do to set things right?"

"Nothing." His eyes appeared to move independently of each other. "People get fucked all the time. Kinda shit no one can do shit about."

"My problem is, I still don't know who the real bad guy is."

"Tell me what you know. I got all night."

Grateful to have someone to talk to who'd actually listen, she talked non-stop for ten minutes or so.

"It's that French guy," he said.

Her jaw dropped open. "How do you know?"

"Theaters are cool in summer, warm in winter, so I go to a lot of movies, see them over and over, and one of the things that comes through loud and clear is that it's always the fancy businessman who shows up pretty close to the beginning." In desperation, he picked up the discarded roach and lit it. "No, wait, I got it. It's this lawyer guy. It's almost always the one you least suspect."

"That would be Sophia, his ten-year-old daughter."

"Yeah, that's it! You got it, babe. And you *are* a babe," he said, while holding his breath to keep the smoke in his lungs. "If a doll can kill people, you know, like Chucky, why not a ten-year-old?"

"Maybe it *could* be de Saint-Juste. He denied knowing anything about it, which is exactly what he'd do if he were the bad guy."

"There you go."

"Of course, it's also exactly what he'd do if he were innocent." She handed him another two twenties. "Buy yourself a decent meal and get cleaned up."

He smiled, showing a snaggle of teeth that looked like an accident in a graveyard. "Mind if I spend it on cigs and a bottle of Jack?"

"Here's another forty, do both."

"You're good people. If everyone were like you, the world would be a better place."

"I wonder."

"No wondering. All the bums would be able to drink themselves to death and not bother anybody."

He was right. It's de Saint-Juste, Ariella said, as Dahlia exited the park. *There's a pay phone, leave him a voicemail. I'll tell you what to say.*

"I can't believe… why would de Saint-Juste have Daniel killed? It makes no sense."

It might make sense to him. He's got a hell of a lot of money riding on that desalination project, he needs to keep the emir happy.

While that sounded reasonable to Dahlia, she had promised herself not to follow any more of Ariella's advice.

"That's about as persuasive as when you told me to douse Marc with wine because he wanted to send me to Creedmoor."

Oh, right, your oath of disobedience, the blank check you issued to your weak mind.

"I've had enough of your *mal mots.*"

Ariella responded with an ear-splitting snit followed by total silence. Fear clutched Dahlia's heart. She told herself to be strong, she was better off without Ariella. Unable to trust her own senses, she couldn't be truly sure of anything, and that insecurity had led her to give too much credence to what might, after all, have been a talkative hallucination. She couldn't allow herself to get sucked back in.

But she hated the silence—and the oppressive loneliness. "Ariella?"

No response.

Her heart felt as if it was being torn from her body still beating. Then she was overwhelmed by loneliness. She'd been prepared to endure Ariella's rampages of psychosomatic revenge, but Ariella's disappearance was almost unbearable. Almost but not quite, Dahlia told herself.

Legs like lead she moved so slowly that at the first light of dawn she was just leaving the park.

All I'm saying is test him. Coming after hours of silence, Ariella's voice was like a hug. *Raise the stakes. If he ignores our message, we'll cross him off our list.*

"Our *list* consists of only two entries: a thus-far-unidentified emir and everyone else in the world."

I still detect a hint of insubordination in your tone.

"Gee, maybe you are omniscient after all."

A ridiculously loud boom of thunder was followed by an atomic-bomb-bright flash. The few pedestrians on the street pulled jackets over their heads and scurried off like sinners attempting to flee Sodom. A lightning bolt struck near Dahlia, shattering the sidewalk. Whether the sidewalk was shattered in the outside world or only in her head was an irrelevant academic question. As she knew from denying the voice's dictates, burning in hell inside one's own head could be at least as unbearable as suffering in the actual physical domain of Beelzebub. Ariella had spoken *ex cathedra*, and when she did, she could not be denied.

What do you have to lose by testing him?

Dahlia hesitated.

Do it!

She put a quarter in the payphone and punched in the Frenchman's number. After a beep that was not preceded by an outgoing message, she repeated what Ariella said in her head.

"Hi, it's Dahlia. I was just speaking to someone in the know who told me you're the one who had Daniel Birnbach killed. I find that a little hard to believe, so I devised a test. If you're really on the right side, put me in touch with Ahmed. Just so you know, I've written down the truth about of Daniel finding the scrolls, what they say, and the efforts to suppress them. I keep the flashdrive on me at all times. So, if you want to the suppress the scrolls, you'll have to suppress me."

Dahlia wasn't thrilled with the last two sentences.

If I'm right about Monsieur, he'll tell Ahmed or one of his emir cronies about our message. That will cause them to escalate and in the process show themselves.

On an intellectual level escalation didn't sound like an entirely good thing, but excitement surged through Dahlia.

We're finally on the right path. Leave more messages.

"I don't know if that's such a great idea."

Dahlia braced herself for the pain that didn't come.

There is a tide in the affairs of men which taken at the flood leads on to fortune. Omitted, all the voyage of their life is bound in shallows and in miseries.

Dahlia hated it when Ariella quoted Shakespeare in that supercilious Oxbridge accent of hers, but she got the point.

DO IT! A giant Nike swoosh appeared in the sky, presumably an attempt at humor.

Not getting the point wasn't an option.

Dahlia left similar voicemails with the UAE, Qatar, Kuwait, and Saudi embassies, and Halliburton and BP as well. If de Saint-Juste didn't know the bad guys, someone did.

But if someone retaliated, she wouldn't know who did it. Also, she realized, it would have been wiser to have said that the flashdrive was somewhere safe under instructions to release it if anything happens to her.

Fortes fortuna iuvat (Fortune favors the bold), Ariella said, quoting Virgil. She might not always act in Dahlia's best interests but at least she was educated.

"Maybe the stupid and crazy as well."

Leaving the park and not looking where she was going, she crossed against the light and almost became a hood ornament on a speeding semi-trailer. Her mood fell like an elevator with a broken cable. She made it to the subway but by then felt as if the train was ascending the Matterhorn, and she was pulling it. The hell with Ariella! As soon as she exited the subway and again had cellphone reception, she'd call de Saint-Juste and ask him to ignore her voicemail. But by the time she hauled herself up the stairs, she didn't see the point. De Saint-Juste would ignore her messages as the rantings of a crazy woman—after all, he'd seen through her ploy of sending an email from Marc's computer. The others didn't even know who she was and undoubtedly got nutty calls all the time. The world was chock full of lunatics.

XVI

Grand Theft Auto

TROLLING OLD CONTACTS, Marc met people for breakfast, lunch, drinks, and coffee but failed to scare up any new business. His lawyer friends complained that business was as slow as it had ever been. He heard no more from Dahlia.

Finally, his phone rang.

"I've given your name to a second cousin of Sheikh Saqr bin Muhammad al-Qasimi," de Saint-Juste said, dispensing, as usual, with hello.

"Who is?"

"The ruler of the strategic UAE emirate, Ras al-Khaimah." De Saint-Juste sounded pained to have to explain something so commonly known. "He died recently, throwing the whole place into some level of political uncertainty. Anyway, one of al-Qasimi's sons is my main contact for my desalination project, and Fahad, your potential client, is his nephew. Frankly, they shipped him here some years ago because he'd become an embarrassment. God knows I wouldn't be dealing with the little creep if I didn't need to keep them happy, but it sounds like he has an interesting case, one that could be quite lucrative for you. I feel bad about having pulled the rug out from under you on the D&S matter and want to make it up to you. Are you available to see him, say around two this afternoon? If not, tell me what works for you."

"Two would be fine. Thanks for thinking of me."

Ominous pause. "One thing, though—are you representing a crazy person who calls herself Dahlia Birn?"

"I'm sorry, but that's really not your business."

"She left me a delusional, vaguely threatening voicemail, invoking your name and her relationship with you."

"She what?!"

"Something about some scrolls and one of the people that fruitcake LaPonte killed."

"Yes, she's obsessed with—"

"If you want future business from me, your representation of her has got to stop."

"Actually, it has, but—"

"If you're no longer working with her, the less said the better."

Marc led into his office Fahad Said, a young man who resembled Rafa Nadal on an astonishingly good hair day.

"May I get you something to drink? Coffee, tea, water?"

"Darjeeling, steeped for three minutes, with a quarter lemon and one and a half level teaspoons of honey."

"Will you settle for Lipton's and sugar? You can control how long the tea bag stays in the water."

After standing on his toes to look down his nose at Marc, Fahad took a deep breath, let it out slow, and in the process blew some errant hairs from his botox-smoothed forehead.

"I'll have the water, cool but not chilled. Either Evian or Perrier would be acceptable."

"Poland Spring from the water cooler or tap?"

"I'll pass, thank you." Fahad sat on Marc's client chair, crossed his legs more daintily than Dahlia had, and said, "I was Ricardo Rodriguez's partner."

He paused to let that talismanic name work its magic on Marc.

"Should I know who that is?"

"Have you at least heard of Tom McKean?"

No one on the face of the planet hadn't heard of McKean. Every one of his books had vaulted onto the bestseller lists, and several had been made into hit movies. Lisa had referred to him as the *Velveeta cheese of lawyer-novelists*, and out of loyalty, Marc had never read any of his thrillers even though he thought he might've enjoyed them.

"Oh, right—Rodriguez is McKean's literary agent, isn't he?" Marc had no idea how he knew that.

"McKean was a nobody until Ricardo discovered him."

"Wasn't he a football star with the Crimson Tide, then an Alabama state senator?"

"Point is, he couldn't get published in a penny-saver. Then Ricardo got him a film deal, for *Hot Red Hurt*."

"George Clooney and Cameron Diaz," Marc said, showing off his cultural awareness.

"Then the publishers came running. Ricardo held an auction that got McKean a $1.5 million advance, practically a record for a first novel."

"You're a literary agent?"

Fahad's face twisted in revulsion, as if such plebian labors were far beneath him.

"Oh, that kind of partner." Apologetic smile. "So, what brings you here?"

"Ricardo passed two weeks ago, massive coronary."

"I'm sorry."

Dismissive wave. "Time and again I told him to drink less, exercise, lose weight, avoid fatty foods, but no. He needed to do everything his own way, wouldn't listen to anyone, least of all me."

"You're here because…"

"I'm his executor and sole heir. Just a couple hours after I woke to find him dead next to me in bed, McKean called. I answered the phone and understandably hysterical, told him what happened. Seems he didn't know that Ricardo was gay, and… well, he's a homophobic cunt." Fahad handed Marc a multi-page letter from a Birmingham, Alabama, lawyer. "I got this yesterday."

The letter claimed that Rodriguez could have gotten McKean another one-quarter of one percent of the gross for the movie made from his thriller *Red Menace* but instead he'd bargained it away in exchange for a part for Fahad in the movie. The letter also gave additional examples of Ricardo's skimming money due McKean and routing it to Fahad. It demanded the return of the $21 million in commissions Rodriguez had received and threatened to sue.

"I should just bin the damn thing, right?" Fahad mimed crumpling it into a ball and tossing it into the garbage.

"Well, if what he's alleging is true… Legally, a faithless agent has to return all commissions he received."

"No, no, no, and no. As Ricardo's heir, I'm entitled to keep getting commissions on existing books and films, that's fifteen percent of everything they take in. Last year commissions were almost seven mil."

Marc took a sip from the now tepid mug of tea that had graced his desk for the previous several hours.

"One-quarter of one percent of the gross is a huge payment for an unknown actor. *Did* Rodriguez use his influence to get you a part in *Red Menace*, even though you had no previous acting experience?"

"Totally false, the lowest sort of slander." He slammed his fist on Marc's desk, knocking over a photo of Lisa. "They wouldn't let me live in Abu Dhabi, exiled me to Riyadh. You have any idea how much acting you have to do if you're gay in Riyadh? Forget about getting bad reviews, they'll actually stone you to death."

"According to this letter, McKean's fee was reduced by exactly the same amount that you received, one-quarter of one percent of the gross."

Annoyed that Fahad neglected to do so, Marc set the photo back in its proper place.

"Ricardo, made McKean a millionaire one hundred times over, Now he's bitching about a few hundred grand." He flicked his wrist to indicate the insignificance of such a small number. "A rounding error, cigarette money."

"But still—"

"McKean's a no-talent, limp-dicked homophobe, trying to screw me." Fahad again slammed his fist on Marc's desk, and Marc steadied the photo. "Last thing McKean wants is negative publicity, and justice is on my side."

Marc held up a hand: *Give me a minute to think.*

"It's in both your interests to settle this quietly. Faced with a lawsuit, McKean might see the light, but if we do sue, we should do it soon and here in New York. I'd rather be before a New York jury than an Alabama one if I'm representing a gay Latino and an Arab against a good ole boy. For that to happen, it would be helpful to be the first to sue. If we can have the case heard here, they might settle in a way that works for you."

"Monsieur de Saint-Juste said you'd handle this on a…" Fahad snapped his fingers. "Contingency, twenty percent of what we collect from McKean."

"McKean is the one threatening to sue. If he recovers anything or if you settle for a wash, there'll be nothing from which to take a contingency, and"—he tapped the letter from McKean's lawyer—"on the surface, at least, this makes a pretty persuasive case."

Fahad pushed a button on his phone and spoke in halting French, his hands waving an incomprehensible semaphore. He listened to the response, then gave the phone to Marc.

De Saint-Juste said, "As we speak, I'm wiring fifty K into your account against a ten percent contingency."

"I was thinking twenty percent."

"If the contingent recovery is greater than fifty K, I want the money back. If it's less or zero, you keep the fifty and I'll find some way to bill it to the desalination project."

"And if McKean gets a judgment?"

"Keep the fifty. McKean won't be able to collect squat from the slimy little bastard, money runs through Fahad like *merde* through a goose."

"Okay," Marc said, not that it mattered—de Saint-Juste had already hung up. "Fahad, do you happen to know an Ahmed? A grandson of an emir, probably in his twenties. He spent some time here, hung out in downtown clubs and formed an attachment of sorts to a very pretty adolescent named Yusef."

Fahad shook his head. "If he made that scene here, Ahmed was a pseudonym. He wouldn't have used his real name."

Marc wasn't surprised. Nothing in Dahlia's case was easy. He hadn't wavered from his decision not to represent her, but if he could help…

After winning her first round in two close sets plus a tie-breaker, Sophia took a 6-1, 6-0 drubbing from the number-one seed. Hugging her opponent, she congratulated her on her superb play.

"I tried, Daddy," she said as she came through the flap in the hanging plastic that separated the court from the corridor.

"You played some terrific points. That girl has a full-time coach and to make time for her tennis, she's home-schooled. I was talking to her coach. Her dad came to watch but stomped out when she lost that one game."

"I wish we still had a car," she said. "The bus and subway take *hours* to get home."

"Not that long," he said. "And think how good it is for the environment that we're taking public transportation. I've got *The Hobbit* in my briefcase. I'll read to you. It won't be so bad."

"Yes it will. I'll start missing Mommy, thinking about how she used to come watch me play and…." Her voice cracked.

A slightly accented woman's voice came from around the corner, where the corridor made a ninety-degree turn toward the clubhouse.

"You really kicked butt that one game, showed that little snot-nose a thing or two."

"Dahlia!" Sophia yelled.

An electric shock of anger burned through Marc's chest.

"Come, I'll drive you into the city and buy you dinner to celebrate Sophia's glorious first-round victory. Now *there* was a match."

"Yes!" Sophia bounced on her toes.

Marc shook his head.

"Marc, I'm so sorry about what I did the other night. I'd gone off my meds, which I should *never* do, but I'm back on them now even though they dampen my enthusiasm and make the world unbearably flat. I just wish—"

"It's okay," he said, not wanting to have this discussion in front of Sophia.

"What do I owe you for the wine?"

"Don't worry about it," he said. "Even with my time charges, the whole thing comes out to less than the five thousand you paid me. We're square."

"Come on, you know that's not what I gave you the money for, and there's no way I don't owe you at least a few hundred dollars."

Hand on the small of Sophia's back, he directed her around Dahlia and along the corridor.

"We want to take the bus," he said.

"No we don't!" Sophia shouted.

"Sophia, please excuse us for a minute, I have something private I need to say to your father." Dahlia receded several steps and with her back to Sophia whispered, "Marc, I get that you don't want to expose your daughter to someone who's been adjudicated criminally insane, but not only was I falsely accused, later exonerated, and certified sane." She looked at the floor. "Well, maybe not sane, exactly, but definitely not dangerous."

"The wine throwing was—"

"Unacceptable, and I promise nothing like that will ever happen again. As I said, I'd gone off my meds, but even that—the worst thing you've ever seen me do—didn't expose you to anything more dangerous than a dry-cleaning bill. I came out here to try to make amends."

She flashed a brilliant smile in Sophia's direction.

"Hey, what are you two whispering about?" Sophia asked.

"My driving you two back to the city and buying you dinner," Dahlia said. "Really, Marc, it's the least I can do."

"Not a good idea."

"Yes it is, Daddy. It's an awesome idea."

Sophia's radar about people was generally accurate. Like many kids, and like her mother, she was good at distinguishing good-hearted people from phonies, but Marc doubted that her talent carried over to psychotics skilled at role playing.

He dropped his voice. "Dahlia, please. I don't want to go with you and don't want to be having this conversation in front of my daughter. If you'd like to talk to me, call me in the office."

They walked though the tiny clubhouse and into the parking lot. In the distance, the bus slowed but with no one getting on or off, didn't stop. The next one wouldn't be by for twenty-five minutes, and that was in the unlikely event that it kept to the schedule.

"Do you hate me so much that you won't even accept a ride from me, after I came all this way to apologize and make things right between us?" Dahlia's voice again caught and her eyes became damp.

He was sure that what she really wanted was to wheedle him into agreeing to represent her further. He reminded herself that no good could come from representing a crazy person. Dahlia's showing up and involving Sophia raised as many red flags as a Stalin-era May Day parade.

A clap of thunder immediately followed a flash of lightning. There was no shelter at the bus stop. The dampness, refracted in the parking lot's halogen light, gave Dahlia's face the sparkle and glow of a model in an ad for an obscenely expensive watch. Another lightning flash made her look demonic, but Marc dismissed that one as an illusion. They quickened their pace.

The lights of a new BMW flashed, and the locks clicked open. Dahlia pulled on leather driving gloves.

She took Sophia's tennis bag and backpack to the other side of the car. Marc thought he heard a zipper open and close. She tossed them into the back seat, then opened the doors.

"Wait! What are you doing?" Marc asked. "I never said I'd—"

"Would it make you feel more comfortable if you drove?" Dahlia asked.

Another flash of lightning, immediately followed by a deafening thunderclap, drowned out his question about whether she'd just unzipped a pocket on Sophia's backpack, not that he had any idea why she'd do that.

Dahlia tossed him the keys. With him driving, he couldn't imagine anything bad happening as a result of accepting a ride back to the city.

"Sophia, would you hand me your backpack, please?" he said. "I think I put my glasses in there."

Dahlia had no reaction to his request, and when he looked in the pockets nothing seemed missing or added. He grimaced. That was the second time he'd suspected Dahlia of doing something she hadn't done.

"Silly me," he said. "They're in my jacket pocket."

"And dinner?" Dahlia brought her hands together as if praying.

Sophia mimicked her.

"If we do, and you say anything inappropriate in front of Sophia, we'll leave. Immediately."

Dahlia stood at attention and saluted. Face bright with excitement, Sophia jumped into the back seat.

The heavens opened, but inside it was warm and dry. He found the new-car smell intoxicating. Dahlia asked Sophia about school, her teachers, and her friends, and she responded with happy enthusiasm. Shorn of her manic intensity, Dahlia was so at ease and so charming that he again found himself liking her. He enjoyed driving such a fine machine, and it *was* true that nothing about her had ever even suggested that she might be a danger to Sophia.

At Amsterdam Avenue and 79th Street, Dahlia said, "If it's okay with you, pull over in front of Nice Matin. Food's good, and we should be able to get in and out pretty quickly."

"Daddy and I have been meaning to go there forever," Sophia said with more excitement than he'd heard in her voice in quite a while.

They started to get out of the car, but then Marc saw the *no parking* sign, pointed to it, and motioned for them to get back in.

"It's okay," Dahlia said. "The police don't ticket in this neighborhood at this time of night."

Marc looked at his watch: 7:45. In fifteen minutes the spot would be legal, probably not a problem. They got out of the car, and he tossed the keys back to Dahlia.

"Anyway, I borrowed the car from a doctor at Creedmoor," she said. "If we get a ticket, the cops will run the plates through their computer, see it's been reported missing, and give the good doctor a call, so—"

"Honey, we're going home." Marc's hand circled his daughter's wrist.

"Come on, Marc," Dahlia said. "I was just joking."

He shook his head. "Even to jokingly imply that you stole—"

"I bought it with the intention of using it for a few weeks and then giving it to you as a surprise—in appreciation for all you've done for me." Although she spoke in a barely audible whisper, Marc thought he heard her add, "And will do for me."

"Daddy, she's giving us a car! Wouldn't it be great to have one again? Oh, thank you, thank you!"

"Show me the registration and the bill of sale," Marc said. "Not that I don't believe you, but I'm compulsive about keeping my records organized."

"Maybe you can just trust me for once," Dahlia said. "Don't you see how unfair you're being? You were angry at me for not telling you the truth, and now that I tell you the truth, you're even angrier. The message you're sending is that I can't win no matter what I do."

"I've no way to know if you're telling the truth, and I suspect you don't know either," he said through gritted teeth.

"She's right, Daddy. You always tell me that if I do something wrong I should admit it and apologize. She did both." Sophia looked confused. "Wait a minute, what did she do wrong? She bought us a car."

"Sophia, she's sick, and it's not good for you to—"

"What's the matter?" she asked Dahlia, eyes wide with fear. "Do you need to go to the doctor?"

"Not that kind of sick," Marc said, wondering if there was anything more insensitive he could have said to a girl who'd recently lost her mother to illness. "But it's very nice of you to be so concerned."

"Sophia, your dad is angry at me because I had a temper tantrum when he and I had dinner. Sometimes I act a little crazy, but the only one who's ever been hurt by it is me—" she turned to Marc—"unless you count getting wine thrown on you as *hurt*." Back to Sophia, "If there's any lesson to learn, it's to always control your temper and before you let yourself get angry, take a minute to think if there's really a good reason for it." Dahlia again turned to Marc. "The transition when I go back on my meds is always a bit tricky, but I'll be good from now on." Hand on her heart. "Promise."

"She promises, Daddy."

He shook his head. "I'm not equipped to deal with—"

"Someone who's been adjudicated criminally insane? That's it, isn't it? It's a profiling thing. Marc, we're people too. 'If you prick us, do we not bleed? If you tickle us, do we not laugh? If you poison us, do we not die?'"

"You are kidding?"

"Yes, Marc, and you should be laughing." She tickled his neck. "See, if I tickle you…"

Sophia was laughing—*really* laughing, for the first time since Lisa died.

Mouth to Dahlia's ear, Marc said, "It's as unclear as everything else about you, but even if there's the remotest chance that you just stole a fifty-thousand-dollar car…"

"I can't believe you'd even suggest… It's a brand-new BMW M6 convertible! No way you can get it for less than a hundred. Well, maybe a little less if you pay cash or…but my point is I wouldn't even think of giving you a ride in a five-figure car. I've got too much respect for you for that."

She smiled. He didn't.

"Something else, did you happen to leave a message with de Saint-Juste—"

"I'm sorry, it won't happen again." Turning her back to Sophia, Dahlia whispered, "I'd never do anything like that when I've taken my meds."

"Why the hell did you—?"

"After the debacle at Canard, I went for a walk in the park, depressed and struggling to come to terms with what I'd done. I met this guy who, in my *unsettled* state, persuaded me that de Saint-Juste might have been involved with Daniel's murder. I wanted to flush him out."

"Why, in your wildest imagination, would de Saint-Juste—?"

"I can't even tell you my thought process. I'll call him and apologize." She took her phone from her bag.

"Please, just leave bad enough alone."

"Did the call cause him to…" The corners of her mouth turned down. "You didn't lose the client, did you?"

"Actually, he sent me a new matter but told me not to represent you anymore."

After a moment's delay, she smiled. She tried to tickle him again, but he hopped backward; she hopped toward him, and he again hopped backward. He couldn't stop himself from grinning at the absurdity of the situation and Sophia's reaction.

"What's going on?" Sophia asked. "You guys are acting weird. I don't understand."

"I don't fully understand it myself," Dahlia said, "but it seems your daddy is scared of me. Scared that if he lets himself get to know me he'll like me."

"Come, Sophia, it's a school night. You've got homework."

"Daddy, it's Friday."

A cop started to write up a ticket for the BMW. Marc made eye contact with Dahlia and tilted his head in that direction. She shrugged and he made a mental note of the license plate number.

"I have just one more thing to say on the subject," Dahlia said. "If after listening with an open mind you still want to abandon me here, then Godspeed and good luck."

Marc rolled his eyes.

Dahlia took from her pocket a crumpled newspaper clipping, slowly unfolded and flattened the paper, then straightened up, as if about to deliver a funeral ovation or an uppercut.

"'Nice Matin gives the Upper West Side a splash of Provençal sunshine and a heady introduction to the cuisine of Nice, home of the *pissaladière, pan bagnat* and, if we are to believe the menu, a whopping big burger topped with *comté* cheese, smeared with aioli and served with a heap of rosemary-flecked fries. It's the best thing to happen to a hamburger since Daniel Boulud worked *foie gras* and short ribs into an all-beef patty. The pleasure is all on the plate, and it carries right through to the desserts.'"

She refolded the article and stuffed it into her pocket.

"To paraphrase the immortal words of *Dirty Harry*, you've got to ask yourself one question: Do I feel hungry?" Her eyes perfectly mimicked the Clint Eastwood squint. "Well, do ya, punk?"

Marc smiled. She might be insane, but she was charmingly insane.

"I feel hungry, Daddy." Sophia sucked in her stomach and cheeks. "I'm starving to death."

Getting out of a place like Creedmoor was a hell of a lot harder than getting in, if only because of the fear of liability if the discharged patient was to then commit a crime. And if Dahlia's meds cured her of her symptoms, he wanted to help but not so much that he'd represent her again. In spite of his uncharacteristic and unsettling ambivalence, he knew it would end badly.

"Fine, let's eat, but two conditions. First, I do no more legal work for you."

"I haven't asked you to do any," Dahlia said.

He put a hand on her shoulder, nudged her a few steps down the street, and squeezed until she winced.

"And no private communication between you and Sophia. I'm mad as hell about how you've used her to manipulate me—"

"*Used? Manipulated?*"

"Don't fuck with me. I'll file a criminal complaint before you know what's happening." Not that he knew of anything criminal she'd done, but it sounded good.

"Got it."

"Okay, let's have dinner," he said.

Sophia clapped.

"You're doing the right thing, Marc," Dahlia said.

"I doubt it, but—"

"I get it. Two conditions. Now, can we all just relax and have a good time?"

XVII

Schizophrenics Can't Lie But They Sure Can Try

Marc enjoyed his burger and beer while Dahlia focused on Sophia, who responded enthusiastically, the way she used to with Lisa when excited about something. Taken out of context, the dinner could hardly have been more pleasant. In context, it would've been greatly improved if his daughter weren't being entertained by a crazy person; not just an ordinary one but someone who'd been adjudicated criminally insane.

Just in case, he had Dahlia's promise that she wouldn't have any further contact with Sophia. And he had the plate number of the car she stole, borrowed, or bought for him. If he combined that with her prior adjudication, he could get a protective order. Although he didn't think he'd have any reason to, he wouldn't hesitate if she broke her promise. But if he had to do that, how would the authorities locate her? He didn't even have her address. While the waiter cleared their appetizer plates and Sophia and Dahlia were deep in conversation, he surreptitiously took Dahlia's fork, wrapped it in a napkin, and slipped it into his inside jacket pocket. At least he now had her fingerprints. Better paranoid than sorry.

Pushing her chair back, Sophia said, "May I please be excused?"

He hadn't heard her utter those words since Lisa died. He needed to be more vigilant about manners. He'd let too much slide.

"I'll come with you." Dahlia stood.

"Nooo." Sophia winked at her.

With his daughter beyond hearing distance, Marc said, "You don't have to answer, if you don't want to, but what did you do to end up in Creedmoor?"

124

"I was a victim of circumstance, unfairly blamed, and railroaded into the place."

She took a long sip of beer. He did the same.

He said, "*The Times* doesn't always get things right, but it was right on about the burgers here."

"It's very nice of you to want to find out more about my bad old days and to get to know me better." She placed a hand on his. "And your clumsy effort to change the subject was even nicer. I hope that one day, when all this LaPonte stuff is behind us, we can be friends, and I can repay your kindnesses."

"You don't owe me anything."

She made a face he couldn't read, then studied the bubbles in her half-empty mug.

Finally, she said, "My father was sent to jail in Israel for gun running, and with my mother dead since I was too young to remember her, he arranged for Daniel to act as my guardian. It wasn't a formal legal thing, Dad just thought I'd be better off if I weren't surrounded by people who knew he was a criminal, or rather one so inept as to get caught. I'm not sure why Daniel even agreed to do it. He and my father weren't really close, he was just one of the people Dad knew best in New York. Dad's third choice, the first two having had the sense to turn him down."

"That explains a lot."

She put a finger to her lips.

"Conditions like mine tend to kick in during adolescence, and here I was living with a virtual stranger, in a foreign country. I took up with an unmusical rock musician, got into drugs, and ran away from home, not that Daniel's place felt the least bit like home. Then Ace—the rocker actually called himself that—shot someone in a botched hold-up. I wasn't even there, but my prints were the only ones on the gun. My symptoms flared up. The D.A.'s shrink diagnosed me as suffering from a schizoaffective disorder, and my Legal Aid lawyer didn't have a counter-shrink examine me. My lawyer, the court-appointed social worker, and the prosecution shrink convinced me that going to Creedmoor would be preferable to ending up in juvie-jail.

"In my condition I barely remembered Daniel, but somehow he found me. He hired a psychiatrist who said I couldn't have shot the druggist, but the district attorney was reluctant to open a closed case. Daniel then tracked down the pseudo rock star's friends and finally, under pressure from them, he confessed. The Creedmoor bureaucrats still hesitated. Even Daniel's handpicked shrink agreed that I'd always be schizoaffective, periodically losing contact with reality, hallucinating, and having precipitous, extreme mood swings. But Daniel persisted until they gave in."

Marc reached out to stroke her arm, but afraid the gesture might be misinterpreted, lifted his glass to his lips. He could only imagine how difficult what she'd gone through must have been for her. It would have been for anyone, but a mentally ill adolescent, alone in a foreign country? He put down his glass and stroked her arm.

"I'm beginning to understand myself well enough to function at a reasonably high level.... Except for the occasional wine-doused friend and misguided attempt at humor about a German luxury car." She took a sip of beer. "I'm still a screw up, but I realize my mistakes soon afterwards and often manage to make them right, if only through the kind of groveling and apologizing to which I've subjected you."

He glanced in the direction of the ladies room.

"That was a terrible story," he said.

"I could improve it, maybe work in some gratuitous sex and violence or better develop some of the characters. Okay, let's see, the Legal Aid lawyer had a lisp and a slight hare-lip, partially disguised by a mustache that made him look sinister, and he and the social worker—the kind of woman who wore cat's-eye glasses with a second pair hanging from a beaded chain around her neck—had a thing going on there. Ace, well, he was just an asshole."

"No, I didn't mean..." He reached for his glass. "You knew that."

"It was unfair of me to lay all that on you, but I do hope we'll be friends. Anyway, you asked, and one of the problems with these damn meds is it's hard for me to lie when I'm on them."

He smiled.

"What?"

"My wife told me that schizophrenics can't lie. You said schizoaffective disorder was similar to—"

"But we can sure try." Her smile illuminated the room, then faded. "Actually, schizoaffective disorder, like any other categorization of psychoses, covers a wide range of symptoms that vary wildly from person to person, and mine are far from typical."

"I wouldn't expect anything about you, even your illnesses, to be typical."

He smiled, communicating that his comment had been an attempt at humor. Their eyes met, and something sweet passed between them.

"But I wouldn't be doing any of this if I didn't believe what Daniel told me." She again placed her hand on his, and he felt a mild electric jolt.

He said, "I appreciate your effort to open up and be honest."

"But you don't fully believe—"

"I don't disbelieve." He smiled.

She returned his smile.

"Huge concession for a lawyer."

"For this one, anyway. And as for our becoming friends…" He wasn't sure why he stopped mid-sentence, and from the increasingly confused look on her face, neither was Dahlia. "I'd like that."

She responded with the brightest smile he's seen from her, other than when she'd been in a manic phase.

"Should I go see if Sophia's okay?" Dahlia asked. "She's been in there awhile."

"Give her another couple of minutes. She's undoubtedly texting her friends about us having dinner."

She saluted.

"I'm still annoyed about your call to de Saint-Juste," he said. "That alone will likely put the kibosh on my doing future work for you."

"Up to you," she said.

"Just for my edification, explain to me why, even under the grip of delusion, you could've thought that de Saint-Juste—"

"Marc, I know. The guy's involved in building an eco-friendly desalination plant, not in killing people, and even if some emir wanted Daniel dead, he wouldn't tell de Saint-Juste about it. Anyway, I told you, I won't be bothering him anymore."

Sophia returned.

The waiter asked, "Would you like to see dessert menus?"

"No, thank you," Sophia said. "I'm full."

"It's up to my insignificant other," Dahlia said.

"I'm fine," Marc said.

On the way out of the restaurant, Dahlia said, "Come, I'll drop you home."

"We can walk, it's just a few blocks," Marc said, to Sophia's muted disappointment. "Goodnight. Thank you for dinner."

"Yes, thanks. It was really fun," Sophia said, "Did you and my daddy have a nice talk?"

"Very." Dahlia grinned, then whispered to Marc, "There is one teensy weensy thing you can do for me."

Marc shook his head.

"May I come by the office tomorrow, say around four? At least give me the chance to talk to you about it."

"I agreed to dinner on two conditions," he said, but gently.

"All I'm asking is that you listen to what I want you to do—something totally innocuous, I promise. You're welcome to turn me down. In fact I don't want you working for me unless you want to, and I'll pay for your time to listen."

He pursed his lips.

She cast a concerned glance at her watch. "Excuse me a sec. I need to make a call, check in with a doctor." She took out her phone, pushed a button, and scowled. "Darn. Out of battery power."

"Here." Marc handed her his.

"Thanks."

She punched in a number and turned her back while she talked, gesticulating and pacing. Turning back to face Marc, she held up one finger.

"Take your time."

Her pacing took her around the corner. She returned seconds later and handed him back the phone.

"Thanks." Her most winning smile. "Tomorrow, your office? Please."

He nodded, feeling as if a puppeteer had loosened the string holding his head up, then jerked it.

She gave him a peck on the cheek, then planted one on Sophia's forehead.

"You're a very lucky girl, Sophia, having such a nice dad."

They exchanged conspiratorial winks.

XVIII

Psychopath or Rectal Ulcer

DAHLIA SHOWED UP at precisely four o'clock: tailored gray business suit, white cotton shirt, and low heels. After telling Marc what a wonderful time she had the previous night, what a terrific kid Sophia was, and how sweet Marc was for agreeing to see her, she said, "I'd really, really appreciate it if you'd meet with Dr. Birnbach's sister, Suzie, and—"

"I thought you had no way to contact her."

"I managed to find a phone number for her. She won't speak to me, but maybe someone with your compassion and gravitas could get through to her."

Marc rolled his eyes. If he continued to represent her, the muscles controlling his eyeballs would get quite a workout.

"I've acknowledged every way I can that throwing the wine at you was unconscionable, but I really thought we'd gone beyond that. It seemed at dinner that there was a real connection between us." She dropped her head. "Or did I misread that?"

"No, but that doesn't mean I'm comfortable representing—"

"Are you ever comfortable?" She smiled, he didn't. "I remember your two conditions, but I'm not asking you to *represent* me, just that you do me a small favor."

"Gee, with your ability to so finely split nomenclatural hairs, you should've been a lawyer."

"Please, Marc, this is the last thing I'll ask you to do."

He raised his eyebrows, exercising another previously underutilized muscle group.

"Well, depending on what happens it could be the second to last."

She slid across the desk a scrap of paper with a number written on it, along with a stack of hundred-dollar bills. He was about to slide it back when he heard Lisa telling him to take the money. But what about the direction from his largest *and only* source of business to have nothing to do with Dahlia? Screw him. Marc didn't let clients dictate what he would and would not do. Once a lawyer lets a client know the client can control him, bad things happened.

"You could do worse things than pursuing justice for a murder victim," she said. "And it's not as if it will take you away from some major project, like curing cancer or saving the world from global warming."

"Fine, I'll listen to what you have in mind, but my instincts tell me—"

"If humans relied on their *instincts*, they'd never have used fire, invented the wheel, or appeared on *Dancing with the Stars*." She paused, no doubt for a laugh; he didn't oblige her. "Marc, one can wallow in self-righteousness for just so long. It's time you got your ass in gear and started focusing on earning a living."

"Someone else once told me that," he said. "I just don't think aiding and abetting you is such a great idea."

Her eyes became damp. Marc wanted to comfort her but didn't know how other than agreeing to do what she wanted.

"Another thing that sets off red flags is that I've got no way to contact you."

"It should make you more comfortable not having my contact information. Now if something were to go wrong, which of course it won't, you'll have *plausible deniability*."

She smiled yet again. In spite of their incandescence, her smiles were becoming tiresome.

She wrote something on a piece of paper from his desk pad.

"Here's my current number. Verizon and I have a love/hate relationship, and with all the deals out there… Well, my phone numbers keep changing. I know this sounds odd but there's no mail delivery where I'm currently living, something about it being an illegal residence as there's no certificate of occupancy."

"Things sounding odd is about the only thing about you that's consistent."

"What could be the harm in having a short telephone conversation and possibly meeting with Suzie Newname?" she asked.

"Newname?"

"She changed her name to protect her daughter from the publicity and went into hiding—might've had something to do with my scene at our brunch and my too persistent efforts after that to get her to talk to me. It was just by a stroke of luck that I managed to get her phone number—she called me by mistake, thinking I was someone else." Dahlia placed on top of the pile of hundred-dollar bills a scrap of paper with a phone number written on it. "Here's thirty-five hundred, enough to pay for your time and make up for whatever I owe you for the wine."

"I told you, we're square on the wine, and it sounds like she deserves to have her privacy protected."

After telling him about her brunch with Suzie and her suspicion that Suzie lied to her about the whereabouts of the scrolls, she said, "My hope is that you'll be able to convince her to turn the scrolls over to you."

"*To me?*" He shook his head.

"Maybe you'll come back convinced she doesn't have them, but she seems to be the best shot." Dahlia rolled a pencil along the desktop. "If you have any better idea, I'd love to hear it."

He shook his head. She balanced the pencil on its eraser. When it fell over, he took it from her and deposited it into a saggy pottery pencil holder Sophia had made in arts and crafts.

"If two people even *might* have been killed because of these scrolls…no way I'll step into the crosshairs of—"

"Right, of course. I…all I want is for you to find out if she really has them and persuade her to turn them over to me. No harm could come from that."

"What about the danger to you?"

"I promised Daniel."

The steely determination in her eyes made it clear that there was no point in trying to talk her out of exposing herself to danger.

"Well, since we're no longer talking about my taking possession of the scrolls… I suppose, if I were to talk to her, I could play on her paranoia—if that's what drove her to go into hiding—and held forth on the scrolls' pivotal role in the deaths of Shustak and Dr. Birnbach and how she'd be better off not keeping them."

Her smile threatened to expand beyond the confines of her face.

"But my guess is that if she ever had them, she's now destroyed them," he said.

"I think not. They were too important to her brother, but we'll see." For no apparent reason, she laughed. "Who'd have thought that beneath that mild-mannered, uptight exterior…"

Annoyed, he nonetheless waited for her to complete the thought.

"You *like* the idea of exposing yourself to a whiff of danger."

He took him a minute to collect his thoughts.

"It's more what you said to me at our second meeting about my need to feel alive," he said. "But mostly if I take on a client, I give him or her my all, my full commitment, that's one of the reasons I've been so hesitant to represent you."

She reached out to touch him, and when he pulled his arm away, grazed a fingernail across the back of his hand.

"You might well be the finest person I've ever met. Except for my dad, who was a convicted felon."

He again rolled his eyes.

"Seems I've given you plenty to think about." She stood.

"Even if Suzie has these scroll fragments and I somehow manage to persuade her to give them to you," he said, "that won't put you any closer to your other goal of getting justice for Daniel."

"I know." Her voice seemed to come from a sad and distant place. "But if I get them to the expert in Israel at least I'll have fulfilled part of my promise to Daniel. Then I can work on getting justice for him."

"Dahlia, I've concluded from a long career before the bar that justice comes in heaven, not on earth."

"Does it? Come in heaven, I mean."

"Okay, fine, I'll talk to her."

Dahlia hopped over to him and kissed his cheek.

"You have no idea how much it means to me that you're disregarding your instincts in order to help me."

He stood up to walk her out.

At the doorway, she turned back to him. "I lied to you again."

"About?" he asked, unsurprised.

"What I said the other day about my meds making me sane. Medication helps some people with my condition but not me. I'd worked through my episodes and now understand them, which I thought was the functional equivalent of taking medication."

"That's kind of like my telling you I'd call Suzie even though I didn't intend to would be okay, because it would be the *functional equivalent* of calling and getting turned down."

"I still think I've kept my promise to be as honest as your average client."

"Possibly." Small wonder he'd lost his commitment to the practice of law. "What else have you been untruthful about?" he asked, having no doubt that there was more.

She dropped her head and whispered, "One of the reasons I tossed the wine at you was that I felt myself falling for you."

"Dahlia—"

She raised her hand. "I'm not coming on to you, just the opposite. I shut those feelings down. The tension between conflicting desires helped set me off. My entire focus has to be on my mission."

He nodded noncommittally.

"With my condition, I've found it useful to dissimulate, and it's sometimes difficult for me to distinguish truth from fiction, but I'm really trying to be straight with you, even if I'm not doing so well at it."

"Understood."

"Really?"

"I sympathize with your struggles and appreciate your attempts at being honest with me, highly flawed though they've been."

"And I like the trust that's developing between us," she said.

"Despite your perpetual efforts to strangle it in its cradle."

"If I didn't know that to be Marc-speak for *I like it too*, my feelings would be hurt."

They both smiled.

The next morning he called Dr. Birnbach's sister.

"Hello." He'd rather have addressed her by her last name, but he assumed Newname wasn't her new name. "I'm Marc Bloch. I'm calling because I'm very interested in the circumstances surrounding your brother's murder. If you could spare a few minutes, perhaps even—"

"How did you get this number?"

"I'm a lawyer. A client, who's outraged over what happened to your brother, gave it to me."

"This *client* wouldn't happen to be the psychopath currently known as Dahlia Birn?" She clicked her tongue. "Oh, crap! My call to that ASH."

"Perhaps her seat isn't in the fully upright position with her tray-table secured, but *psychopath* isn't quite fair."

"Would you prefer *rectal ulcer*?" She made a tsking sound. "Sorry, that might've been a bit extreme."

"LaPonte got away with murder. Don't you care?"

"My brother's dead. Whatever happened after that doesn't matter to me."

"You think you're the only one who's ever had to deal with the death of someone close to you?" To his embarrassment his voice cracked. "Dahlia cares enough about what happened to your brother to pay me to find out more about his murder. I'd think you'd approve of what she's trying to do."

Suzie sighed.

"You said your name's Marc Bloch?"

He spelled it for her.

"I'm Googling you. Call me back in fifteen minutes."

Apparently he was golden on Google. When he called back, she asked, "Can I trust you not to tell Dahlia when we're meeting or even that we're meeting?"

"Yes. May I report to her what we discuss?"

"If, after we speak, you think it appropriate," she said.

"Okay."

"Tomorrow morning, at eleven. You know Larchmont at all?"

"Not really, but I'm sure I can find my way." This time he'd check Google Maps.

"There's a little park on the Long Island Sound, Manor Park."

"I'll be there. How will I know you?"

"You won't. How will I know you?"

"I'll be on a bench—if they have benches, otherwise I'll be standing—reading the *Financial Times*. That's the one printed on salmon-colored paper."

"Okay, word to the not-so-wise. Stay away from Dahlia Birn between now and then."

Marc tossed a pen at the wall. It shattered, leaving an ink stain the shape of Argentina.

XIX

Truth Isn't What It Used To Be

PUFFY CLOUDS DARTED across a cordial blue sky. Third-world nannies pushed first-world babies in strollers. A school-cutting skateboarder did flips off benches. No one looked like a potential Suzie Newname. Marc yawned. He had to get more sleep.

A henna-haired, middle-aged woman, slim and not unattractive, slid from behind an ancient oak.

"Mr. Bloch?"

"Suzie? Hi. I appreciate your taking the—"

She reached into his jacket and ran her hand across his chest and sides.

"I hope you're checking for a wire," he said.

"Let's walk." She glanced left, then right. Probably ingrained habit rather than a specific fear.

Marc told her about his meeting with LaPonte and her story about the dossier.

"You believe her?" Gray eyes narrowed.

"Sounded like *she* believed it. I'm interested in hearing your take on it."

"She's too self-righteous to lie," she said, voice flat and tired. "But there's no limit to the tripe she can persuade herself of—or conjure up an angel to do the persuading."

They walked along a narrow spit of land. Marc surmised that at least part of the reason for her choice of route was that the noise from the wind and waves would confound all but the most sophisticated listening devices, not that he had the slightest idea why anyone would've wanted to eavesdrop.

"I'm not paranoid, Mr. Bloch," she said as if reading his mind. "But protecting my daughter is paramount to me."

"Protecting her from..."

"Publicity, blow-back from the trial…your *client*."

"Oh, come on."

"Mr. Bloch, the difference between your opinion of her and mine is that I've known her longer."

"LaPonte also seemed to dislike Dahlia beyond all proportion."

"It's impossible to dislike Dahlia beyond all proportion."

"Please, Suzie, I don't get it. It seems the only reason you agreed to meet me was to warn me about her."

"Not that I know you well enough to care, but I guess I see Dahlia as fallout from Daniel's…*misadventures*, and feel some small sense of responsibility."

"I grant you that she has a unique ability to be infuriating, but the degree of your hatred…I'm getting tired of feeling like everyone but me knows what's going on."

Suzie turned to retrace their steps. Marc followed.

"Dahlia mentioned someone called the Snowman," he said.

She stopped mid-stride. Her eyebrows rose and she twisted an absent wedding ring.

"You know how little children have imaginary friends? Well, he's Dahlia's imaginary enemy. He's supposed to be some sort of *agent provocateur* acting on behalf of a foreign espionage agency."

Yet again, Marc didn't know what to think, beyond that there was more to the Birnbach killing than he'd ever know, or want to know.

He followed her off the macadam path as they snaked between seaweed-covered rocks on a narrow rock-strewn beach.

"The way you reacted to my mention of the Snowman, it seemed he was more than just an imaginary bogeyman."

"He is. He's an imaginary bogeyman through whom Dahlia performs deeds too terrible even for her to do."

"These terrible deeds?" he asked.

She shook her head.

"I'm more confused than I was before I came here," he said. "You want to warn me, and I thank you for that, but please give me something of substance."

They stopped walking and turn to face each other. Finally, she sighed.

"Dahlia and I had talked several times over the phone and had what started out as a pleasant brunch together," Suzie said. "While she didn't seem to be playing with a full deck, I liked that she was so totally dedicated to obtaining justice for Daniel, who'd come through for her in a big way some years ago. Over coffee and dessert she asked me about some secret scrolls Daniel supposedly discovered. When I had no idea what she was talking about, she accused me of lying, shoved me down, and turned the table over on me."

Marc let out an audible sigh of relief. He'd feared that Suzie would tell him something awful that Dahlia had neglected to reveal. While Dahlia's brunch freak-out had been extreme, at least she wasn't hiding something even worse.

"Dahlia said Daniel showed the scrolls to her and told her you'd know where they are," he said, keeping his tone non-confrontational.

"I hope you don't believe that any more than her other bullshit. As far as I know, those supposedly secret documents or whatever the hell they are don't exist."

Suzie broke eye contact, her nostrils flared. Her smile looked forced, as only the muscles around her lips moved—the exact non-verbal cues Dahlia had described that had made her think she was being lied to.

"You and Dahlia agree on one point: Daniel wasn't a pedophile. So why was he killed if not for the scrolls?" They again stopped walking and stared at each other. "There's also that Professor Shustak, the one who died soon after Daniel showed him the scrolls."

She again broke eye contact. "Maybe that's why, if they actually existed, I wouldn't want to find them."

"My guess is that you fear that if you give Dahlia or the Snowman the scrolls, they'll kill you on the spot, just so there are no witnesses."

"Has occurred to me," Suzie said after a pause of several seconds. "I mean on the hypothetical chance that I were to find something."

"Wouldn't you be better off passing this hot potato along, perhaps to someone other than Dahlia or the Snowman?"

"Mr. Bloch, my only concern is protecting my daughter and myself."

"If you stumble upon two sets of fragments of ancient scrolls, each about three and a half feet long, one in Aramaic, one in Hebrew, arrange to meet me secretly, pass them on to me, and then go into hiding for a reasonable time… I'll make sure neither Dahlia nor anyone else knows I have them until you're long gone. Or give them to someone else, have him or her pass them on to me after you leave town." Aghast that he'd become so caught up in the effort to persuade her that he'd just offered himself as hot potato holder, he said, "Something for both of us to think about."

"Why are you doing this?" she asked.

He sighed. "In part out of a desire to see justice done, in part out of a deeply ingrained compulsion to do the best job I can for my client."

And a desire to feel alive.

"You understand the risk you're taking?" Suzie asked.

"I guess I don't. Maybe I don't scare easy." To fill the ensuing silence, he said, "It doesn't sit right with me that the scrolls are all that important. It *does* seem, though, that someone manipulated LaPonte to kill your brother and that the scrolls are a key piece in the puzzle."

"Maybe I agree with you, but I guess I scare easier," she said. "I can't afford to take such risks. I'm a single parent of a young daughter."

Marc felt as if he'd been socked in the solar plexus. It took all his concentration to continue walking with her along the path.

"Thinking about it a little more, there's no reason why you should give me the scrolls," he said. "Have an intermediary deliver them directly to Dahlia."

"No way I'll deal with her."

"Again, I just don't get this hostility of yours."

She stared at him. He stared back, waiting for her to respond.

"After the brunch incident, I made it clear that I wanted nothing more to do with her, but Dahlia kept pursuing me."

"She can be persistent." He smiled to convey that he considered her persistence to be an amusing quirk, rather than a character flaw that could subject her and everyone around her to grave danger. But he was unsure what he really thought.

"Finally, she left me a voicemail, saying that if I didn't give her the scrolls, the Snowman would make me give them to him, perhaps going so far as torturing my daughter while I watched. She clearly enjoyed describing that torture in pornographic, stomach-turning detail. I pulled Alexis out of school, and we've been in hiding ever since."

"You don't really think Dahlia intended that as a threat?"

"You know damn well that's exactly what I thought and what anyone in my position would've thought. She was talking about my daughter for Christ's sake. By the way neither law enforcement nor the private investigator I hired have ever heard of this Snowman person."

"How could you know that? From what I understand *the Snowman* is only a name Dahlia uses based on his birthmark. You don't have a real name or much of a physical description."

"The way Dahlia describes it, that three-ball birthmark is pretty distinctive, not that anyone other than her seems to have seen it."

He swallowed. She took a deep breath.

"You believe that someone manipulated LaPonte into killing your brother, right?"

She nodded.

"Then there has to be a Snowman or someone like him."

"If there is a Snowman, that's an even better reason for me not to be involved. Maybe I'm just an old scaredy-cat but I prefer not to antagonize hit men—almost as much as I like to steer clear of psychopaths."

Marc sighed. Dealing with this mess was like playing checkers with a three-year-old who kept changing the rules.

"It seems a lot of effort went into murdering Daniel and making it look as if he was killed because of his sexual transgressions," she said. "Whatever real-world value they might have, if some well-financed nutcase believes these pieces of parchment, or whatever the hell they are, are worth killing for, then they're worth killing for."

He nodded.

"Alexis and I are moving again in a couple of days."

"That's—"

"A shitty way to live. Hopefully, the time will come when I believe Alexis is sufficiently out of danger, so I can send her to a real school and she can again have friends and a normal life. What I'm trying to tell you is, even if you have a death-wish I'm sure you can find a less unpleasant way to pack it in."

Marc swallowed hard.

"You still want the scrolls?" she asked.

"Me? I never... wanted them." But having stupidly put the idea in her head, he realized he wasn't going to easily dislodge it. "This conversation has given both of us plenty to think about."

"If I somehow find those scrolls, the only one I'll give them to is you, and you'd have to promise not to tell Dahlia or anyone else that you have them for at least twenty-four hours." Suzie pulled her coat around her and began walking away. "Don't follow me."

After watching her get into a gray Honda with dirt-obscured license plates, he began the trek to the train station.

While walking, he called the number Dahlia had given him and a computerized voice told him that voicemail was full, giving no indication that it was even was hers. Then he called John Cooper, the private investigator he'd recommended to her, and gave him the license plate number of the midnight blue BMW Dahlia was driving and asked him to check it out. He also checked his phone to see what number Dahlia had called the night of their Nice Matin dinner, but there was no record of that call.

XX

Checkmate

JUST AS SOPHIA put his queen in check, Marc's phone rang.

"I found out who that car is registered to." Cooper sounded annoyed.

"Tell me." Marc wondered why he had to ask.

"You."

"Me what?"

"Please, Marc, don't play games with me. The car is registered to you."

"Someone with my name?"

"And your address and a signature that looks a lot like yours. A parking ticket was issued two nights ago on Amsterdam and Seventy-ninth, paid on line a few hours later."

"The car wasn't reported stolen?"

"No, Marc, you didn't report it stolen."

"Yeah, thanks."

Because he didn't want to worry Sophia or have to explain something to her that he didn't understand himself, he made an effort to keep the anger out of his voice.

"Cooper, you ever hear of someone called the Snowman?"

"Sounds like a handle for a teenage coke dealer."

"What about the name Dahlia Birn?"

"She had something to do with that LaPonte lunatic?"

"That's right."

"Someone asked me to check her out."

"Who?"

"Marc, you know I can't tell you that."

"And?"

"Nothing. She's a ghost, but not a friendly one."

"Daddy, you shouldn't be on your phone when we're playing. Move already."

"Thanks, send me a bill." He disconnected and moved his queen out of danger.

Three moves later Sophia put him in check again. His phone rang, and in spite of her dirty look, he answered it.

"So?" Dahlia asked. "Did Suzie crack like a walnut when subjected to the full force of your cross-examination skills?"

"Seems there are several things you neglected to tell me."

"I don't want to disturb you at home. Do you have time to see me tomorrow, say eleven?"

"Sure. I'll ask my questions then."

Even before Dahlia took a seat in Marc's client chair, he said, "Suzie told me that the Snowman's a figment of your imagination."

"I'm fine. How are you? And sure, I'll have some water, thanks so much for asking."

"I checked out the registration of the BMW."

"Oh, gosh, I'm so sorry. I wanted it to be a surprise, but I accept your apology. Sure, you were wrong to get all bent out of shape about the car being *stolen*, but hey, don't worry about it. Everyone makes mistakes."

"What about your mistake in putting the car in my name?"

"Not a mistake. I want to give it to you, I just need it for another few weeks."

"Get it out of my name!" He got up to shut his door, so he wouldn't disturb others if he had to shout again. "Do you happen to have the registration?"

"Not with me."

"Well, get it."

"Next time I see you." She spit out the words.

Fine, now both of them were angry, although he considered the possibility that he should have been angry not at her but at himself for practically telling Suzie that he'd take possession of the scrolls.

She closed her eyes, took a couple of deep breath, then, in a calm quiet voice, said, "Please report on your meeting with Suzie."

He did.

"Marc, you can't possibly believe I'd even implicitly threaten a child. I can be… *temperamental*, but has anything you've seen to date shown me to be violent or sadistic?"

He shook his head.

"You think Suzie has had the scrolls all along and will decide to give them to you?" Her knuckles turned white as she griped the edge of his desk.

"Probably."

"I'm surprised you offered to take them."

"Heat of the moment, but I intend to back off from that offer."

"Just pass them on to me as soon as you get them," she said. "Better yet, let me handle the pick-up, then you won't even have to be there."

"I told her I wouldn't tell you when or where the transfer would take place and I'd give her and her daughter twenty-four hours to disappear."

"You'd be safer if you just gave them to me."

"But that's not what I told her I'd do."

Staring at the photos of Lisa and Sophia, he wondered how he'd let this go as far as it had. He reminded himself that he hadn't agreed to do anything… yet.

"The Snowman *does* exist. I've seen him." She told him about their run-in at LaPonte's news conference.

He tented his fingers.

"Sounds like he could've just as easily been a hallucination, and as far as his response when you asked, 'Who died and made you king?' Well, you do have auditory hallucinations."

She grimaced, her lips moved as if she was having a conversation with herself—or Ariella—and struggling to come up with an appropriate response.

"I can't explain how I know it, but I'm sure."

"Because Ariella told you?"

Her cheeks turned red.

"Dahlia, you do realize that if I had the scrolls, and the Snowman or anyone armed or threatening were to show up and demand them, I'd give them to him."

"I'd expect nothing else, but…" She smiled as if she'd just had one of her damn epiphanies. "You don't really believe there's any danger in holding the scrolls overnight?"

"Depends what you mean by *any*. I don't know how anyone would know I had them. From what you said, this Snowman only learned about Shustak from his department blog and about Birnbach from Yusef. So maybe I'll decide that my duty to you and indirectly to Suzie might outweigh the risk…." He held a hand up. "But I'm still thinking it through."

"The scrolls are the key to everything. Vance confirmed that—"

"I don't buy it." He shook his head. "It sounds like the scrolls, or rather the *scroll fragments*, are basically nothing until they're fully authenticated and… Some years ago an entire gospel turned up, the Gospel of Judas. In it he was a hero doing Christ's bidding. It caused a ripple of controversy, spawned a book or two but no murders, no rioting in the street, no wars."

"How do you explain the murders of Daniel and Professor Shustak?"

"I don't."

"These people will continue to kill until someone stops them, and I seem to be the only someone willing to try."

"I can't judge that, but I admit I'm starting to find this interesting and it seems you're not doing anything nefarious and in your own mind you're fighting for justice."

She raised her neatly trimmed red eyebrows.

"In *my own mind*?"

"Black roots are starting to show in your hair and brows."

"If the legal thing doesn't work out for you, I'll retain you as my colorist." She bit her lip. "Anyway, the significance of the scrolls doesn't matter. I promised Daniel I'd take them to Israel for authentication and I can't do that if I don't have them."

"Suzie might not call me."

"You did make a persuasive case to her?"

"Yeah, I did great."

She stood. "Thanks for everything. I really appreciate it."

"I'll let you know if I hear from Suzie, if the number you gave me works."

"Dial it."

He did and somewhat to his astonishment heard a ringing from her bag.

She kissed him on the forehead. He stood to walk her to the reception area, but at his door she stopped and turned toward him. He waited. And waited.

"My quest isn't just to find the truth, get justice for Daniel, and take the scrolls to Israel," she said finally. "It's also to find out whether I'm capable of seeing things clearly enough to deal effectively with life in all its complexity. It's become a do-or-die test. If I pass, I really believe I'll be able to turn my life around."

"It's not a good idea to invest so much of one's self-worth in something that to a great degree turns on factors beyond one's control."

"Everything I've tried to do to date has failed. I need to prove to myself I'm not so crazy that I can't succeed."

"I get it. There are days when I find it next to impossible motivate myself to do anything much beyond caring for Sophia."

"Sometimes everything we do seems about as productive as painting a burning house. Spend an hour listening to the news, and it becomes clear that's what we're *all* doing." She ran a finger along his cheek. "But I didn't see you as defeated. It took some effort to get you motivated. Once I did that, though, I had the feeling you enjoyed doing what you did for me, and when we talk you seem quite engaged."

"Maybe so." He chuckled but couldn't imagine what he found amusing.

She stepped so close to him that he felt uncomfortable, particularly when she tilted her head and parted her lips.

"I value our friendship—the friendship we're growing into," she said, then stepped back.

He realized he was okay with her wanting to kiss him, particularly since she hadn't done it.

"You're scintillating company," he said. "Scintillating to the point of being exasperating."

"I hate being sanity-challenged, but I guess many people would love to be as smart and attractive as I am. So, like everyone else, I have to play the hand I'm dealt."

"Well, maybe you're now on the right track."

"When you see the Snowman lying dead on the floor, his employer in cuffs, and me, scrolls in hand, bound for *Eretz Yisrael*, then you'll know for sure."

Her phone rang. She checked caller ID, scowled, kissed him on the cheek, said "Moustache," and hurried toward the reception area.

After she left, he realized she actually said, "Must dash."

As anticipated, McKean's lawyers made a motion to move the New York suit to Alabama and consolidate it with the one they'd brought in his home state. Taking Marc's suggestion, the judge ordered McKean to give a deposition in New York two weeks hence, when Marc could interrogate him under oath about the extent of his contacts with New York. Because Marc had filed his case in New York before McKean's lawyer had filed in Alabama, she ruled that if McKean had come to New York on business enough times and spent sufficient time there, the case would proceed in New York. If that happened, McKean would probably want to settle quickly and quietly, perhaps even paying enough for it to be a windfall for Fahad. And Marc.

His phone rang. *Unknown number,* according to caller ID.

"Mr. Bloch?" A whispering tubercular wheeze.

"Yes?"

"Grand Central waiting room, the one you enter via 42nd Street. I'll be in disguise but reading the *Financial Times*. Sit next to me. Don't acknowledge me, don't even look at me. When I get up, I'll leave the paper behind. Take it but be careful—there'll be a box under it, containing what you want."

He waited, hoping for more of an explanation. All he heard was her breathing. If this had been a movie, he'd have heard a gunshot, followed by a death moan.

"Is all this cloak-and-dagger stuff really necessary?"

A long pause.

"Daniel and I used to have a hiding place in the woods when we were kids. I took my daughter there, to show her where I grew up and how we used to play. In an old stone wall I found a thick brass cylinder with some plastic-protected documents rolled up in it and a note telling me not to look inside but if something were to happen to him to give it to someone I trust. Someone other than law enforcement."

"Slow down a minute, Suzie. Behind a loose stone in a wall, really?"

"It's a little Hardy Boys, but we were kids."

"Daniel's been dead almost a year now, and you just discovered this?"

"Let's say I came to realize it was in my interest to do it and you needn't take literally that it just happened or that a stone wall was involved."

"Why are you doing this?"

"I want to get rid of the damn things, put distance between me and them."

It suddenly all seemed so real, scary real.

"I'm surprised you'd want Dahlia to have them. When we met you referred to her as a *rectal ulcer.*"

"It's not what I want but what Daniel wanted. There are two export certificates in with them. Don't ask how I know that."

"Suzie, I don't... This sounds like something I shouldn't be involved with."

"I'd greatly appreciate your help." Heartbreakingly pleading tone.

After the threat to her daughter and murder of her brother, the woman deserves a break and so does her daughter.

"Well..." He sighed.

"Please wait twenty-four hours before telling Dahlia you have them. Also, promise you won't give them to the police."

"Not to worry. I'm honorable to a fault."

"Whew! You have no idea what a big load that took from my mind."

"When would you like to meet?"

With there now being more than a whiff of danger, he could hardly believe he'd said that, but it seemed his interest in finding the truth and getting justice for Birnbach—or his interest in helping two damsels in distress—had overridden his survival instincts. But if anyone were to ask for the scrolls, his response would be: *Here! Take them! So glad you asked!*

"What time do you have?" she asked.

"One-thirty."

"I'll see you in two hours."

XXI

Light as Dandelion Fuzz

DAHLIA FLOATED OUT of Marc's office light as dandelion fuzz. She loved Marc. How could she have been so lucky as to meet such a wonderful man? She loved everyone she glided by. She hovered over some, basking in their beauty, brilliance, or determination. At a bank she changed three hundred-dollar bills into tens, cheerfully noting that her supply of money wouldn't last more than a couple of months or, if she flew to Israel to deliver the scrolls, a mere two weeks or so. As she continued to drift downtown, she handed a ten to everyone who looked as if he or she might need it.

Sure it was *possible* that Suzie would decide not to give Marc the scrolls, but he was so brilliant he could persuade her, and he was so thoughtful and nice he'd certainly agree to take them.

SHE'D SOON HAVE THE SCROLLS!!!!!!

That night she didn't sleep. With life so glorious, why would anyone waste time sleeping? Years before a therapist had advised her to always get a full seven to eight hours and to eat three meals a day. How did therapists even make a living? They couldn't empty pee from a boot if the instructions were written on the heel.

She did floor exercises for hours. Double flips, even a triple flip. Moves she could barely do, even as a kid when she was in intensive training, now seemed effortless. Occasionally she blew a landing, even flopped down hard on her back. Each time that happened was funnier than the last time. Finally, she was laughing so hard she could barely move.

She'd soon have the scrolls. She wasn't a fuck-up. To the extent she was crazy—wrong word; she was different—it only made her more charming, gave her more of an edge; cutting edge that's what she was. What had that handsome genius called her? Oh, right, scintillating. She said the word several times. So poetic. She made up a song using only that one word and sang it, switching tones, melodies, and styles, until she dissolved into giggles.

Sunlight slanted through the skylight. The night had flown by on gossamer wings of...oh never mind. It was the super, special scarlet morning of a sure-to-be-superlative day. "The first day of the rest of my life," she said, marveling at the profundity of the phrase.

She checked her phone—or more accurately Marc's phone, via the bug she'd installed in it after the Nice Martin dinner. She'd done that for his own good, to make it easier for her to protect him. She had no intention of letting Marc take the scrolls without her and her Beretta hovering nearby. But he'd gotten no calls since the one from Suzie. Poor boy. Her next project would be to get him some more friends. Perhaps she'd create a Facebook page for him, have him friend the world. Also, she'd be his friend. A very good friend, if she had her way.

Having neglected dinner, she considered breakfast, but staying still long enough to eat it would've been a colossal waste of time and energy. Instead she went out for a walk to enjoy the glorious day. The wind coming off the river could hardly have been more invigorating, and the patterns in the old ice-and-soot-blackened snow could hardly have been more fascinating. A lovely pedestrian, weighed down by coat, hat, and scarf, gave her a long look, presumably envious of the freedom she had in her short skirt, spiky heels, and tight T-shirt. Why walk when she could summersault? The ice cut up her hands a little, but that was part of the fun.

Her phone rang, or more accurately Marc's phone. She listened to the call. BINGO!

She had to get to Grand Central. Sprinting home, she slipped, skidded, and smashed down on her ass, but no harm it was already cracked. She laughed. What a delightful sense of humor she had!

Now that she'd succeeded in putting her craziness behind her, she'd soon figure out how to catch the Snowman—Ariella had confirmed that he was the killer—and his handlers. And, no surprise given her brilliance, a plan sprang from her mind, like Pallas Athena emerging from Zeus's head fully grown and battle-dressed.

Ariella guffawed.

Dahlia, you're not just funny, you're a funny classical scholar!

The unexpected compliment made Dahlia positively glow with pleasure.

You know what the gamblers say, "lean into a good streak." Let's leave a follow-up message for Monsieur la Grenouille.

Dahlia punched in his number and repeated Ariella's words as she spoke them. "You told me that Ahmed said his political bedfellows don't care about the scrolls, but I have reason to believe that might not be true. You'd be doing them a great service by telling them that Marc will soon have the Birnbach scrolls, and I'll have perfect copies. And be sure to tell them that if anything bad happens to Marc or his daughter, I won't rest until I've blighted their crops, struck down their herds, and poisoned their wells—literally and figuratively."

After Dahlia hung up, Ariella said, *Not to worry, when the time comes I'll help you with the blighting of crops and striking down herds. It's easy once you get the hang of it.*

Dahlia delighted in Ariella's whimsical side. Under her direction, Dahlia left a message—basically the same but more detailed—with the United Arab Emirate cultural attaché to the United Nations.

On the subway to Grand Central, it occurred to her that the voicemails might've been a shade irresponsible, but if de Saint Juste or the cultural attaché tell the evil emir about them—even if they didn't know him as the evil emir—that would get a response, which would reveal him as the malefactor. Otherwise they'd disregard her messages as the ravings of a lunatic and no harm would be done. Under the law of unintended consequences, the good, bad, and neutral results break down to roughly a third each. One-third positive results, she liked those odds.

She wasn't happy about having put Marc at risk—particularly as blighting crops, etc., was beyond her range of expertise, and Ariella didn't always come through with her promises of assistance. But no worry, she'd be able to make sure no harm came to him. The bugs she'd placed in his phone and Sophia's backpack were working fine, so she could always be within a few minutes of where he was. Just to be super-safe, she intended to take the scrolls from Marc sooner than the twenty-four hours he'd promised Suzie. As soon as she got them, she would leave voicemails announcing that fact with the cultural attachés of Qatar, Kuwait, and Saudi Arabia, the president of Halliburton, the heads of all oil companies working in the Persian Gulf, and Dick Cheney—while she couldn't see how Cheney was involved, his involvement wouldn't surprise her—and Marc would then be off the hook.

If the emir, or whoever engineered Daniel's murder, had thought Daniel and Shustak were problems, he was going to see her as a catastrophe on a par with blood, frogs, gnats, pestilence, wild beasts, boils, hail, locusts, and the slaying of their first born.

He's already suffering from the second plague if he's dealing with de Saint-Juste.

Dahlia noted with pleasure that Ariella was enjoying herself. Spreading the joy, that was what she was all about.

XXII

A Bad Case of the Deads

SEEING NO ONE resembling Suzie, Marc sat next to a black woman with a blond wig, dark glasses, and a big-brimmed floppy hat. Her long loose coat appeared to cover broad shoulders and a large bust-line—one hell of a disguise if it was Suzie. At least she was reading the *Financial Times*, looking down on it spread out on her lap in a way that could conceal a box. After a couple of minutes she glanced at her watch and got up, leaving the paper behind.

Once she was out of sight, he waited a minute or so, then picked up the newspaper and saw a wide cylindrical Federal Express box. He read the front page, or rather he tried to; his hands were trembling and his vision was blurred. He was frightened but his primary emotion was anger—at himself for having given in to his compulsion to serve his client, help Suzie and her daughter, and, perhaps, flirt with danger. It hit him that the lack of a spiritual dimension in his life made him feel empty, and on an unconscious level he'd wanted to take the scrolls to have contact with something authentically holy. Consciously he knew damned well that nothing he'd done had brought him a nanometer closer to God and that getting involved in something with no upside and considerable downside was as bad as it sounded; worse because as a sixty-year-old single father of a ten-year-old he had responsibilities, chief among those being not to do anything stupid and dangerous. He craved redemption, needed to feel alive and virile, but he'd get none of that if he were dead and Sophia an orphan.

He folded the paper, stuck it in his briefcase, and carried the tube under his arm through the main waiting room. No one seemed to be watching him.

A big guy, coming from his blind side, smashed into him.

"Outta my way, motherfucka," he said, then staggered off.

149

Marc checked his pocket and briefcase. Nothing missing. His heart was pounding.

It took him a few seconds, but he realized that although he was frightened and annoyed, he was also excited. His rational self—the one he was ignoring ever since he'd met Dahlia—told him to drop the box in the nearest trash receptacle and if he wanted a thrill, to take up something safer, like clearing land mines in Afghanistan. Lisa had often commented on his self-destructive streak. His refusal to incriminate those who worked for Peter and his insistence on paying all of the firm's obligations had arguably fallen into that category. But he'd felt he was merely doing the right thing, and dammit, he still did.

He rode the escalator into the MetLife Building, exited at 44th Street, and walked a block west to pick up Sophia's tennis racket at Grand Central Racket, where he'd left it for restringing—she'd been thrilled that she'd finally broken a string, a step toward being a *real* tennis player and a symbol of her burgeoning power, even if she'd had the same strings for almost a year.

With walls hung floor to ceiling with tennis, squash, and paddle-ball rackets, the narrow shop featured two stringing machines and barely room to hold a few customers. A TV tuned to CNN, volume on mute, hung from the ceiling.

"Hey, Woody!"

"Hi, Marc." Big smile, handshake. "Got you right here."

While Woody ferreted through a pile of rackets, Marc glanced at the screen. LaPonte!

"Turn up the sound, please."

Looking for the remote, Woody said, "Wheels of justice grind slow but fine."

"What happened?"

"You haven't heard?"

"I live under a rock. Tell me."

"Mary LaPonte—the nut case who offed the two pedophiles? Well, someone shot her last night, point-blank, in the head." Woody formed his hand into a gun and squeezed off two shots. "Did it as she was leaving a bar after getting a phone call. No witnesses. She had a bodyguard, but he was taking a leak. Why she left without him…"

Marc felt dizzy.

"You okay, Marc?"

"Yeah, just…tired."

As he walked back to his office, the tube under his arm seemed to throb, as if it contained a beating heart.

With LaPonte's murder he suspected Dahlia wouldn't be coming for the box any time soon. He was about to call the police when he remembered his promise to Suzie. Anyway, he had no information that would've been helpful. Dahlia had said he'd be better off without her contact information, and she might have been right. Certainly *she was* better off. The box might've contained evidence, but he wouldn't know unless he looked in it, and he'd heed his instinct's admonition not to do it. That instinct also directed him to throw out the box, but he wasn't about to destroy possibly important evidence in a murder investigation.

No, it was more than that. Religious Jews kiss even an ordinary prayer book if it falls to the floor, and there was no way this irreligious Jew was going to discard a part of the Torah. Even if the scrolls turned out not to be an authentic part of the Torah, they probably were over two millennia old and handwritten by a scribe who'd made serving God his life's work. While it was in his best interests to destroy them, one couldn't always act in his best interests and still look at himself in the mirror. Good fathers didn't besmirch their souls.

Where to put the box until he determined what to do with it? He considered removing the scrolls and tapping them behind the huge photo on his office wall, but he didn't want to open the tube or look at its contents. Well, he *wanted* to, but he was damn sure he was better off not doing it. He went into the firm's file room and slipped it into a stack of similar boxes of varying sizes, part of a huge document production in a long-dormant litigation.

Having learned, from interrogating LaPonte's bodyguard, of Marc's Shay's Lounge meeting with LaPonte, a pair of NYPD detectives came by his office. He told them what he and LaPonte had discussed.

"What did this Dahlia Birnbach tell you about Ms. LaPonte?" asked Detective Mary Thomas, a broad-shouldered, short-haired woman with a beer gut protruding over too-tight black pants.

"Regrettably, I have to invoke the attorney-client privilege."

"We have reason to believe she's about to kill again."

"Then you're way ahead of me. I don't know that she ever killed anyone. I don't even know where she lives."

"And you didn't find that strange?" asked Thomas's partner, a tall, solidly built, baby-faced man who'd introduced himself as Detective Santos.

"Of course I did."

"You do know that impeding a police investigation is a felony, as is lying to a police officer?" Thomas said.

"Yes, my wife and I used to watch *Law & Order*, back when it was set in New York."

"There must be something else you can tell us," Santos said.

Marc had never quite understood what the expression *butter wouldn't melt in his mouth* means, but he thought it applied to Santos. On the other hand, lead would've melted in Thomas's mouth, and she looked as if she was about to spit it into his face.

He shuffled through some papers on his desk. "Here's a phone number she gave me. I haven't tried calling her, but I suspect it's a prepaid phone and no longer operational."

"Call it," Thomas said.

He got the voicemail-is-full recording again and held the phone out so the detectives could hear it. Then he told them about his meeting with Suzie—communications with non-clients weren't covered by the privilege. Marc's mention of the Snowman gave Thomas the opportunity to dig deep into her apparently inexhaustible supply of snorts, smirks, and snarkiness.

"If you hear from this Dahlia again, you'll call us right away?" Santos said.

"Of course."

They handed him their cards.

"Oh, one more thing," Thomas said, her attempt at a casual tone failing miserably. "We'd like to take a look at your car."

"My car? I don't have a… Oh." Marc told them about the BMW.

He started to give them the license plate number, but Thomas cut him off. "We already have it."

"Why did you ask about the car?" he asked.

"Please, Mr. Bloch, don't play dumb."

"I'm not playing. I don't know."

"You'll know soon enough."

The detectives exchanged looks heavy with portent and left without so much as a goodbye.

Marc's underarms were soaked with sweat. *We have reason to believe she's about to kill again.* Maybe that was just the kind of thing cops routinely said to squeeze information out of witnesses. Or maybe they actually had evidence that Dahlia killed LaPonte and will kill again? No, he didn't believe that. Sitting quietly at his desk, he hoped for a useful thought.

XXIII

Dahlia Feels Wanted

"MARC HAS THE scrolls!" Dahlia shouted. "Marc has the scrolls!" She couldn't recall ever being happier. Even the ecstasy of yesterday paled by comparison. It was six a.m. Another night without losing time to sleep, and she was pulsing with energy. "Marc has the scrolls!"

Double front-flip...and she stuck her landing!

Yesterday she'd watched the Grand Central transfer, making sure Marc was safe. Today she intended to protectively tail him as he dropped Sophia off at school and went to the office. Then she'd stop by his place—well, break in—get the scrolls, and leave voicemails, announcing she had them, for everyone she could think of with a connection to the UAE. Voila! Marc would be out of any danger.

To get the weather, she hit the power button on the remote. "I have to decide which blood-red T-shirt to wear," she said out loud, then gave in to the giggles.

She'd been laughing so much lately that her stomach muscles ached—quite pleasantly.

A picture formed on the screen—a drawing of herself, resembling a police sketch but more like a Roman death mask.

She dropped the remote.

Thinking it was a hallucination, she screamed, "I forbid it! Be gone!"

She shut her eyes, and when she opened them, saw an ordinary Toyota ad. Thank God! She changed channels and got a Geico commercial. She loved that spokes-gecko. She went to the bathroom to brush her teeth.

On her return, though, the television wasn't cooperating. It showed a picture of LaPonte. Deciding to take the hallucination head on, mano a mano, she turned up the sound.

The anchorperson said, "The police have what they're calling a *solid lead* in the execution-style killing the day before yesterday of child-welfare advocate Mary LaPonte."

Child-welfare advocate? What the fuck? This wasn't a hallucination, Dahlia's hallucinations weren't that stupid. Anyway, she didn't have visual hallucinations, not like this.

Wait, had he said *killing?*

"The police have released a sketch." The death mask returned to the screen. "The woman, who goes by the name Dahlia Birn, is considered armed and highly dangerous. She's known to have stalked Ms. LaPonte, having attended one of her news conferences armed with a concealed handgun. Anyone seeing her is advised to immediately call the number on this screen. She's believed to be driving a midnight blue BMW M6 convertible with New York plates, MC 17565."

Her mood crashed like a satellite knocked out of orbit by a meteor. The heat of re-entry blistered her skin and singed her hair.

Marshalling her self-control, she took hold of the remote, pushed the channel-changing buttons, and for greater effect, swung it as if it was a Star Wars light saber. But the other news channels carried the same story. It was not a hallucination.

LaPonte dead? Dahlia wanted for murder?

How could she have ever thought she was capable of fulfilling Daniel's mission? How could she have ever thought she was capable of anything?

She fell to the floor, like a puppet with its strings cut. Some hours later she managed to climb into bed, exhausting herself in the process.

She had to get up. She needed to get the scrolls and protect Marc.

Don't be stupid. You can't protect anyone, best thing you can do for him is stay as far away as possible. You've done quite enough harm already.

"But you told me we'd keep him safe."

That was before I knew what a screw-up you were.

Dahlia sobbed but soon lost the energy to do even that.

XXIV

The Dark at the End of the Tunnel

BLESSEDLY MARC HAD work to distract him from events over which he had no control and little understanding.

He didn't think Dahlia killed LaPonte. But...

He was sitting in the office conference room, with McKean across the table from him, flanked by a team of three lawyers. A court reporter was at the head, ready to transcribe Marc's questions, McKean's responses, and the lawyers' objections. Although Fahad didn't have to be there, he'd told Marc that he wanted to attend. A half-hour after the 9:30 scheduled start, however, he still hadn't appeared, and McKean's lawyers insisted that they begin the deposition without him. Fine with Marc, clients only mucked up the litigation process.

An hour into his examination, Marc had developed enough evidence of McKean having done business in New York to persuade the court to let the case remain there. He'd made multiple visits to the city to meet with his publisher and Rodriguez, his now-deceased literary agent. He'd also spent a month there working on a book, *Red Revenge*, in which his hero, an Alabama lawyer and former state senator, uncovered a conspiracy by a group of New York investment bankers to destroy the economy of the South. McKean had spent his formative years in Alabama and still maintained a home there, but he hadn't actually lived there for several years, preferring his one-hundred-fifty-foot yacht or his twenty-thousand-square-foot home in Jackson Hole. While most writers couldn't make a living, it appeared that a select few made a killing.

"Do you enjoy coming to New York?" Marc asked.

"My publisher puts me up in the Ritz-Carlton. What's not to like?"

"You've earned, what, about a hundred and ten million from your books and the movies made from them?"

"I don't know the exact number, but that's ballpark."

"And you like coming to New York because you're comped on hotel rooms?"

Squiggly smile. "I guess so."

The conference room phone rang. Since Marc had told the receptionist he didn't want to be disturbed, except in an emergency, he feared the worst, but it turned out that she was just calling to say that Fahad was on his way in from the reception area.

Accompanied by a man wearing a thin-lapelled suit, white button-down shirt, and narrow tie that made him look as if he'd just stepped off the set of *Mad Men*, Fahad handed Marc a change-of-attorney form. Fahad's new lawyer introduced himself around the table and asked for an adjournment to get up to speed on the case and complete the deposition at a mutually convenient future date.

He then turned to Marc. "I gather this de Saint-Juste fellow is unhappy that you're doing work for someone named…Delilah? He asked that you give me the retainer he sent you, less your time charges for work actually done, less twenty percent to cover the inconvenience to Fahad in having to retain me."

"You're kidding."

"Hey, don't shoot, I'm just the messenger."

"Right."

"He told me not to leave here without a check and the file."

"No problem. I'll be right back."

Marc slammed the door behind him.

He telephoned de Saint-Juste. "What the hell?"

"I told you I can't afford to have a lawyer associated with me who is working for a psycho."

"Nothing to do with you or what you told me, but I'm done representing her."

"I heard otherwise."

"You what?" Marc yelled, but de Saint-Juste had hung up.

De Saint-Juste called back seconds later.

"I appreciate all the good work you've done, and I respect you personally."

"Oh, that's real comforting."

Marc slammed the phone down. He broke a pencil in half, then in quarters. Furious and without work or any immediate prospects, he called Martha to tell her that he'd pick Sophia up at school and that she could take the afternoon and evening off.

"What are you doing here, Daddy?" Sophia asked. "Aren't you supposed to be working?"

"Can't a guy take some time off to spend it with his favorite daughter?" She smiled. "What should we do?"

"Whatever you want."

"I asked you first."

"How 'bout we walk home the long way? It's a beautiful day...for February."

"It's March, Daddy."

"Still it's a beautiful day for February, but if you'd rather go to a movie or shopping... You could use a new pair of shoes."

"No, you decided. We'll walk."

She took his hand, causing his anger at de Saint-Juste to begin to dissipate. Her backpack over his shoulder, they headed west and cut through Lincoln Center. Arriving at the path along the river, they walked out on a pier. The cold wind tossed Sophia's hair, and Marc had a brief glimpse of the beautiful, confident woman she'd become. She'd done a remarkable job of dealing with Lisa's death. The school psychologist had told him to expect some acting out, but there'd been none. Even her sleep problems and crying jags were mostly over. Although she'd been more reserved than she used to be, she'd begun to make new friends that Marc preferred to Talia, who was too materialistic and sophisticated for his taste. He had to admit, though, she'd been a good friend to Sophia. Although he'd heard stories about her being mean to other girls, she'd never turned on Sophia or suggested that the two of them gang up on someone else, something Sophia would never do, he hoped.

At the boat basin, Sophia asked, "Should we cut through here and take the short way back?"

"Good idea. I'm getting a little tired," he said even though he wasn't.

Approaching the horizon, the sun cast weird elongated shadows and the sky looked red and swollen as if infected. Father and daughter circumvented the Boat Basin Café and headed for the tunnel under the West Side Highway.

A large, swarthy man blocked the tunnel exit. They tried to go around him but he stood in their path, forcing them back.

"You got something I want." He spoke with an accent Marc couldn't place. Middle Eastern? Russian?

The mugger punched him in the face, fist moving so fast that Marc didn't even see it coming. Sophia screamed. Marc staggered backwards. Regaining his balance, he pushed Sophia behind him. They backpedaled. The thug followed.

"I've got about fifty bucks in cash," Marc said. "You can have it all. My watch was a present from my wife; I'm not prepared to part with it." He immediately regretted saying that. What's the watch compared to Sophia's safety?

The man shoved him. Sophia screamed again.

"I don't want your fucking money."

A mugger who doesn't want money? Oh.

"I have something that originally belonged to a Dr. Birnbach," Marc said, playing a stomach-curdling hunch. "If that's what you're looking for, you can have it."

"Where is it?"

"I'll take you to where I have it." Marc was determined to sound calm. "I just need your assurance that once I do, you'll leave us alone."

The man stepped toward them and drew back his fist.

"Doesn't work that way. Until you give me that box I'll hurt you worse and worse." The man glanced behind him. Perhaps he was looking out for the police, but Marc had the impression that he was expecting someone, and how did he happen to know it was a box? "My only *assurance* is that once I have that box the pain will stop, maybe permanently, depending on my mood."

"Okay, just let my daughter go home, then I'll take you to the scrolls."

"Neither of you leave my sight until I have the package and know the contents are genuine. Once I do, I'll decide what to do with you."

In no position to negotiate, Marc had no choice but to give the thug what he wanted and hope that once he got it, he'd clear out.

Sophia emerged from behind Marc. "You bully!"

The thug darted around Marc but skidded on the muddy ground, and Marc managed to block his access to Sophia, at the cost of a glancing blow to his ribs.

The thug again looked behind him.

"Expecting someone?" Marc asked, struggling to sound calm and think clearly. The longer he stalled, the greater the chance that someone would see them and call the police.

"Yeah, I'm having a cocktail party. Serving bloody Marys made with real blood, bloody Blochs I'll call them." Apparently pleased with his wit, he grinned.

"How do you know my name?"

The thug shoved Marc.

"Take it easy, I said you'll get it, just…"

The thug's eyes narrowed to dark reptilian slits.

Once he gets the scrolls, he's not going to let either of us live. Our best chance is here in the open where a dog-walker or jogger might see us and call 911.

"If you're good, I'll make it quick and painless."

"Run," Marc whispered to Sophia.

Trembling with fear, she shook her head. He gave her his most commanding look.

The thug grabbed one of her arms and slapped her across her face—hard enough for blood to spurt from her nose.

Hatred took control of Marc's mind and body. His senses sharpened. He shifted his weight to the balls of his feet. He could only hope something from his year of martial arts classes had stuck.

"For the last time, let her get out of here," Marc said, his voice quiet, his tone as calm as he could make it. "The package isn't an issue. I'm more than happy to part with it."

The thug snickered, then pulled back and hit him square on the chin. Marc's head smashed into the tunnel wall. Pain burst upon his brain like a brilliant light in a pitch-black room. His knees buckled. The man steadied him. Sophia's face formed into a silent scream.

"Don't even think about losing consciousness," the thug said. "You've got nothing to look forward to but pain."

Marc dodged and blocked, but the methodical controlled punches found his kidneys and other organs. They were mostly glancing blows, thanks to his evasive moves, but some found their mark. Struggling to focus, Marc gauged how much speed he'd lost over the years—too much. With each agonizing breath, he sucked in blood. Yet he realized the man was holding back, toying with him. Hitting to hurt but not hard enough to cause lasting damage, not yet. Could be he was taking it slow, amusing himself until whoever he was waiting for showed up.

Marc raised his hand. The man stopped hitting him. Marc paused for several heaving breaths, and spit up blood. He'd intended to say something but now realized it would've been pointless.

"When I'm done with you, I'll take your keys and toss your apartment, then your office."

Sophia started crying. Marc realized that things would only get worse from here. He had to take his best shot.

He shifted his weight to his front leg and brought his right knee up toward his attacker's balls. The thug blocked the blow with a hard rabbit punch before Marc's leg came within a foot of its target. Marc's slow roundhouse left got within two feet of his face, but the thug caught the fist in his huge paw of a hand and squeezed.

Marc bent his knees and turned his shoulders, as if he was setting up to hit a cross-court winner. Enjoying himself, the thug squeezed harder.

Uncoiling, Marc jammed his right index and middle fingers into the thug's eyeballs. The space between them and his skull felt like jelly. Marc twisted his wrist, and yanked down. The thug's hand released Marc's and flopped to his side.

Marc pulled his fingers from the oozing cavities.

Before his adversary had a chance to gather his wits, Marc shifted his weight from back to front foot and put his entire 166 pounds behind his karate punch. The bully's windpipe crunched like a cockroach smashed by a stiletto heel. A hard right to the man's solar plexus doubled him up.

Grabbing the thug's hair and one of his ears, Marc slammed his head into the wall. His body went limp. Marc let go, and the thug fell to the ground, his breathing shallow.

Marc raised his leg to break the guy's neck but seeing Sophia, reconsidered. He carried her out of there. Barely aware of passing through the park and crossing Riverside Drive, he felt lightheaded, almost high.

"You okay, honey?"

"I think so," she said, her voice robotic. "Is he...dead?"

"No, but he won't bother us again." But his friends would.

"It was like a movie." She sounded far away.

"Yes, that's.... a good way to think of it."

"Your face is bleeding, Daddy."

"Yours too. We need to wash up good when we get home."

"And use a lot of Neosporin." Distant stare like a shell-shocked infantryman. "Mommy always told me not to worry, because you're very brave and very strong."

"You're very brave too."

She cuddled into him.

"'Even though I walk through the valley of the shadow of death, I fear no evil; for Thou art with me; Thy rod and Thy staff, they comfort me. Thou preparest a table before me in the presence of my enemies.'"

"What did you say, Daddy?"

"Oh, nothing, really."

"Yes, you did, you were sort of mumbling, something about walking through Death Valley."

"Oh, I must've been talking to myself. It's nothing."

Reciting the 23rd Psalm was so out of character and so contrary to what Lisa would've expected of him that he didn't know how to explain it. But if he were going to turn to religion—turn back to the religion of his childhood—he'd do it out of conviction, not sudden desperate need.

Finding himself in their apartment, he wasn't quite sure how they'd gotten there. He remembered leaving the tunnel but nothing that followed. His stomach turned inside out, and he barely made it to the toilet to vomit, empty his watery bowels, and vomit again. He took a couple of Tylenols with codeine and went to care for Sophia, who, having politely waited until he finished, did her own vomiting, while Marc held her hair away from her mouth.

"There are some very bad people in the world and very bad things happen sometimes, but we're safe now and everything's going to be okay," he said, wishing he could've come up with something better than platitudes.

"I know, Daddy," Sophia said, but her tone and facial expression showed that she felt anything but safe and doubted that things would ever be okay again.

"May I do my homework now?" She sounded like the Talking Barbie she'd used to have. She sat at her desk, opened her notebook, and methodically arranged her pencils as Marc drifted into the far reaches of the living room. Her intense focus on her homework and total concentration concerned him. Concern? He was worried sick. Was she blocking everything that happened this afternoon?

Once Sophia went to sleep—it took extra reading and several off-tune lullabies, but still he feared she'd gone down easier than she should've—he called John Cooper. He told the investigator what had happened and answered his questions as fully as he could, which wasn't all that fully.

"Did you call the police?" Cooper asked.

"I guess I should have.... I wasn't thinking straight. Not thinking at all. Let me do that right now." His face felt warm. How the hell could he have neglected to call? "A pair of detectives visited me a couple weeks back in connection with LaPonte. I have their cards.... They're in the office—the cards, I mean—but I guess I could call the precinct or something."

"Having not done it right away, maybe now you're better off not doing it," Cooper said. "Particularly since you're not at your most coherent. Wait until we have a chance to talk face to face. When can we get together?"

"I need to be with Sophia, but I can come by at nine a.m. if that works for you."

"Be better if I swing by the crime scene...the site of the event, now, then come over. I think we should talk tonight. See you in an hour or so?"

"Great, thanks."

Marc called a locksmith and had another set of locks installed on his door, then devoted himself to sweating and shivering. He knew someone else would be coming for him, someone who'd be armed and unlikely to be suckered into letting his guard down so he could be felled by a surprise poke in the eye.

He wanted to pray but wasn't sure what to say. It felt wrong to ask God for help, and he didn't see the point of praising Him.

XXV

Life Expectancy of a Suicidal Mayfly

MARC HAD DEALT with Cooper over the years but mostly on the phone. He was surprised to see how big he was, having to turn sideways to get his shoulders through the door. With his huge shaved head and one diamond earring, Marc would've found him scary if he hadn't had all the scare scared out of him earlier.

"Have you grown or have I shrunk?"

"Steroids, HGH, lifting."

"Be careful."

"I've got a doctor supervising my program. I know just what I'm doing." He smiled. "You look like shit."

"I feel worse than I look."

"I was all over that tunnel," Cooper said. "There's no sign of violent activity. Thought I was in the wrong place or this was a reprise of the BMW incident, but then I noticed the walls had been cleaned and the mud scraped smooth."

"So even if I wanted to go to the police, there'd be nothing to tell them."

Marc led him into the living room, and they both sat on the couch.

"Walk me through exactly what happened. Slowly, and don't edit out any details you think might be unimportant."

Marc did.

"He made clear to you that even if you gave him the box, he'd kill you?"

"Clear enough."

"If what he really wanted was the box, why tell you that up front? Makes me think the point was to send you a message, scare the shit out of you."

"Mission accomplished." Marc tried to keep focused. "But why?"

"How did he know you'd be coming through that tunnel?"

"No idea. I'd planned to spend the entire day at work and only changed my plans when I got unexpectedly taken off a case. I called the babysitter an hour or so before I picked up Sophia, and it was only a few minutes before we met the thug that Sophia and I decided to cut through the tunnel and take the short way home."

"Sounds like the guy wasn't in shape to clean up after himself, so whoever did that... Means he wasn't working alone."

Marc took a series of shallow breaths, since deep ones hurt like hell.

"He knew my name. I had the feeling he was waiting for someone to show up. Maybe the Snowman." He shook his head. "I don't know even know if there is a Snowman."

For the next several minutes, Marc rambled on, less coherently than he'd have liked, about the history of his representation of Dahlia.

"When we spoke a few weeks ago," he said, "you told me someone hired you to investigate her."

"And that I couldn't tell you who."

"Come on, circumstances have changed a bit here."

"I still can't, because I don't know. His or her voice was electronically altered, a commercial messenger delivered my fee in cash, and my client called me from a blocked phone to hear my report."

"Sounds like it could've been Suzie."

"Or Dahlia, checking on what was out there about her."

"I think I once gave her your number."

"From what I could see, there's no one in any law enforcement computer with a snowman birthmark on his cheek."

Marc swallowed a pair of codeine-infused Tylenols. "So, what should I do?"

"Might be a good idea to hire a bodyguard, at least until this all sorts out."

"Anyone you'd recommend?"

He grinned, showing off a perfect set of teeth. "I know a big, tough-looking character, licensed to carry. He's an expert marksman." He slid back his jacket, revealing a shoulder holster.

"What hours can you work?"

"Twenty-four seven, long as you need."

Marc would have to invade Sophia's college fund, but if he didn't she might not make it to fifth grade.

"What do you think about my taking Sophia out of state?" Marc asked, after pouring Cooper a drink.

"Before we do anything, I'd like to have a better idea of who we're dealing with and what sort of resources and agenda they have."

Feeling guilty about keeping Cooper up so late when they'd have to wake up in the morning in time to get Sophia off to school, Marc yawned.

"I need to get some sleep. That couch folds out into a bed. You'll find it surprisingly comfortable."

Long after midnight, Marc, hearing Sophia scream, bolted toward her room. He smashed into a large immovable object and tumbled to the floor.

"Sorry." Cooper extended a hand.

"DADDY!"

"Go back to bed, John. I'll handle this."

It took Marc some time to calm Sophia sufficiently for her to lie down and lay her head on his lap.

"I dreamt there was a giant in the apartment. He pretended to be our friend but really wanted to hurt us."

"I'm hiring a huge man to protect us, honey."

"No! You can protect us."

"I just want you to be super-safe."

"I don't want to be super-safe. I want to be with my daddy! No one else!" She sat up, so much for calming her.

"For a little while, you'll have both of us."

Her face reddened. She glared at him, perhaps a prelude to throwing a fit. Marc met her gaze with his own unyielding one, and their face-off ended with her returning her head to his lap.

After not more than five hours of sleep, Cooper went grocery shopping for them, while he checked out the area for anything suspicious. When he returned, Sophia pointedly ignored him.

Marc read to her while Cooper made what Marc had told him was her favorite breakfast—cheddar and mushroom omelet with well-done bacon on the side and fresh-squeezed orange juice. This mollified her a bit.

"We should stay home today," Marc told her.

"Do we need *him* around?" She pointed to Cooper.

"We want him here to help us if something happens."

Her upper lip quivered. "Is something going to happen, Daddy?"

"No. The bad man knows enough not to come after us now. I just want to be extra careful."

"What if the bad man has friends who are mad at us?"

"That's why we have Mr. Cooper."

She returned to her eating, or rather spreading the food around her plate and taking the occasional forkful.

"I don't feel good," Sophia said.

"What's the matter, honey?" Marc's stomach cramped, his head throbbed, and his chest hurt every time he breathed.

"My tummy." She distended her stomach and folded her hands across it. "My head, too." Her most serious face. "I don't think I should go to school."

"Okay, as I said—"

"Also, maybe you shouldn't go to work."

"Yes, I told you..."

"Oh. I forgot."

She never forgot anything like that.

Marc went from the dining nook into the living room to consult with Cooper. Although Marc was still within her line of sight, Sophia shrieked.

He ran back to the dining nook.

"I'm not going away." He hugged her. "I just need to speak to Mr. Cooper for a couple of minutes. I'll be right there." He pointed. "Would that be okay?"

She pulled her head back: what do you think?

"Just for a couple of minutes."

Reluctant nod.

Marc returned to Cooper, who said there was nothing online or in the newspapers about a Riverside Park confrontation or anything new about the investigation into the LaPonte killing.

Marc paced the circumference of his living room rug.

"If he really wanted that box, he'd have let Sophia go. Any sort of disguise, even as simple as one of those balaclavas movie terrorists wear, would've made him unrecognizable to her."

"There are therapists who treat both children and their parents," Cooper said. "I met a particularly good one, while working on a thermonuclear divorce earlier this year. I'd be glad to give you his name."

Marc rubbed his chest. It did nothing to ease the pain. Lisa would've already made a doctor's appointment for him and one with a child psychologist for Sophia. Among other things, he had a couple of bruised ribs, one of which might've been broken, but a doctor would have probably just give him Tylenol with codeine, which he already had, and tell him he would feel better in four to eight weeks. Sure, if he lived that long. As for Sophia, he could tell she was traumatized, but it seemed best to wait a few days and see how she did.

"Why would he want to scare us? Why not get the box and be done with it?" Marc asked.

"Daddy! It's been a couple of minutes. I counted to a hundred and twenty."

He rushed over and sat next to her.

Five whole days crept by and finally neither Marc nor Sophia could stand to spend another hour holed up at home. Marc walked Sophia to school, with Cooper hanging back, looking out for potential trouble. Marc had arranged for Sabrina to drop Talia off at the same time he and Sophia arrived, and thanks to Talia's enthusiasm over seeing her best friend, the drop-off went fine.

Around noon, the phone rang.

"Hello, Mr. Bloch, this is Ms. Mungoli, the school nurse."

Marc's stomach twisted. Seeing his face turn white, Cooper rushed over.

Turned out Sophia had a belly ache. When Marc showed up at school, she claimed to be feeling better and said she didn't want to go home.

"My tummy hurt, but I wasn't really that sick," she said. "I just had to go into the bathroom to cry for a long time."

He told himself it was a good sign that she was showing some emotion, and maybe it actually was.

Tuesday was a quiet day, and on Wednesday, bowing to a weird compulsion to discuss something with Sophia as they walked to school, Marc suggested that Cooper take the morning off and join them for afternoon pick-up at school.

On their walk he asked Sophia, "Do you have any interest in having a *bat mitzvah?*" His voice trilled up.

"Isn't that only for Jewish girls? Mommy wouldn't like that."

"She'd have no objection to your being exposed to religion. She believed in learning and understood that religion is a sort of *philosophy*. You could start with religious school and see how you like it. One step at a time. I mean, if you're interested."

"The girls in my class that go say Hebrew school's dumb. They just fool around."

"No education is dumb. People who fool around and don't learn from it are dumb. But it was just a passing thought."

She stopped and turned toward him.

"Why? I mean now?"

"I just told you—"

"Daddy, you're like Mommy and me, you don't have *passing thoughts,* and if you do, you don't waste energy putting them into words."

Looking at her, he shook his head. *She sounds about twenty-five years old.*

"Well… it's about where you come from, our family's history. Our Jewishness goes back three thousand years, unbroken. That's a very long time. They—I mean, *we*—went to a whole lot of trouble to hold onto our heritage. In almost every generation some despicable group tried to wipe us out, but the pharaohs, the crusaders, the Spanish kings, the czars, the Nazis, to name just as few, are all gone, and *we* are still here." He shook his head again. *I sound like my mother. Next thing you know I'll spit every time I mention one of the oppressors.* "As for why now? I'm not quite sure myself, something to do with Mommy dying and then the fight in the tunnel.... Hard to explain, but I'm slowly starting to feel…"

Thank God he had enough sense not to say he was starting to feel *mortal.*

"Do you think Mommy was wrong and there really is a God?" Quizzical look.

"No way to know, but what I do think is that the religious, or rather the *spiritual,* side of life is important, more important to me than I'd thought. Mommy's interest in philosophy was a sort of substitute for that, one that worked fine for her, but wouldn't have worked for me. I need something more and neglecting that side of life, I think I might have been selling myself short. Does that make any sense to you?"

"Sort of, maybe. I think it might be a little important to me, too."

"I probably shouldn't have even mentioned it until I'd thought it out more."

Suspicion narrowed her eyes. "If you want me to… I like school. It might be fun to learn Hebrew."

"Only if you decide it's what you want to do."

"Can I think about it?"

"Of course. I will, too."

She seemed happier at drop-off, running up the steps with something akin to enthusiasm.

Marc too was healing, but slowly. Among other things, his digestive system was still a mess. Halfway home his stomach cramped so painfully that he went into a coffee shop to use their bathroom.

He neglected to lock the door properly and it opened, then locked. Dahlia!

"I just wanted to thank you for not forking me."

XXVI

All Forked Up

"WHAT?" MARC SHOUTED. "What do you know about what happened to me in the tunnel."

"The fork with my fingerprints that you so sneakily took from Nice Matin," Dahlia said. "If you believed I killed LaPonte, you'd have given it to the police. Thank you for believing in me."

"I forgot I had the fork." His voice sounded as if it was coming from far away.

He needed to learn about the tunnel attack—*but does she even know about it?*—and how to keep Sophia safe, also, whether he was standing face-to-face with a homicidal maniac.

"You're not the forgetting type."

"When I mentioned the tunnel, you didn't seem surprised," he said, beginning to recover his equilibrium.

"Nothing surprises me anymore."

Marc stepped into her space, leaned forward, and dropped his voice; most people would've found this intimidating, but Dahlia? He had no idea.

"How did you find me here? And more to the point, how did that thug happen to—"

"I'm sure you meant to say, 'Thank you for cleaning up the scene of the fight.' You're quite welcome, think nothing of it."

"YOU!?"

Dizzy and beginning to hyperventilate, he took shallow breaths.

"Marc, get a grip." She pushed her arms downward: lower your voice. "Beyond this flimsy door is a public place, and we're wanted for murder."

"*We're* not wanted for anything."

"Well," she said, "given the alleged involvement of your car and your withholding of evidence… Maybe in your case it's just obstruction, but a very public arrest wouldn't be good for your fragile career. I understand that tunnel thing was somewhat traumatic, particularly with Sophia there to watch, but—"

"She was more than *there*. She was hurt and her life was threatened." So much for keeping calm. Marc was so furious he might even have hit her, if his hands hadn't already hurt so much.

Dahlia's face turned from joyous to miserable. "I tried, but…" Her voice cracked. "The news story that I'm the prime suspect in LaPonte's murder sent me into a funk, and—"

"Wait, how the hell did you know Sophia was there?"

"I saw little footprints in the mud." She sighed. "Marc, I really didn't mean to annoy you, just before. I've been a bit off-kilter lately. Even as I listen to what I'm saying now, I know I'm not controlling myself very well, but I will, I promise."

"You saw her footprints?" he sputtered.

"I arrived at the scene just a few minutes after you and Sophia left. Being seriously depressed and having to keep under the radar slowed me down. I'm really sorry."

"And you happened to go there because?" he asked, so quietly he practically whispered, but still his voice shook with rage.

"I'm watching out for you, or trying to. I should never have…" Her voice again cracked, and her eyes became damp.

He again leaned forward, so his face was inches from hers. "Dahlia, you need professional help."

"That's why I hired you." She grinned, actually *grinned*. "You're one of the best professionals around."

He shoved her. She staggered, her lower back banged into the sink.

"Someone, the Snowman no doubt, told the police I'd taken a gun to one of LaPonte's news conferences, claimed to have seen your car leaving the scene of LaPonte's murder, and talked to a police artist." Her rapidly mutating tone indicated no reaction to his aggression. "The cops don't know where to find me, but still…I'm just managing to stay one or two steps ahead of them."

"Before you sprout fangs and wings and flap off into the night to kill someone else, explain this: I had the feeling the thug in the tunnel was waiting for someone. Also, I offered to give him the damn box that Suzie gave me, my only condition that he not kill Sophia and me after I gave it to him."

"Yes! Just as I thought." Her incandescent smile made Marc want to punch out her lights. "You were just bait. With me on their tail, the box wouldn't have done them much good. I'd nab them as soon as they got it. So, counting on my out-sized sense of loyalty, their plan, pretty much the mirror-image of mine, was to ratchet up the pressure on you, figuring that if they tightened the screws hard enough, I'd come to your rescue and BAM!"—she smashed her palm on the wall—"they'd have both the box and me."

"Your sense of loyalty?! You're loyal like herpes."

"The Snowman and whoever he works for want the box, but they want *me* too," she said, her tone pedantic and undistorted by emotion. "The box does them little good so long as there are people around who've seen what it contains and know what they did to Daniel, Shustak, and Vance. They plan to get rid of anyone who's seen the scrolls—which is me." She pointed an admonitory finger. "Don't look inside the box."

"And if this Snowman—if there really is such a person—is anything like you claim, he'd just believe that I didn't peek?" Marc said, feeling silly that he was responding to her ranting as if it was worth taking seriously.

"I hope so."

Hands clenched so tightly that his fingernails dug into his palms, he asked, "How did *they* even know about the box?"

Mona Lisa smile, as if she was not only in on a joke Marc missed but she and she alone got the joke behind the joke.

"I've been leaving voicemails about the scrolls for all the potential masterminds: the embassies of the Persian Gulf countries, oil companies, money men, and Dick Cheney, to see how they react. I even told de Saint-Juste and through him his emir pal."

"Oh, please! Listen to yourself. Why the hell would anyone who got your crazy-grams have anything to do with Birnbach's killing?"

"Please, one question at a time—you *really* don't want me to go into overload mode. I thought you wanted to know why you were attacked."

"Fine, go with that one."

"I set it up so no one can find me. The only connection they have to me is through you."

"Oh, come on, Dahlia, how would they—whoever the hell *they* are—even know about me?"

"I told them I have a copy of the scrolls, and in each of my voicemails I mentioned you and implied a great connection between us," she said, matter-of-fact tone, as if that were what anyone would've done. "You know, to set a trap for them. I'd planned to swoop down as soon as you were attacked."

"You...*what?*"

"Did you also ask about my importance?" She paused, but Marc didn't respond. "Yes, I think you did. They killed LaPonte partly because they feared she might tell the truth about how they euchred her into killing Daniel, but mostly because of me. I'm known to have *harassed* her, so it wouldn't be beyond belief that I'd kill her. After shooting her, they called in an anonymous tip about my car—well, your car—leaving the scene. If the cops find and arrest me, they'll Jack Ruby me, before I have a chance to talk."

"Dahlia, they don't have to discredit you. As a certified lunatic, you're already discredited."

Her lips trembled and she stared off in the distance. "If they didn't care about me, they'd ignore my messages, but no, each time I leave one they escalate."

Marc pressed his throbbing temples.

"Last time we spoke, *they* consisted of Ahmed, his grandfather, and maybe some of their hangers-on. Have they now metastasized to include all the Persian Gulf countries, oil companies, money-men, whatever that means, a former vice president, and even de Saint-Juste? What about the International Zionist Conspiracy, the Catholic Church, and the Freemasons?"

"I've given this a lot of thought."

"No doubt with the help of Ariella."

"Lose the cynical condescending tone. She's actually been terrifically helpful."

"Well, that certainly adds to your credibility."

"I should never have told you about her." She shook her head. "So fine, forget about anything she said. Professor Vance explained the whole thing. Ahmed, his emir grandfather, and the other members of their party want the scrolls, so the pro-Iranian faction can't use them as the basis for a jihad." Her tone was so patient and put-upon that someone listening might've thought Marc was the crazy one. "You've seen for yourself how the Internet has been buzzing with rumors. I've been disseminating my voicemails widely to make sure they reach the emir."

"What if word of the scrolls reached the bad guys through Shustak's blog, not Yusef's conversation with Ahmed?" Marc asked. "Then there'd be no reason to believe the emir is even involved."

"Yes, exactly, that's why I need to cast a big net. Still, I'm with Professor Vance. I'm certain it all goes back to the so-called *moderate* faction in the UAE."

"That's not what he said. Also, if these scroll fragments were legitimate, don't you think the Israelis would be showing interest?"

"Why do you think the Snowman pushed Vance down the stairs if he wasn't onto something?"

"I've no reason to believe that there even is a Snowman. Dahlia, please, stop, think. It's just not plausible that people are being killed over a few unauthenticated scraps of parchment."

"Let me tell you a story."

Marc rolled his eyes.

"Please, just listen. I *need* you to believe me."

She tugged at his sleeve, desperate, and damn it he felt the tug deep in his gut. If only she weren't crazy.

"My grandmother lived on the green line, the line that separated East and West Jerusalem before the '67 War," she said. "One day she hung her laundry on a clothesline. A gust of wind blew a pair of her panties into no-man's land. She wanted them back, so an international commission was convened."

"Okay; there was an international incident over her underwear. I still don't see—"

"After considerable debate, the commission ruled that my grandmother could have her panties back if she could prove she'd bought them prior to Israel's independence in 1947. My point is, in the Middle East some things have greater significance than they might elsewhere. Never underestimate the capacity of the region for ridiculous behavior in the face of preposterous provocations."

"There might have been a time when I'd have found that story interesting."

His fury over the tunnel incident began to fade. One of the few things he was sure of about this mess was that she hadn't had him attacked. Still, she should've known that her stupid voicemails might get him attacked, not that he could be sure that anybody she called had had anything to do with the attack.

"Maybe the Snowman exceeded his mandate when he killed Shustak and had Daniel murdered and now both the murder *and* the scrolls need to be covered up. That can't happen as long as I'm picking at the scabs. The emirates have done very well, exploiting the status quo. Now they fear anything that might upset the diamond cart." She grinned. "That's like the apple cart only on a more elevated financial level."

"Yeah, I got the joke."

"As Professor Vance confirmed, political careers will rise and fall depending on how this plays out, and the emirs value their positions more highly than they value a few heathen lives."

"Okay, fine, maybe someone somewhere might care about the scroll fragments, but—"

She motioned for him to come closer, then whispered in his ear, "With Ariella's help, I had a breakthrough. I'm seventy-five-percent certain de Saint-Juste is the bad guy."

Marc's head jerked back.

"WHAT?"

"The desalination plant he's building over there is the world's third largest construction project. Huge bucks on the line there. It all makes sense, he needs to please his United Arab Emirates friends."

He shook his head. He'd been considering the possibility that there might've been something to her speculation, but it was beyond belief that de Saint-Juste had had anything to do with Dr. Birnbach's death or the tunnel attack.

"I first came to you not because I wanted a lawyer but because I wanted you to introduce me to him," she continued. "When you refused, I sent you out for tea and emailed him from your computer, and he—"

"You what?"

"Please, Marc, try to stay focused, this is important. He agreed to see me right away. At first I thought it was because of the glowing recommendation from you that I'd written, but it became apparent that he only saw me because the email mentioned Daniel and the scrolls. He pretended to call Abu Dhabi and speak to Ahmed, who denied everything."

"So because he denied it, it has to be true?"

"It was after two a.m. in the UAE. Looking back, I realize that de Saint-Juste was speaking gibberish—I know enough Arabic to know that what he was saying made no sense, but at the time I was so happy that he seemed to be taking me seriously that I didn't focus on the strangeness of it all. My subsequent messages contained phrases that would only have pushed his buttons if he feared I was on to him. Otherwise he'd have dismissed me as a pesky lunatic."

Although he understood that no good could come of it, Marc said, "A client of mine told me that if this Amhed were in the country, hanging out in downtown clubs, drinking, doing drugs, running around with pretty boys, he wouldn't be using his real name."

"Yes! That explains why I've had such trouble finding him." Self-satisfied smile. "De Saint-Juste knew exactly who I referred to when I mentioned Ahmed, and on the phone he called him Ahmed, not some other name. Now, I'm ninety-percent sure he's in on it. Don't you see it all makes sense?"

"Here's what makes sense to me, Dahlia. You take the damn scrolls and stop involving me in your intrigues."

She made a whistling sound and shook her head.

"You do at least understand that Daniel and Shustak were killed because—"

"There have to be easier, less risky ways to discredit unauthenticated ancient artifacts than killing people."

"But—"

"There were many copies of the Torah, all hand-copied. Why would this be the one that indicates an error? Why isn't *it* the aberration?"

"Oh. I never thought of that." Her thin, hurt little girl voice. "What about the offers on the Internet, Daniel's and Shustak's murders?"

"You're so committed to this fantasy about the scroll fragments that you're not thinking straight. This has to end badly." He exhaled though closed lips. "De Saint-Juste, really."

"Marc, with all these law enforcement types swarming around the LaPonte killing, it might be a while before I'm able to help you. So I'll need you to hang in there, know I'm on my way, and not do anything stupid in the meantime."

"That's a shame, seeing how great you've done keeping me out of danger so far."

"You're so damn fickle," she said. "I thought we were friends."

"Please just take the damn box. That way it and you will be together, and you and this Snowman can fight it out without me, mano a mano, spy vs. spy, bad personality against worse personality."

Her eyes fluttered, her shoulders slumped, and the corners of her mouth turned sharply down, but seemingly by dint of great effort, she pulled herself together.

"I intend to get the scrolls and confront the Snowman, just as soon as I get law enforcement off my butt long enough to give me room to maneuver."

He took a series of deep, slow, calming breaths. At least they would've been calming if he didn't have several bruised ribs.

"I'm going to throw the scrolls out."

"You don't want to do that. It could get you— or worse, Sophia— killed."

"DID YOU JUST THREATEN—"

"Of course not. Relax."

He stood rigid, fists clenched.

"Come on, Marc, deep breath."

She breathed deeply, like a yoga instructor demonstrating.

"Good, now again," she said, although he hadn't done it the first time. "Great. Glad we got through that. Phew." Theatrical wipe of her brow. "So, anyway, the next thing we need to do is—"

"*We* don't have to do anything. No way I'm going to be part of…whatever it is you're planning." Deep, painful breath. "I should just turn over that fork."

"If it makes you feel more comfortable, by all means do it."

"Please, take the box and get out of my life."

"You can't be serious."

"Deadly serious! My daughter and I have been beaten and threatened, and I'm two feet away from a psychopath wanted for murder."

"A person who suffers with schizoaffective disorder is not a psychopath. Look it up in DSM-IV if you don't believe me." Her voice cracked and her eyes became damp.

"Dahlia, you need to turn yourself in and get help."

She stared off into infinity, and her lips moved. Marc waited.

"I know our friendship will bounce right over this little speed-bump," she said. "But I've got to tell you, I'm getting the feeling that you and I aren't quite on the same page."

"More like not on the same planet."

"Okay, sure, I understand why you want to be out of harm's way, but do you at least believe—?"

"I believe that if you continue working so hard to piss people off, you'll succeed in stirring up a shitload of trouble for yourself and for me as well." He held eye contact, then speaking slowly and enunciating each syllable, said, "Hear this, Dahlia, I don't want to have anything more to do with you. You're not to call me, come see me, use my name in voicemails. Don't even *think* about me." He shook her. "Got that?"

Going limp, she stared back in damp-eyed disbelief.

"Please, you have to believe me." She pulled at his fingers, eyes pleading, desperate. "I need someone on my side."

"I'm not going to expose myself or my daughter to any more—"

"I told you I understand that. All I'm looking for is your friendship. Your emotional support." Tears formed in her eyes. "Is that too much to ask?"

"I'm sorry, Dahlia, but yes, it is."

"But...I don't think I can function without you." Her voice cracked and trembled. A tear rolled down her cheek. "Even Ariella has deserted me."

"That's a plus."

"Please."

He felt awful, but he shook his head.

Her phone rang. She looked at it, then shut it off.

"Gotta go," she said. "We'll talk when you're feeling...calmer. Not to worry, I understand. This is stressful for all of us."

She ran out.

When he got to the street, he saw no sign of her, just a green Ford pulling out, tires screeching.

Seconds after she disappeared, a dozen police cars showed up and helmeted, body-armored SWATers armed with automatic rifles took positions around the entrance to the coffee shop. Marc watched until they stood down, stowed their weapons, and heads bent, shoulders slumped, returned to their cars. Seemed there was no reason for Marc to alert Thomas and Santos that he'd seen Dahlia.

As soon as Sophia was doing her homework, Marc told Cooper about his conversation with Dahlia. He concluded, "The woman's nuts—and dangerous. There never was a way I could've helped her, I was foolish to try. I'm lucky to have gotten out of it with only some bruises and a temporarily traumatized child."

"I'm glad you're finally coming to your senses."

They sat in silence, turned on the TV news, then turned it off again.

Marc said, "It's been over a week since the park confrontation. Can we assume the threat to Sophia and me has receded?"

"What do you think?"

XXVII

The Worst Things in Life Are Free

AFTER JUST BARELY avoiding the SWAT team and somehow making it back to her, or rather Yusef's, apartment, Dahlia fell to her knees.

"Ariella, help me."

Then she remembered. Like Marc, Ariella had deserted her.

Like the heroine of a Victorian novel, she took to her bed. Staring at the ceiling for hours—days?—she neither ate nor slept. She yearned to hear Ariella's voice, which only made her feel more pathetic. With no one to talk to, she'd never felt so bereft, so totally alone. Telling Marc she couldn't function without him sounded melodramatic, but it had been perhaps the second truest thing she'd ever said, the first being that she was a fuck-up.

It was Ariella's fault! Dahlia had left those voicemails at her command and with her assurance that she'd keep Marc safe. If Ariella hadn't kicked her when she'd been down, telling her she was a screw-up who couldn't protect anyone, she might've been able to make it to the park in time to protect Marc. But all that was beside the point. Ariella had warned Daniel that getting the scrolls and bringing his killers to justice would be beyond her abilities. If only he hadn't had such faith in her, such misguided faith. Because of her the Snowman now knew Marc had the scrolls. He'd have no trouble finding Marc. He was going to get them and probably kill Marc and even Sophia in the process. No, she couldn't blame Ariella or Daniel, this one was on her.

Right-o, you ungrateful bitch.

"Ariella, you're back! Thank God! I need you."

Of course you need me. Without me, you wouldn't remember to brush your teeth with the fuzzy end of the toothbrush.

"Help me find the Snowman. We need to stop him before—"

Get a grip, the Snowman's just a figment of your imagination.

"WHAT!? You told me—"

I told you? Incredulous snort. *I've heard of rewriting history but that's like saying Pearl Harbor attacked the Japanese.*

"You're just picking on me. You always do that when I'm down." She sniffled. "It's not fair."

That she'd regressed to sounding so child-like only made Dahlia feel worse.

I've had enough of you blaming me in order to avoid taking responsibility for the consequences of your own actions. Yusef made an obscure comment about a birthmark on some thug's cheek. You then concocted this whole—

"No! You said…" Dahlia couldn't remember exactly what Ariella had told her about the Snowman. She couldn't think. She barely had the energy to cry. "I saw him at LaPonte's news conference, saw his—"

You're sure of that? Absolutely positive? Might that birthmark have been a hallucination or even a trick of the light? As for his comment about Shustak and Daniel, you do tend to hear what you want to hear.

Dahlia began trembling.

"What about the Beretta he put in my bag?"

Gee, didn't you bring with you a gun just like that when you moved here from Israel?

"No, well, I did but…I lost that one."

O Creedmoor, we're coming home to you.

"Why are you being so mean to me?"

You complain when you think I lie to you, now when I tell you the truth I'm being mean.

"I have to keep my promise to Daniel." Dahlia trembled as if she was sobbing. Her tear ducts felt like they were about to explode, but she couldn't cry. "I have to protect Marc and Sophia! What are we going to do?"

There is no we.

"NO! I need you."

No you don't. It's all my fault, remember? I commanded you to leave those voicemails, failed to support you when you were depressed.

"I took that back, admitted it's all my fault."

Oh, I'm sure you'll come up with something on your own. No, right, you don't want me to lie to you. Well, you can still blame Daniel for being foolish enough to count on you.

"Please."

Of course if I wanted to I could get you out of this mess, but you'd have to promise to follow my commands to the letter.

"Yes, anything."

Anything? Ariella whispered. And whispered.

"You're the crazy one!" Dahlia yelled. "I'd never do that."

Fare thee poorly.

"Wait!"

Silence.

"What possible reason could there be to—?"

Do I really need to explain that with Marc willing to do anything to help you, you can take down de Saint-Juste?

"Is de Saint-Juste really—"

You told Marc you were ninety-percent sure.

"I'm asking you."

And I'm not answering, next thing I know you'll be claiming it was all my idea, like with the Snowman.

"I'm not doing it, much too dangerous... Actually, it's outrageous, out of the question, no way! If all I were risking were myself, maybe, but..." Dahlia took a deep breath. "There is medication I could take to get rid of you."

Remember the meds they gave you at Creedmoor, how they made you feel half dead?

"If it's a choice between my being half dead and maybe making someone else fully dead—"

Sooner or later you'll change your mind. You really have no choice.

"I won't."

Okay, go with God. Ooops, no, you just cut off that option. Vaya sin dios, go without God.

"Stay! Please. Let's talk about it."

Silence

"We've always discussed... Come back!"

The silence and the accompanying loneliness thickened until she could barely breathe. She screamed.

Silently.

XXVIII

Rolls and Jam

MARC CALLED DE Saint-Juste. "You have time to meet with me? Today, if possible? I'm in sort of a jam."

"Can't. My plane leaves for Abu Dhabi in forty-five minutes. Can we do it on the phone?"

Marc sighed. "I'd prefer to talk to you in person. When are you back?"

"Not sure. What's the subject matter?"

"Dahlia."

"*Mon Dieu*! Marc. Didn't I tell you—?"

"Yes, and you have no idea how right you were," Marc said. "She seems to think you had something to do with the murder of Daniel Birnbach, the archaeologist who—"

"*Oui*. I know more than I'd like to about your friend and her delusions."

"I was attacked in the park, my daughter witnessed—"

"My God! Are you all right?"

"Better than I deserve to be. I'm concerned, though, about what'll happen next, and given her obsession with you, maybe you should be concerned as well. Perhaps we can work together to avoid a further tragedy."

"We can talk in the car on the way to the airport. My driver will swing by and pick you up in eight minutes."

Marc wondered whether de Saint-Juste was being so accommodating out of concern for Marc's welfare or his own.

"Thank you. I'm at home." He gave him the address.

Marc couldn't see how de Saint-Juste expected to make it to Newark or Kennedy in forty-five minutes, let alone clear security and board, but that wasn't his problem.

Precisely eight minutes after de Saint-Juste disconnected, a charcoal gray Rolls Royce—Marc believed the Rolls people called the color *anthracite*—pulled up in front of Marc's apartment building. A gray-uniformed driver hopped out and opened the door. Typing so fast on his BlackBerry that his thumbs were a blur, de Saint-Juste didn't acknowledge Marc.

The limo headed up the West Side Highway, and de Saint-Juste held up one finger, indicating he'd be with Marc momentarily. As the Rolls turned off for the George Washington Bridge, de Saint-Juste directed his attention to Marc, his gaze so intense Marc feared it would singe his eyebrows, and this was his *casual* gaze. Staying in character, de Saint-Juste didn't comment on Marc's bruises.

"Speak," de Saint-Juste said, in the sort of tone that was usually followed either by an award of a dog biscuit or a smack on the nose with a rolled-up newspaper.

Marc relayed Dahlia's theory that de Saint-Juste was responsible for the killings. De Saint-Juste glanced at his BlackBerry, facial expression and body language displaying nothing beyond indifference or perhaps boredom. Marc feared he'd be even more difficult to get the truth out of than Dahlia.

"I credit you with enough intelligence not to believe any of that," de Saint-Juste said.

"Of course I don't believe Dahlia's speculation about your involvement. Still, it does seem that my mugging, the murders of Shustak, Birnbach, and LaPonte, and the attack on Professor Vance are connected and have something to do with those scroll fragments."

"Those scrolls that Dahlia rambled on about? What do I have to do with—"

"Nothing, I'm sure, but given what happened to me and Sophia, seems I should check out every angle, and Professor Vance did provide some support for Dahlia's theory about the emir."

"I assure you that neither I nor anyone I work with in the UAE could care less about these scraps of parchment." Disparaging snort. "Emirs tend not to be murderously passionate Torah scholars."

"You should care that she suspects you. She's quite resourceful and persistent."

"She must be, having murdered two people and thus far eluded the police."

"I can't believe she—"

"Once her calls became nuttier and more threatening, I had her investigated." He handed Marc a bound file. "Prepared by Wickman & Taft."

"Never heard of them."

"You wouldn't. They're one of the two or three top investigative agencies in the world, but they're not on the Internet or in the phone book. If you have to ask who they are, you can't afford them. By comparison to their bills, Davis & Stearling's look like rounding errors. Unfortunately, I can't let you keep a copy of their report. I had to sign a non-disclosure agreement—they're hypersensitive about their work-product going only to their clients and certain specifically designated law enforcement personnel—but feel free to peruse it in the car."

"Plain manila cover no logo, not even a designation who prepared it."

"They're Wickman & Taft, they don't need a logo or a designation." De Saint-Juste flipped through several pages. "You might want to start here, on the list of her calls to me." He pointed to the top of the page.

"What? That's my cellphone number."

"The calls came from your phone."

"Couldn't have."

"Wickman & Taft aren't paid to be wrong."

De Saint-Juste took a call while Marc read. The report detailed Dahlia's illness and symptoms, covered her confinement in Creedmoor, her ejection from Mossad training, and her attempted strangling of the Israeli gymnastics coach. It hinted at a sexual relationship between her and Dr. Birnbach.

"We should put these guys on the Birnbach killing," Marc said, in the tone he'd use if he were joking.

"I wasn't aware there was any question of who killed him."

Marc hesitated, but then relayed LaPonte's claim had that she'd been given a dossier on Birnbach and his belief that the file had been a fabrication. De Saint-Juste didn't look up from his BlackBerry.

"There's also the question of whether Professor Shustak fell in front of the train or was pushed," Marc said.

"Not according to Wickman & Taft." De Saint-Juste flipped through several pages.

As he studied a blurry surveillance photo of the subway platform showing a tall woman with spiky hair, his stomach spun like a yo-yo flying off a broken string. The resemblance *was* striking. According to the verbiage that followed, she'd purchased a MetroCard with a credit card the morning Shustak died and used that card to enter the station four minutes before his death—three seconds behind Shustak.

Before Marc had a chance to express his disbelief, de Saint-Juste said, "If she'd shoot a Mossad agent, who knows what else she might do."

Marc flashed on his conversation with Dahlia where she'd told him about her inability to resist Ariella's commands. Yes, he had a lot to think about.

The Frenchman turned to the section on Professor Vance. It said he'd left his office several seconds after Dahlia and had been pushed down the stairs. No one had entered the building after she had.

"Why would Dahlia…? This makes no sense."

Marc didn't mention that Vance had agreed to identify the emir via his brother-in-law in the American embassy and that Dahlia had had no reason to interfere with that effort… Or had she?

"If everything crazy people did made sense, they wouldn't be crazy."

De Saint-Juste turned some more pages and showed Marc that an anonymous caller had claimed to have seen Dahlia's car—or as Dahlia would've said, *Marc's* car—leaving the scene of the LaPonte shooting.

"In one of her messages for me, Dahlia claimed you have the parchment fragments." De Saint-Juste's laser gaze. "If that's true, I'd think you'd have enough sense to turn them over to the authorities."

"They were taken from me before I had the chance," Marc said, sensing that this was one of those occasions where honesty was *not* the best policy. "I'd left them in my office. Between the time of the attack and my return to the office, they disappeared."

"Disappeared?" De Saint-Juste's eyebrows rose like crows in the background of a van Gogh, the most emotion, other than disdain, Marc had ever seen him display. "I gather we can assume that Dahlia has them?"

If Dahlia was right about de Saint-Juste, Marc realized he'd just put her in even greater danger than she was already in. She'd probably like that. Certainly Ariella would.

"I'm done making assumptions," Marc said. "My interest begins and ends with keeping my daughter safe and extricating myself from this mess."

"If only you'd come to your senses earlier."

"Seemed the least I could do was warn you."

Since Marc had been attacked and those in league with the attacker likely weren't done with him, de Saint-Juste's welfare was low on Marc's list of concerns. The Frenchman, though, was sufficiently self-involved to believe otherwise.

"Thank you, but I'm fully capable of protecting myself." He tapped the window, and it sounded as if he was hitting a granite wall. "An anti-tank grenade would barely dent the paint-job."

The Rolls turned into Teeterboro Airport. The driver showed ID to an armed guard, who waved them through. They crossed the tarmac to a private plane the size of a Boeing 737. In fact, it *was* a 737, anthracite, with the same coat of arms that had been on the shield in de Saint-Juste's office. Unlike Wickman & Taft, it seemed he needed a logo. The chauffeur opened the car door for his boss. De Saint-Juste stepped out and ascended the stairway to the jet. The stairway rolled away and the plane taxied down the runway, precisely forty-five minutes after Marc's call to de Saint-Juste.

Marc helped Sophia with her homework and when she was in bed shared what he'd learned with Cooper. After several calls to friends in the Bureau, Cooper confirmed that Wickman & Taft were who de Saint-Juste had said they were.

"I assume that when Dahlia contacts you again, you'll immediately call the police?" he said.

"I assume Dahlia won't contact me again."

Marc poured each of them two fingers of Jameson's Irish Whiskey, neat.

"When we've talked before, I had the feeling that you didn't fully believe that Dahlia was the bad apple here," Cooper said.

"I still don't. Some things in that report didn't ring true."

Cooper's brow furrowed. His eyebrows would've lifted and met, if he'd had any.

"What do you need to think about?" Cooper leaned toward Marc, an intimidating move from someone with his bulk. "I don't know how to make it any clearer than de Saint-Juste did. If Dahlia would shoot a Mossad agent under the command of her Ariella voice, she's capable of most anything, particularly when under pressure, which she quite obviously is."

Cooper leaned back, his expression that of a lawyer who'd just scored a key point on cross-examination.

"That's clear all right." Marc sipped his drink. "Thing is, life is muddy and nuanced. Things that are neat and clear often tend to be false. What's his motivation to put together such an airtight case?"

"If I were threatened by a crazy woman—"

"She told him I had the scrolls and she wasn't going to rest until she got justice for Dr. Birnbach. Was that a threat? Would he have even cared, if the scrolls meant nothing to him? If most people were threatened, they'd go right to law enforcement."

"*Most people* don't have the kind of scratch he has." Cooper dropped his voice and spoke slowly as if talking to a child or a dimwit. "Dahlia's pursuit of her fantasy that an emir muckety-muck in the government of de Saint Juste's biggest customer had Birnbach murdered could cause ripples in his deal. Likely he'd want those ripples smoothed out privately."

"Like how he had that thug tried to smooth me out?"

Cooper rolled his eyes.

"Come on, Marc, does that make any sense to you?"

"Not much, but de Saint-Juste's report makes too much sense. That's why I said I need to think it out."

They each sipped their whiskey.

"Inspired by her Ariella-voice's *jealousy* she threw wine in your face. It's not so hard to believe that, under pressure from her hallucinatory voice, she'd escalate."

"Murder's an awful big escalation," Marc said.

"Maybe yes, maybe no. She blames this non-existent Ariella for her bad acts. From there, it's a small step to make up this Snowman and maybe even act in his name. That was Suzie's theory, right?"

"Yeah...trying to make sense of a crazy person..."

"Your problem is that you like her, you can't believe she's truly evil, and you enjoy thinking of yourself as the kind of person who helps people in need. You suffer from a classic bird-with-a-broken-wing complex."

"That may not be my biggest problem, though." Marc smile. "May I freshen your drink, Herr Doctor Freud?"

Cooper shook his head.

"You know how a hypnotist can make a person do all sorts of nutsy things but can't make them do something, like murder, that they know is wrong?" Marc said. "There are lines people won't cross."

"I don't know the first thing about hypnosis, but I do know that psychopaths sometimes hear voices commanding them to kill and they can be incapable of resisting them."

"I'm inclined to go with my heart and my gut—"

"For a smart guy, you can be awfully—"

"Yes, Lisa used to find that frustrating, too, but you know what? I don't think she'd believe Dahlia's capable of murder either."

Copper looked like he was about to respond but instead emptied his glass and put it in the sink.

XXIX

Sleazy Does It

MARC WAITED AT the foot of the steps as the kids fanned out of school. Cooper surveyed the scene from a few yards back.

A teenager with a familiar mop-top haircut began to cross the street against the light. Cabs came to screeching halts. A woman with long dark hair and a short tight dress that showed off a too-familiar curvy body grabbed his arm and yanked him back. Then they darted across the street.

"That's Justin Bieber and Kim Kardashian!" Talia yelled. "Let's go meet them."

Talia and a bunch of girls shot across the street, ignoring the green light and the phalanx of cabs bearing down on them. Mothers and caregivers went wild trying to restrain their charges or pull them out of harm's way. Some kids hid but most watched, finding the whole scene riotously funny and using it as an excuse to scream as loudly as possible and generally run amok. Marc searched for Sophia.

Finally, she tentatively stepped out on the sidewalk, glanced at Talia, then Marc.

Everything was white.

Marc tried to sit up. Pain burst into his brain like a flash of brilliant light. His hand drifted to an egg-sized bump on the back of his head and came back dripping with blood.

"Mr. Bloch. Mr. Bloch, can you hear me?" a man asked.

Cops, police cars, flashing lights, crime scene tape.

"Wha... What happened? Sophia? Sophia! SOPHIA!"

"Mr. Bloch, calm down, please. You need to focus. We have to talk." The

186

man stuck something in Marc's face. A detective badge, maybe. "Time's of the essence."

Sophia? Where's Cooper? Marc turned to look behind him. Cooper was being attended to by a squad of paramedics. As there was a neat red hole in the back of his head and a large jagged one in his forehead, their concerns were forensic, not medical.

"Mr. Bloch, I'm Detective Lopez," the man said, kneeling by Marc. "Your daughter is missing. The FBI are on their way."

"Missing as in...*kidnapped?*"

"We think so. There was pandemonium. No one saw it go down.... Please take a moment to collect yourself, then tell me everything you remember."

The words spilling from Marc's mouth served as a fragile barrier between him and the awful truth. Sophia was in grave danger. Cooper was dead.

"Justin what's-his-name and that Kim woman?" he asked when his monologue ended. "Maybe there's a connection."

"Professional celebrity look-alikes hired over the phone," Lopez said. "Both paid in cash via a messenger they can't ID. Both were stoned stupid. Given their condition, I'm not sure they could identify their mommas."

"NO!" Marc screamed. Looking concerned, the detective made a palms-down gesture. Marc screamed louder. Drawing stares.

A pair of FBI agents and three technicians accompanied Marc back to his apartment. They put listening devices on his landline and BlackBerry and told him that in most kidnappings there was a ransom call within eight hours and that "the prognosis is good."

"Is...is that true, or just what you guys...always say?" Marc needed all his concentration just to form simple words.

"More often than not, we recover kidnapping victims unharmed."

More often than not wasn't reassuring.

While the others searched his apartment, talked and texted on their phones, an agent who'd introduced himself as Hugh Jodl interrogated Marc. Marc felt nauseous. His head ached. The pain behind his eyeballs would've been unbearable if any physical misfortune could've competed with his agony over Sophia. Over the next few hours, he haltingly told Jodl everything he remembered from the time he'd met Dahlia forward. He talked so long that when he was done, he felt as if he'd vomited, and maybe he had; he couldn't remember.

But he *could* remember that Cooper was dead because he'd dragged him into this.

Jodl sent an underling to Marc's office to retrieve the scrolls and asked Marc about former clients of Nichols & Bloch who might've held a grudge.

Marc told him he was certain that any who'd been ripped off by Peter realized that not only had Marc had nothing to do with it, but also he'd done his best to make things right. Still he gave Jodl a couple of names to check out. Whenever Marc's BlackBerry beeped, everyone jumped, but it was only SPAM except for one call from a law school buddy about a new case, which Marc ignored.

Jodl finally ran out of questions, leaving Marc even more frightened if that was possible.

"So what now?"

"We wait."

Marc's chest constricted, making it difficult to talk. He couldn't allow himself to become so depressed that it compromised his ability to focus.

"Please, there must be something more...proactive you can do."

"We're doing everything we can. Take a break, then we'll go through your story again."

"A break?" Marc laughed idiotically.

He paced, forced himself to think through everything that had happened. He had to think clearly, but how the fuck could he do that? He allowed himself a few minutes of sitting in the bathroom feeling bereft, then berated himself for giving in to weakness. Everything that had happened was his fault. He'd known Dahlia was crazy and that getting involved with her would lead to no good.

He told Jodl about his Rolls Royce conversation with de Saint-Juste.

"Why didn't tell you me about this before?"

"I didn't want to prejudice you against her."

"Oh, sure. That makes sense." Jodl shook his head just like Marc used to when a client would say something unimaginably stupid.

Jodl called de Saint-Juste, leaving a message that he would like to see the Wickman & Taft report and politely advising him that if he didn't receive the report by morning, he'd subpoena it.

"Let me see your phone."

Marc handed it to Jodl, who passed it on to a techie in an FBI windbreaker. Removing the battery, he located a card that read Marc's GPS chip, monitored his calls, and could be used to route calls from elsewhere through his phone.

"Very sophisticated little device," the techie said. "But easily acquired, if you know where to look."

"I guess we now know how Dahlia knew I was in that coffee shop bathroom," Marc said. "I just thought of something. When she gave us a ride back from the tennis tournament, she took Sophia's tennis bag and backpack to the other side of the car. She seemed to take longer to open the door than necessary, and I might've heard a zipper open and close."

Jodl asked the techie to check Sophia's backpack, which the kidnapper had left behind. Sure enough, he found another GPS chip stuck to the inside of one of the unused pockets.

"Seems Dahlia was planning this for quite a while," Jodl said.

Marc shook his head. "I don't think so. I can't believe she'd..."

"You have any idea who else might've done it?"

"The Snowman," Marc said and immediately felt stupid.

"The one with the supposed three-ball birthmark on his right cheek, whom no one but Dahlia has ever seen and who Suzie said was Dahlia's alter-ego?"

"I just..." His throat clenched. "She likes Sophia. She really knows how to talk to her."

"Maybe she liked her too much." Jodl swallowed as if trying to recapture his words. "Did she have any legitimate reason to route calls though your phone, monitor your calls, or plant a GPS chip in Sophia's backpack?"

Marc shook his head.

Time crept by. The agents dozed. Marc paced. Agents in the field called in. They'd located several people who'd seen, or thought they'd seen, Sophia being tossed into the backseat of a car. The tall, thin perpetrator had worn a long dark coat. The witnesses, though, disagreed on the person's gender. One thought the car was a blue BMW, another was certain it'd been a black Lincoln town car. A security camera that should've recorded what had happened had been disabled that morning. Several more videos of the celebrity-manqués turned up on YouTube but none yielded anything of use.

Marc started shivering. He draped a blanket over his shoulders but it didn't help.

More for distraction than out of any hope that it'd lead to something, he asked, "Would it be possible for you to have someone in the Bureau contact the State Department and put us through to our embassy in the UAE or Saudi Arabia? That way we could check out this story about these political factions."

"You can't be serious," Jodl said.

"Just trying to check out every lead."

"It's hardly a lead."

"It is if Dahlia didn't kidnap Sophia. Please?"

Jodl rolled his eyes, but eventually he had on the phone an assistant something or other in the U.S. embassy in Saudi Arabia. The man very much doubted that the scrolls would've been of such interest that either side would've risked the political fallout from killing a U.S. citizen on our shores to obtain or suppress them.

When they got off the phone, Jodl said, "The more we go over this, the more we return to the same place. You seem hesitant to believe it, but everything points to Dahlia as the kidnapper."

"There's no motive," Marc said. "I know her, and she wouldn't do it."

"In her delusional world, kidnapping your daughter probably ties in to her battle with this Snowman," Jodl said. "Even if there actually is a real Snowman who killed Dr. Shustak and Dr. Birnbach, which I very much doubt, he's likely long gone. Hired killers don't hang around after they do their work."

"Dahlia is infuriating and has more than a couple of screws loose, but I don't think we should dismiss the possibility that the Snowman might be real."

Jodl touched his fingertips together, forming a steeple.

"Even if someone other than Dahlia killed Shustak and even Ms. LaPonte—although there, too, the evidence points to Dahlia—I see no reason why the killer would've grabbed your daughter. It's a completely different MO for one thing."

"I…" Marc couldn't put together a coherent response.

"Come morning, if we don't hear from the kidnapper, I'll bring in a forensic psychiatrist and a profiler. Maybe they'll be able to help us get inside her head."

They sat in silence, dejection having made it difficult for Marc to talk or even get up from the couch, not that he had anything to say or anywhere to go.

A techie carrying a laptop came over to them. "You need to hear this. A call to 911 made a few hours ago, in front of the Ethical Culture School."

He hit some keys. Jodl and Marc leaned forward, straining to make out what had been said over the background traffic noise.

"I saw a tall woman with spiky red hair and a nose ring throw a bag over a little girl's head and toss her into a fancy car, dark blue, a BMW, I think it was."

Marc's jaw fell open.

After a triumphant glance at Marc, followed by a penitent head bend, Jodl turned to the technician. "NYPD have any more info on the call?"

"Just that it came from a payphone a few blocks away from the school and the caller hung up before he could be questioned."

An even more unpleasant silence descended.

"You told me there's usually a ransom call within eight hours," Marc said. "It's now been eleven."

"Maybe we got a kidnapper who's not a clock-watcher." Jodl shook his head. "Sorry, I didn't mean to be flip. It's been a long day."

"Does not having heard from the kidnapper decrease the odds?"

"Everything you've said indicates that whoever grabbed Sophia did it to put pressure on you. Seems the next step will be for the kidnapper to make contact."

"Unless something went wrong, like"—Marc's voice cracked—"there was an...accident along the way, and Soph didn't make it."

"Let's not jump to conclusions." But Jodl's tone indicated that if he hadn't jumped to a pessimistic one, he'd gotten there via small steps.

Marc was certain Dahlia would run rings around Jodl, and that a forensic psychiatrist and a profiler would just waste time coming up to speed, while Sophia's life hung in the balance.

Oh, God, please see to it that Sophia is all right.

At Jodl's suggestion, Marc went to bed. He had no expectation of sleeping but his pacing, moaning, and sighing had been disturbing the agents' and forensic people's rest. He hadn't known he'd been moaning or sighing, but he had no reason to doubt Jodl. Certainly, Jodl and the rest of his team would be more effective if they got some sleep.

Although the evidence that Dahlia kidnapped Sophia was overwhelming, his instincts told him she hadn't done it, not that those instincts had been so reliable lately. If only he could find Dahlia and confront her. Maybe alone in his bedroom an idea would come to him.

XXX

Hope Sung in the Key of Lunacy

MARC TOLD HIMSELF that even if he couldn't sleep, lying still with his eyes closed would be somewhat restful. It was pure agony. He imagined Sophia tied to a chair, hungry, terrified…if she was even still alive. What could he do to help her?

He willed himself to think through, yet again, everything that had happened since he'd met Dahlia. There might have been a seemingly insignificant snippet of conversation he'd neglected to tell Jodl that might yield a useful clue. He couldn't focus. But he had to. He remembered conversational bits and from them began meticulously to reconstruct entire conversations. Nothing helpful, though. According to Dahlia, her voicemails had caused *them* to escalate; perhaps she'd done something that caused the kidnapping. If only he could talk to her.

Covering his face with his pillow, he screamed, then beat the pillow and mattress with his fists.

Jodl had said all they could do was wait for the kidnapper to get in touch with them. But the kidnapper had to know the FBI would be all over any phone call.

Dawn brought a flash of clarity. Suddenly he knew how to find Dahlia— have her find him.

Carrying his shoes, he tiptoed into the living room. Jodl was snoring on the couch; Marc had neglected to tell him that it pulled out into a bed. Another agent was asleep on cushions from the back of the couch. Marc looked in on Sophia's room, and pain exploded behind his eyes. A techie was sleeping on her bed, another on her floor. Marc found the GPS chip from her backpack on the dining area table, along with his phone and the card Dahlia had put into it. He slipped the chip into his pocket. After trial and error, made

192

difficult by the semi-darkness and the need to be quiet, he figured out that the card slid under the battery. He reinserted it into his telephone, turned on the phone, and put it, too, in his pocket. Then he took the FedEx box, tiptoed out of the apartment, and quietly closed the door behind him.

Now, whoever had been tracking him would know his phone was on and that he was on the move. To alert anyone monitoring his calls he left a voicemail for a former client who never checked his messages. "Just calling to let you know I've broken away from the FBI and am on my own."

As a testament to the toll anxiety and sleeplessness had taken on his judgment, he walked two blocks along Riverside Drive before realizing how stupid he'd been to cut himself off from FBI support.

No harm done. There was no sign of Dahlia...or the Snowman. He was so far around the bend he was ready to believe anything, even that the Snowman might exist. Actually, he believed nothing except that he needed to get Sophia back safe and sound. The best way to do that was to trust in the FBI. They were professionals with decades of experience dealing with kidnappings. He turned back toward his apartment building.

A green Ford drove by slowly; the driver seemed to be checking out the area but was probably just searching for a parking spot.

A slow-moving Lincoln town car came to a stop. A door opened.

"Get in, please, Mr. Bloch."

"Who are you? Where do you intend to take me?"

"I'm José, your driver." Gap-toothed grin. "I told to pick you up, then wait instructions." He tapped the Bluetooth in his ear. "I told to drive away, if you not get in right away or if anyone with you or watching."

Marc hesitated, then climbed in. He knew this was dangerous and stupid, but the time to worry about his conduct from that angle would've been before he'd agreed to take possession of the scroll fragments. Perhaps when he'd first lain eyes on Dahlia.

"You have package?"

Marc pointed to the FedEx box.

The driver made a U-turn, then a sharp left in front of a bus, then a right as the light changed from yellow to red. After another U-turn, he gunned it through the light and went around the block. The green Ford made a U-turn behind him, blocking the view up the street. The driver turned onto Broadway and took a left onto 81st Street. Another passed around the block, and he pulled into a loading zone ahead of a bakery delivery van that cut off the lines of sight from down the street.

"What the hell are you doing?" Marc asked.

"Taking evasive action. Now wait further instruction."

Marc's phone rang.

"Are you okay?" Dahlia said. "I was so worried."

"DO YOU HAVE SOPHIA?"

"Of course not. "

"Is she okay?"

"I certainly hope so."

"I want to speak to her. NOW!"

"Don't worry, I'm on the case."

"Stop fucking around! Where is she?"

"Come on, Marc, the Snowman has her. You know that."

"Fine, put *him* on the phone."

"If he were here, one of us would be dead. Turn off your phone, lie back, and close your eyes. I'll see you soon."

"The FBI's listening in." They should've been, but in his overwrought stupidity, he'd made that impossible.

"That's why you need to turn off the phone. NOW! No, wait! One more thing. I paid the driver, you don't even have to tip him." She paused, but he could still hear her breathing, so he waited. "I'm running out of money, though, so if we don't succeed today, I might need a loan."

He turned off his phone—having chosen this path he'd stay on it, however risky.

After a few minutes of aimless driving, the limo stopped at a light at 68th Street. A yellow cab with its off-duty light on pulled up next to them.

"You get in to that one there," the limo driver said.

He did. After making a sharp u-turn, the cab headed uptown.

"Where are we going?" Marc asked.

"Morris-Jumel Mansion, Manhattan's oldest house. In 1776, it was headquarters to the father of the country, General George Washington."

"Washington Heights? I thought we were going to Long Island City. Or was that a ruse?"

"Not to worry, I'm already paid."

"By whom?"

"Bike messenger."

At 110th Street and Central Park West, a cherry red BMW M6 convertible, with *MYTOY* vanity plates, pulled up next to the cab. Dahlia, wearing a long black wig, motioned for Marc to get in. Anger shot through him like a high-voltage electric charge, but he did as he was told.

She made a sharp right onto 110th Street.

"How do you like the new color?" she asked. "I probably should've asked you before painting it, seeing it's your car and all, but I wanted it to be a surprise."

Marc didn't respond.

The corners of her mouth turned down.

"I'm afraid I have some bad news." She bit her lower lip. "All my fault, but I don't know what to say beyond I'm sorry."

Marc swallowed hard.

"You've gotten a bunch of parking tickets. They're in the glove compartment, with your license plate. I put the current one on just for today, after liberating it from a Toyota." She adjusted her driving gloves. "Nothing to deal with now, but when you get the chance. It'd be a stone drag to have this beauty towed."

He clenched his fists and willed himself to stay calm enough to think clearly.

"I've got the scrolls." He spoke quietly, enunciating each syllable. "Take me to Sophia."

"Here's the plan, we drive around until the Snowman finds us. After that…" She held up a hand. "I know that's not as proactive as you might want, so if you have any better idea, I'm happy to listen. Problem, of course, is we don't know where he is."

"Or if he really exists."

He turned the wheel just in time to avoid an old lady hobbling across the street.

"Marc, this really isn't a great time for you to joke."

"Talking to you is like trying to explain to a rock what it's like to be a tree. Please, Dahlia, you have to come to terms with your…disability before you do any more damage."

He reminded himself that despite the mountain of inculpatory evidence, he didn't really believe she'd kidnapped Sophia.

"So, as I was saying, before your gratuitously hurtful remark…" She knocked his hand off the steering wheel and glanced ahead of her, a pained look on her face. "We hang out and wait for the Snowman to find us. We hope that rather than killing us on the spot, he takes us to Sophia and the guy he works for, then—Bang!—we turned the tables on them. I still need to work out the details of the turning-the-tables part, but worst case we just improvise."

"If there were such a person, your *hope* that he won't kill us on the spot would seem wildly optimistic."

"Maybe you're right. We have to be more proactive. Give me your phone."

Seeing no alternative but to play along, he did. While weaving through traffic she turned on the phone and scrolled through his contacts. Tires screeched as cabs swerved to avoid her. Marc was buffeted from side to side.

"*Bonjour, Le Petit Mort*. How's the tiny member hanging? Oh, too small to hang? Well, *bonnes nouvelles*. Marcus dumped the Feds, took the scrolls, and went rogue. A regular little Sarah Palin manqué we've got. So, anyway, he and I are out driving around, and I had a sudden urge to call and say *bonjour*."

She turned off the phone. "As I told you in the bathroom, he's the bad guy. It's not enough that we stop the Snowman. To put an end to this horror, we've got to get to the head of the organization and chop it off." She made a chopping motion.

"All I want is to get my daughter back!"

"You really think the Snowman will hand her to us, just because we ask politely?" She made a tsking sound. "Oh, I'm sorry, that must've been another one of your little jokes. I get it, you're telling me I need to relax a little here. I can't be at my best if tense."

As with their bathroom encounter, Marc couldn't tell whether her perky tone and excessive self-enjoyment were calculated to annoy him, to distract him, or if her thoughts were so muddled that she said whatever came into her head in response to her flip-flopping moods.

After another series of deep breaths, he suppressed his fury sufficiently to put together a coherent sentence and maintain the semblance of a conversational tone.

"Why would the Snowman want to kidnap her?" he asked.

"I know in my gut I'm right. You have to trust me."

"Not going to happen."

"You do understand that this all has to do with the scrolls?"

"You're wrong. The FBI agent and I spoke to someone in our embassy in Riyadh, who confirmed that there's no way a political group there or in the emirates would risk the political repercussions of killing an American citizen on American soil just to suppress, or recover, these scraps of parchment."

"Yes!" She pumped a fist in the air. "I could just kiss you all over. That's exactly what I thought."

Finally realizing that logic would get him nowhere with someone so mired in her own insanity, he had no response.

"That's why they needed to use de Saint-Juste, so they'd have deniability." Still grinning over Marc's revelation about the conversation with the embassy and with her cadence quickening with each word, she said, "Beautiful day for a drive. Spring has sprung high as an elephant's eye."

"Dahlia!"

"Sorry. But not to worry, when we confront the Snowman I'll be cold as ice, hot as fire, hard as rock, sharp as a tack, high as a...no, not that." With an abrupt swing of the steering wheel, she turned down Fifth Avenue. "I've been fighting this fight for so long and now, being so close to the goal made me a little silly."

"DAMN IT, DAHLIA, STOP FUCKING AROUND AND TAKE ME TO SOPHIA. NOW!"

"Marc, we're working together toward a common goal here, please try to be a little more collegial."

He slapped her across the face, grabbed the wheel, and shoved his foot down on the brake. She stared at him, looking surprised and hurt.

"Dahlia, you're insane."

"Yes, but we'll work around that." She floored the car, leaving a patch of rubber. "Marc, you have to cut me some slack here, if only because of my condition. Ever hear of the Americans with Disabilities Act?"

His fury turned into...something strange and indefinable. Words came into his head that he didn't know he remembered and hadn't spoken for fifteen years, not since his mother died. He repeated them to himself, "*Yis'ga'dal v'yis'kadash sh'may ra'bbo, bolmo dee'vro chir'usay v'yamlich malchusay, b'chayaychon uv'yomay'chon uvchayay d'chol bais Yisroel, ba'agolo u'viz'man koriv; v'imru Omein.*" Tears streamed down his cheeks. "May the great Name of God be exalted and sanctified, throughout the world, which he has created according to his will. May his Kingship be established in your lifetime and in your days, and in the lifetime of the entire household of Israel, swiftly and in the near future; and say, Amen."

Dahlia pulled over. Hand over her mouth, eyes wide, she looked stricken.

"Sophia isn't dead, Marc. She'll be fine. I promise."

As if he'd been awakened from a deep sleep, he blinked repeatedly.

"You just recited the first part of the mourner's Kaddish, the prayer for the dead," she said.

His cheeks felt warm. He thought he'd only said it to himself.

"I don't know why, the words just came to me," he said, not addressing Dahlia but trying to understand what had happened to him. "I should've said them for Lisa, even though she didn't want me to. Should've? Who knows? I sure don't. I guess it was for Lisa, to finally say goodbye. Seems I have a spiritual side I need to be better in touch with." He swallowed hard. He could hardly believe he'd shared with her his most private feelings or even that those *were* his feelings. "But for now all I want is Sophia."

Dahlia placed her hand on his thigh. "I'm so sorry for what I'm putting you and Sophia through. If I had any other way..."

He shook his head. Last thing he wanted from her was pity.

"You have to know I wouldn't hurt Sophia." Her voice cracked.

He stared into her deep, liquid green eyes; only they were no longer green but gold-flecked yellow-brown. He felt as if he'd crossed some sort of line and was in a rational conversation with a dear friend. The mourner's Kaddish? He was losing it, or maybe he'd already lost it. Still, feeling a compulsion to conclude the prayer, he did so, this time making sure he didn't speak or mouth the words.

After looking to see that the way was clear, Dahlia eased back into traffic.

"You think de Saint-Juste is behind this. Call, offer him the scrolls," Marc said. "Whatever their significance, they can't be worth more than Sophia's life."

"He only acts through the Snowman—so he'll have deniability."

"Didn't you say he reacted to your voicemails?"

"We *can't* just give them the scrolls. They want me too. I've written it all down." She took a flashdrive from her bag. "I told them I have the flashdrive and always keep it with me, along with a copy of the scrolls. I'm telling you so you know you're not the only bait here."

Marc struggled to come up with a diplomatic way to articulate the obvious solution.

"I'd offer to trade myself and the scrolls for Sophia," she said, as if she'd read his mind. "But now *you* know too much for them to let you go free."

Marc buried his head in his hands.

Dahlia parked the car at a bus stop at 65th and Fifth Avenue and started to get out of the car. Marc didn't move.

"What's the matter, lose your nerve?"

"Sill thinking it through," he said.

"You were attacked in the tunnel just a few days after I told de Saint-Juste that you had the scrolls. That's what finally convinced me."

Marc fixed her with his most hostile stare.

"If I could've thought of any other way…" She again put her hand on his thigh.

He shoved it away, but…

"De Saint-Juste showed me a report prepared by top-flight private investigators. It made out a pretty convincing case that you killed Shustak and LaPonte and pushed Vance down the stairs."

"That he'd go to the trouble of creating a phony report confirms that he was the bad guy."

"Other than my gut feeling that you'd never hurt Sophia, that's what opened my mind to the possibility that you might be right."

"My schizoaffective disorder might've gotten the better of me at a couple points back there, but now I know I'm on the right track."

"Dahlia, you might be too crazy to know whether you're on the right track."

"Let's hope not," she said. "By the way, Ariella and I have had a falling out."

"Killing to suppress the scrolls still didn't make sense to me, but something's going on, and de Saint-Juste..." Marc gave her a long look. "I like you with long black hair."

She tilted her head as if trying to discern if *he* was the crazy one.

"I've worn it that way all my life. I cut and dyed it when I went underground, after LaPonte's news conference, where the Snowman planted a gun on me and called the cops."

"De Saint-Juste showed me a photo of you on the subway platform when Shustak was pushed. You had short spiky hair. The investigative report said that you purchased a MetroCard that morning, with a credit card you, that morning and used that card into enter the station three minutes before Shustak's death."

"I'm crazy, but I'm not stupid."

"That's pretty much what I thought."

She took the FedEx box, got out of the car, and said, "It's the bait for our trap." She grabbed a Frisbee. "A useful prop." She got out of the car. "Hope you don't mind this is an illegal parking spot."

He followed.

XXXI

The Snowman Cometh

IN HER LEATHER mini-shirt, skin-tight red *come and get it* T-shirt, and stiletto heels, Dahlia got plenty of looks. Even the leather bag swung so rakishly over her shoulder and her black leather gloves seemed provocative. None of those looks, though, came from anyone even vaguely threatening.

When they arrived at the Central Park Sheep Meadow, Dahlia, Frisbee in hand, cocked her arm.

"Go, I'll hit you on the run."

He took the Frisbee from her and dumped it in a nearby trashcan. Her shoulders hunched, and she seemed to shrink and collapse into herself.

"I'm a screw-up." She sniffled. "All this work, all this effort and all I accomplished is getting Sophia kidnapped. I should never ever have left those voicemails no matter what Ariella threatened. Not only did they get you attacked, they let them know they could get to me through you."

Tears wet her cheek. She began to shake.

He hugged her.

"You've done great," he said. "Avoiding the police for months, getting the scrolls, manipulating me to do your bidding. That's extraordinary, even for someone who's not sanity-challenged." He leaned back so that he was looking into her red-tinted eyes. "Now, if we can only find Sophia…"

Tears still coming, she gripped onto him, like four-year-old Sophia used to when scared by a large dog. He held her close, stroked her long, black hair, and rubbed her back. Comforting a crying child was a well-practiced talent. She stepped back. Snot formed a bubble in her left nostril. He handed her a Kleenex—when he'd stopped carrying baby-wipes, he switched to tissues.

"My instincts may be all screwed up, but I'm sometimes remarkably perceptive about people." She bit her lip. "At least I think I am."

"You are...sometimes."

She grinned and brushed strands of tear-soaked long black wig-hair from her face.

"De Saint-Juste lives over there." He pointed to the Time Warner Center at the southwest corner of the park. "He might still be in Abu Dhabi, but let's go see."

Taking his hand, she started running toward the building. Like a reluctant dog on a leash, he allowed himself to be pulled along.

Calling up to de Saint-Juste, the concierge told him that Dahlia Birn and Marc Bloch were there to see him. He listened to de Saint-Juste's response, then told them which elevator to take to the penthouse. One of several penthouses, apparently, because Canard's private rooms occupied another.

As they were being whisked upstairs, she whispered, "See, you think he'd let us just waltz up there if it wasn't a trap?" Her self-doubts seemed to have vanished.

"A trap... Yeah, that's great news," he said, his mood deteriorating in direct proportion to the improvement in hers.

"The moment of truth is but seconds away," Dahlia said, bouncing on her toes like a little kid.

A butler opened the door and offered them a seat in a cavernous three-story living room with floor-to-ceiling windows. Wearing a blue pin-striped suit, open-necked white shirt, and pale blue paisley ascot, de Saint-Juste emerged from one of the two doors leading to the rest of the apartment.

"Ms. Birn, do you mind telling me what this intrusion is all about? I'm this far from filing a criminal harassment complaint against you." He held his thumb and forefinger close together. "I let you up only because Marc is with you, and I feel for his predicament. One I suspect you have a great deal to do with."

Impressing Marc by how well she put her case together, Dahlia set forth her theory about de Saint-Juste working with the emir to find and suppress the scrolls and how the trail of death led to his door.

But then she veered off. "In World War II, the French heard a couple explosions from somewhere around Belgium and the entire country collapsed like a soufflé. Their only injuries came from getting shot in the back or turning an ankle, while running away. They were the only country whose own police helped round up the Jews."

Mercifully cutting off Dahlia's tirade, de Saint-Juste said, "Marc, I'm terribly sorry about what happened to your daughter and I'd be glad to help if I can, but aligning yourself with this crazy person..."

"See, he didn't deny it." Dahlia raised a triumphant fist.

"Of course I do. Has the FBI approved of this idiocy?" He took a phone from his pocket.

Dahlia pulled a gun from her bag and shot the phone out of his hand. With the silencer on, the pistol made an eerie whooshing sound. Her second shot took off the tip of one of his fingers.

De Saint-Juste stared at his wound, then screamed in agony.

"Dahlia!" Marc yelled. "Enough! Give me my phone."

"Marc, sit, make yourself comfortable." Her voice icy calm, she sounded insanely at ease and confident. "Killing him might take a while. I intend to draw out the pleasure, payback for what he did to Sophia."

"Where *is* she?" he asked.

Pointing the gun at the butler, Dahlia motioned for him to take a seat as well. Face already chalk white, he tumbled to the floor. Scanning the room with her gun, as if she considered all present to be mortal enemies, she took Marc's phone from her bag with her free hand and composed a text. De Saint-Juste sucked on his bloody finger. He'd just lost the very tip, but it didn't seem that *just* would be a word he'd use in describing his injury.

Sitting straight, he said, "I never...you can't believe that I'd..."

"Dahlia!" Marc yelled. "You want to spend the rest of your life back in Creedmoor? You need to let me call the FBI or this is going to get much worse for you very quickly."

An insane grin planted itself on her face.

"DAHLIA. THE PHONE. NOW!"

"Calm yourself, Marc. It's about to get interesting. I was practicing on his finger, now I'm going to go for a really small, thin target." She took slow and careful aim at de Saint-Juste's crotch.

"She's crazy!" de Saint-Juste shouted. "Marc, please, can't you see she's crazy?"

"DON'T!" Marc yelled.

"Please don't," de Saint-Juste whimpered.

Marc grabbed her arm. She knocked him away with an elbow to the chin that left him seeing stars.

A door opened and a tall, swarthy man blocked the doorway. He had a port wine stain on his cheek that resembled a snowman. And a large gun in his hand, aimed at Dahlia's head.

"Ah, nice to see you again. It's been far too long," Dahlia said, her tone so cool and unruffled that a confused look passed across his face.

She somersaulted. One of her shoes flew off. He shot. No silencer on his gun, the noise shook the windows. It seemed his shot hit the shoe, which smashed into the wall.

Moving so fast, Dahlia was more shadow than form. She rolled behind a chair.

The Snowman shot again. Dahlia screamed.

Marc, de Saint-Juste, and the butler dove behind the nearest pieces of furniture. Peeking out, Marc saw only a blur of movement and heard only gunshots, some suppressed, some ungodly loud.

Dahlia shoved a chair across the floor.

The Snowman's gun barrel followed the unexpected movement.

She shot. A hole opened in his head. He staggered forward, then back, then fell forward. The force of his hitting the floor sent a vase tumbling from a table thirty feet away. Shattering, it sounded like another gunshot.

Blood oozing from her left shoulder, Dahlia calmly shot de Saint-Juste in the crotch, picked up the FedEx box, and tossed the gun in a high parabola. Marc reflexively raised his hand to catch it.

"NO!" she yelled.

Marc twisted out of the way, and the gun crashed along the floor.

She said, "Don't get your prints on the murder weapon."

Extending his foot, he nudged it toward himself.

"Not that that would've been a problem for you," Dahlia said, her insane grin threatening to surpass the confines of her face. "You'd have handled it with aplomb, or maybe a banana. My God, all this fun has made me giddy."

"Sophia?" Marc said, his voice so high he hardly recognized it. "Where is she?"

"I'm sorry, I've got to run. Oh, hey, don't worry about me, it's just a flesh wound." She pointed to de Saint-Juste and whispered to Marc. "His, too. I aimed low. He's more scared than anything else. He'll live to stand trial."

"SOPHIA!" he yelled.

"A swarm of police is about to descend on this place—the gunshots." She spoke rapidly, her words running together. "They'll want to retain the scrolls as evidence. I gave my word to Daniel."

She put a gloved hand on the doorknob.

"What about *Sophia*?" Marc said.

"I'm truly sorry, but I *really* have to run. Ask Monsieur Froggy. My shot softened him up for you." She threw him a kiss. "Give my love to Sophia. I'll be in touch. I meant it when I said I want us to be friends, and as you've seen, I tend to get what I want."

She sent a quick text, tossed him his phone, and shut the door behind her.

She opened it again, tossed him the car keys, and said, "Sometime when you're out on the open road, think of me." She again shut the door behind her.

Marc remained sitting for a moment, stupefied, but de Saint-Juste's moaning focused his attention. From the location of the hole in his pants, well below the zipper, it appeared the shot had been just a glancing blow, not that a glancing blow down there was anything to smile about. Fingers to de Saint-Juste's neck, Marc checked his pulse. Rapid but strong. His skin was neither pale nor clammy. He was in pain but neither dying nor about to go into shock, at least not for the moment.

"Where's Sophia?"

"Call an ambulance now!" he screamed, clutching his crotch.

"You're in a piss-poor negotiating position," Marc said. "Where's my daughter?"

"How the hell would I know? Do I look like a fucking nanny?"

"Hey, I've got all day." Marc tossed the phone in the air and failing in his intentionally clumsy attempt to catch it behind his back, let it fall to the floor. "Gosh, hope I didn't break it. I mean with yours ruined and all."

"You've picked the wrong guy to fuck with."

De Saint-Juste took several breaths, trying to manage the pain.

"Looks like you're not going to be doing much of that for quite a while." Marc smiled. "I'm sure you'll tell me about Sophia, when you're ready. In the meantime, as long as we're chatting, tell me why you did it. Shustak, Birnbach, LaPonte, the scrolls, I want to know it all."

Non-committal blowing sound.

Marc stuck his face within inches of de Saint-Juste's. "Answer me!"

"Anglo-Saxon pig."

"*Judenswine*," Marc said. Three months ago he wouldn't have defined himself as Jewish and certainly wouldn't have corrected someone. "But let's not digress."

Marc turned toward the butler and pointed to his chair. The servant nodded in response, indicating no intention to move. Tapping his foot, Marc again faced de Saint-Juste.

"You know what it's like to have a client you need to keep happy," de Saint-Juste said. "Once Ms. Birn figured out what had gone down, she had to be dealt with." He glowered at Marc. "Now, call the ambulance. I'll send lots of business your way, make it up to you."

"My daughter's missing."

"You just let her kidnapper waltz out the door," de Saint-Juste said. "If you let me call down to security, we still have time to stop her before she leaves the building. This is your last chance. Once she leaves, who knew where she'll go. The police have been looking for her for months without success."

Marc's heart stopped. He could only hope that wasn't true.

"So it was all just business?"

"I stand to make almost a billion dollars from the project. That's hardly *just* business."

"*Stood* to make."

"They value loyalty and can't boil water without hiring a foreigner to show them how to do it. Then they lose the recipe and have to be shown again." He pointed to the huge mound of dead Snowman. "They suggested him." Gallic shrug, or rather an attempt at one. Cool as he tried to be, he couldn't quite pull it off. Getting shot down there had to take a toll on one's equanimity. "If he fucked up, it's on their heads. The jackass was supposed to get the scrolls, not get anyone killed. Now *please* call the ambulance, I'm bleeding like a stuck pig here."

Hard as it was with his daughter still missing, Marc continued to affect nonchalance.

"Just one more question, and I'll call an ambulance—unless, of course, you answer it wrong." Marc paused for a five count. "Ready?" Another pause. "Where's Sophia?" Marc sat. "Gosh, that sure looks like a lot of blood for a little fellah like you to lose."

"Christ!" De Saint-Juste called toward a partially opened door. "Sophia. Sophia, you can come out now." He said to his butler, "Maurice, please go get Sophia, tell her it's okay to come out now. Marc, you'll see she's fine. We treated her very well. Bringing her here for leverage was the Snowman's crackpot idea. I had nothing to do with it."

Marc held his breath.

The butler receded into the inner reaches of the apartment, closing the door behind him.

An agonizing few seconds later, a different door opened.

"Daddy!"

He held out his arms. Sophia sprinted toward him and plopped onto his lap. It was as if she'd been away for months and as if she hadn't been gone at all.

"Are you okay?" he asked.

He ran his hands over her body, checking for bruises, found none. He hugged her.

"Yeees. Now I am." She glanced at the mound of flesh that used to be the Snowman. "Daddy, I don't like seeing dead people."

"We need to stay here for a few minutes, while I talk to the police, then I'll drive you home in our beautiful car."

"*Our* car?" Tentative smile.

"Long story."

"Guess what, Daddy. I read over a hundred pages of *The Hobbit*. I threw a fit and made them buy it for me." She showed him the book.

His phone rang.

"You have Sophia? And she was all right?"

"Yes, Dahlia."

Marc stroked Sophia's hair.

"Again, I'm sorry I dragged you into all this, but I saw no other way," Dahlia said. "By the way, you texted reporters from the *Post*, the *Times*, and the *Wall Street Journal*. They're on the way."

"You texted—"

"If you put just the tiniest spin on the story, you'll be the hero and get all the business you can handle."

"Oh, yeah, that's just what I'm thinking about now."

"Have I ever led you wrong? Don't answer. But now that I've recovered my mojo, sky's the limit, and guess who'll be my lawyer?"

"Things still don't make sense."

"Welcome to the real world." He could practically hear her smile. "I never thought *I'd* be able to say that to someone."

"Could you find a phone number for Ahmed, the guy Yusef told about the scrolls?"

"Probably, now that the Mossad and I are going to be friends again. Why?"

He disconnected and went back to hugging Sophia. He had no idea how Dahlia intended to get the scroll fragments out of the country and back to Israel, but he was sure she had that all worked out. Maybe they'd even turn out to be legitimate and historically significant, but he still didn't think they would.

The police arrived, and he told them that Dahlia had said something about wanting to take the scroll fragments to an expert at the Smithsonian in Washington and that she might take the Metroliner. The Beretta? That had been Cooper's. In the horror of the kidnapping, Marc had forgotten he had it. Luckily Dahlia knew how to use it in self-defense and in defense of Marc and Sophia.

A scrum of reporters arrived at the door a few seconds behind the police, who kept them away from the crime scene. Joining them in the hallway, Marc thought Lisa would be proud of the way he played it. Hell, if he were to land two or three decent-sized cases, he'd be as busy as he wanted to be. Curiously, he looked forward to again having a busy law practice. He felt happier... lighter than he had in a long time. A large part of that was relief over getting Sophia back and delight that she was all right, but it was more than that. He was tingling, as if from an inflow of testosterone. He would rebuild his law practice and have a hell of a lot of fun doing it.

A photographer for the *Post* took a terrific picture of Sophia sitting on his lap, looking up at him adoringly. While his editor would make the decision, the photographer suggested, *My Daddy's the Best* as the following day's headline.

EPILOGUE

Marc knocked on the door to the Presidential Suite at the Pierre. Two business-suited, closely cropped men with military bearing politely walked him through a metal detector and scanner, then asked him to make himself comfortable on a plush couch.

A trim, handsome, Semitic-looking man entered, smiling warmly. Marc stood.

"Should I address you by your *nom de club*, Ahmed, or would you prefer—"

"Kahlil is my given name, but Ahmed's fine. I associate it with the good times I've had in the States." He extended his hand. "So nice of you to contact me, Mr. Bloch. The people of the UAE owe you a great debt. I still cannot believe that Monsieur de Saint-Juste did such terrible things."

A dark-complected boy in gold-threaded robes came in bearing a jewel-inlaid golden tray that held two tiny golden cups.

"Won't you join me in some strong Turkish coffee?" Ahmed asked.

The boy handed Marc a tiny cup, gave one to Ahmed, bowed, then exited, along with the bodyguards. Marc and Ahmed sat.

"I insist on paying you for your time," Ahmed said.

"Not necessary."

"It is to me. He handed Marc a ten-dollar bill. "A token payment is legally sufficient to establish attorney-client privilege, is it not?"

"I suppose you'll be able to talk more openly if our conversation is privileged." Marc took the money. "Some time back, I had the opportunity to read the contract for de Saint-Juste's desalination plant. I noticed the morals clause."

"Yes, we are a highly moral people."

"All the time Dahlia was telling me about these killings because of the scroll fragments it didn't make sense to me." Marc sipped the mud-thick coffee. "Then I realized you never cared about those scrolls."

"Yusef told a compelling tale. With certain *enhancements* I added, to increase the entertainment value, my father, grandfather, and their friends found it quite fascinating. We shared it with de Saint-Juste and perhaps embellished the importance of the scrolls, but only to make for a good story. We simple desert people have always been great storytellers." He extended his arms. "But, of course, no one suggested that he kill anyone."

"No one had to, once you introduced de Saint-Juste to a murderous psychopath with poor judgment and a reputation for excessive zeal."

"He asked us to find someone who might help him with various only vaguely articulated tasks—none of which, I assure you, involved murder, kidnapping, or intimidation." Ahmed shrugged. "English being neither de Saint-Juste's nor my first language, there might've been an unfortunate miscommunication."

Marc stroked his cheek while his thoughts coalesced.

"So now, you'll invoke the morals clause in the contract and confiscate what he'd built so far, while he'll be prosecuted on a murder-for-hire charge."

"We owe our people a profound obligation to ensure that our country's business is conducted on the most moral level."

"And in the most profitable way for those in charge."

"We are starting to get the hang of Anglo-American capitalism. Red in tooth and claw, as the great English poet once described it."

"Alfred Lord Tennyson was referring to nature."

"But still, capitalism is supposed to be Darwinian, is it not?"

"I suppose I should congratulate you as the new developer for the project."

"Again, please understand, we didn't mean for anyone to get killed."

"Just for de Saint-Juste, via the Snowman, to do something sufficiently criminal to justify your taking him off the project and confiscating what he built."

"Sharia law is very strict, particularly as interpreted in the UAE, as provided in the contract." Ahmed raised his coffee cup, as if expecting Marc to touch it with his in a toast. "When Dr. Birnbach was murdered, we thought American justice would take its course. When it didn't, we lacked enough evidence to justify taking over the project, without time-consuming, expensive, and embarrassing litigation. Thank Allah, blessed be His holy name, for your persistent friend."

Not obliging him, Marc said, "She made a persuasive case for the significance of the scrolls."

"The Middle East may be unstable, but it's not *that* unstable." He looked

Marc up and down as if performing a metal scan. "I'll be having considerable legal work in this country. We need a whole lot of cement and pipe. There are bound to be disputes a good litigator can help with."

"Not interested."

"Please give it some thought. I'm now rich enough not to need to cut corners. I want someone honest, who will keep me on the straight and narrow."

The conversation becoming disturbingly reminiscent of meetings in which Dahlia had tried to persuade him to represent her, Marc put down his cup and stood.

"There's no need for me to take up any more of your valuable time."

"You'll give my proposal some thought?" Ahmed held out a business card. "When you're ready, send me a retainer agreement, including whatever clauses you need to make yourself comfortable."

Marc took the card.

"I'm rarely comfortable."

"These days, no thinking person can be. The human condition is to always be struggling fruitlessly while all collapses around us."

"But along the way, some of us gain control of a multi-billion-dollar construction project or two."

"Thank Allah, blessed be His holy name."

Once outside in what passed for fresh air in New York, Marc received a text from Dahlia:

● *My real contact info below. I look forward to our getting together soon—*
He didn't read the whole message but didn't delete it.